BOUND TO FALL

A Colorado High Country Novel

PAMELA CLARE

BOUND TO
FALL

PAMELA
CLARE

BOUND TO FALL

A Colorado High Country Novel

Published by Pamela Clare, 2022
Cover Design by © Jaycee DeLorenzo/Sweet 'N Spicy Designs
Photo credit: mrbigphoto/Shutterstock

Copyright © 2022 by Pamela Clare

ISBN: 979-8-9854351-1-5

This book is dedicated to my beloved daughters-in-law, Angela and Courtney. Thank you for being a part of my family and making my sons so happy.

Acknlowledgements

Special thanks to my sister, Michelle White, and to my younger son, Benjamin Alexander, who have done more than anyone to support my writing journey. Additional thanks to Jackie Turner, the best catcher of typos in the known universe. Where would I be without you? Thanks, too, to Shell Ryan for her friendship and support.

Many thanks to my readers in the Pamela Clare Readers Group, whose love and support makes it all worthwhile. I hope you love Sasha and Darius' story as much as I do.

Chapter 1

September 15
Scarlet Springs, CO

SASHA DILLON SENT a quick text message to Nicole Turner, her best friend, to tell her where she was going. Years of doing search-and-rescue work had taught her that there was no such thing as being too safe. She always told someone where she was going and when she expected to return.

Going for a ride. Caribou loop. Back in two hours.

She strapped on her helmet, climbed onto her trail bike, and pedaled through Scarlet Springs toward the highway. She wanted to get in another conditioning ride, and the Caribou loop was both strenuous and beautiful, with steep switchbacks and views of the high peaks that stretched all the way to the Divide. So much of rock climbing was leg strength and endurance, and a good ride improved both while giving her upper body a much-needed rest.

Next week, she would pack up for the long flight to Bratislava, Slovakia, where she would defend her title at the sports climbing world championships. Though she was excited to see her international climbing friends again, she wasn't a fan of long international flights—or flying in general. She felt safer roped in on a two-thousand-foot cliff than she did strapped into an airplane seat.

Sasha pedaled hard, savoring the rush of wind in her face and letting her mind go, the stress of the upcoming competition melting away. She'd promised herself years ago that she would leave competitive sports climbing if it started to feel like work. Climbing was supposed to be fun, even at the professional level. If competition became too stressful, she would quit and go back to climbing for the joy of it.

A red fox darted across the road ahead of her.

"Hey, little guy."

It glanced her way before disappearing into the pines on the other side.

Sasha loved living in the Colorado mountains. She'd grown up in San Jose, California, where both of her parents still worked as software engineers. But life in the suburbs of Silicon Valley, with its traffic, industry, and boutiques, had been too mundane for her. She'd take a snowy conifer forest over palm trees and traffic jams any day.

The sound of an engine approached from behind.

As a battered, black SUV roared by, the man on the passenger side stuck out an arm, his middle finger raised. "Suck my dick!"

Jerks.

How unhappy he must be to treat a stranger that way.

She glanced at the Colorado license plate and memorized the number.

Sasha had tried to grow a thick skin when it came to harassment and sexism. The world of professional sports was rife with it. From men whose egos were bruised when she climbed better than they did to random creeps on the Internet who threatened her because she was a successful, single woman, she dealt with jerks almost every day.

Forget them.

She turned her mind away from the guys in the SUV and focused on her ride. She was in the best shape of her career, and the exertion felt good—the sweat on her face, the rush of air in her lungs, the nice burn in her quads and glutes.

A truck engine.

Sasha glanced over her shoulder to see a white truck with the words *RANGER* and *Forest County Parks and Open Space* painted on the side. She smiled, waved. Austin Taylor, a park ranger and a good friend, waved back as he passed.

Like Sasha, Austin was a Rocky Mountain Search & Rescue Team member. Founded by Megs Hill and Mitch Ahearn, two legends of the climbing world, the Team conducted hundreds of rescues every year, saving dozens of lives and earning the reputation of being the best high-risk SAR team in the nation.

Not that Sasha was biased or anything…

She had joined the Team after its volunteers had rescued a buddy of hers who'd broken both ankles taking a whipper on *Desdichado*, a route in Eldorado Canyon State Park. Sasha hadn't been there to watch them work, but she'd heard about it. When she'd learned who managed the Team…

Megs Hill had always been her idol.

Sasha downshifted as the road sloped more steeply uphill. She passed the sign that marked Scarlet's town limits, the turnoff for Caribou just ahead on the left. Then she saw it—the black SUV.

Damn.

It sat in a vehicle turnout, just ahead to her right, engine running, windows down, heavy metal blaring. She would have to pass them to reach the turnoff, and for a moment, she thought about turning around and finding a different route today.

To hell with that!

She couldn't let those rat bastards bully her into changing her plans. She checked for traffic and then crossed the road, riding on the left shoulder, putting some distance between herself and the jerks in the SUV.

This time, they said nothing as she passed.

She relaxed into her ride, now only a hundred feet or so from the turnoff. More than once, she'd seen a moose—

The roar of an engine. Tires squealing on asphalt.

She glanced over her shoulder to see the black SUV cross the centerline, heading straight toward her.

What the…?

Were they freaking insane?

On a surge of adrenaline, she turned her handlebars toward the forest, instinct driving her toward the cover of trees. But this side of the highway had a steep five-foot drop from the road to the forest floor. She would have taken her chances and ridden her bike over the edge, but the SUV was too fast. Its bumper hit her rear tire and sent her hurtling over the handlebars, her scream cut short when she struck a tree.

Bone snapped. Brakes shrieked. The forest floor rushed up at her, drove the breath from her lungs when she hit, landing face down.

Men's laughter.

"Die, bitch!"

She fought to inhale, pain exploding in her side. As the world went dark, she heard them drive away.

———

IT WAS pain that roused Sasha as she fought to get air into her lungs.

Stay awake, or you'll die here.

She raised her head, spit pine needles and dirt from her mouth, and struggled to sit up. But the pain in her ribs and chest was unbearable, and it was all she could do to roll onto her back. Without the breath to scream or cry for help, she lay there, feeling as if there were a fifty-pound weight on her chest. She knew what that meant.

Pneumothorax. A collapsed lung.

Your phone.

Where was it?

It was zipped into the right pocket of her cycling shorts.

She tried to reach for it with her right hand, but pain stopped her, her wrist clearly broken. But retrieving it with her left hand was impossible because it forced her to reach across her body, putting pressure on her collapsed lung and ribs that must be broken. She steeled herself against the pain and tried with her right hand once more. The zipper wasn't completely zipped, the gap at the top large enough for a fingertip. Gritting her teeth, she worked her finger inside, pushed the zipper down, and drew the phone out with two fingers, dropping it onto her chest.

She took it with her left hand, searched her contacts, and called Megs.

Megs answered, the familiar sound of her voice putting a lump in Sasha's throat. "Hey, Sasha, what's up?"

Dizzy from pain and lack of breath, Sasha managed to get out only a handful of words. "Help me! Hit … by car … near … Caribou turnoff. Can't… breathe."

Then the world went dark again.

———

DARIUS SILVA POURED himself a cup of coffee, relieved that today's action had gone so well. After nine months of hard detective work, the son of a bitch who'd murdered Reina Hernandez was behind bars.

"Way to go, Silva." Julian Darcangelo clapped him on the shoulder as he passed. "I'm glad that bastard is off the streets."

"Thanks, man."

As a detective with Major Crimes Investigations, Darius didn't work directly with Darcangelo. Still, the man had a reputation for getting the job done, and Darius respected that. If even half the shit people said about him was true, he was a badass.

Darius made his way down the hallway toward Conference Room 2 for the debriefing, nodding to those who congratulated him along the way.

"Congrats, Silva."

"I hear you got him. Well done."

"Good work, man."

He got paid to catch bad guys, but if his fellow cops wanted to make a big deal out of it, he would let them.

Darius had been with the Denver Police Department for a little more than a year now. He'd moved to Colorado after a decade with the LAPD's Threat Management Unit, chasing down the stalkers and psychopaths who targeted celebrities. The work had been rewarding at first. But after a decade of working with movie stars, directors, models, and singers, he'd decided most of them were as obsessed with themselves as the unhinged people who stalked them. Everything he'd loved about his job had become everything he'd hated about it, and he'd known it was time to go.

After LA, Colorado was a breath of fresh air. Though Denver had the conveniences of a big city, it was close to world-class skiing and endless miles of pristine wilderness. Best of all, there was no celebrity culture. It had been more than a year since anyone had demanded he run press releases by their publicist or treated him like staff or sat through an intake interview naked.

The conference room door stood open. Chief Irving, with his gray crew-cut and suit jacket, sat at one end of the table. Marc Hunter, the SWAT captain whose team had assisted with the arrest, sat a few chairs down, still in body armor.

Darius took the seat across from Hunter. "Thanks for your help today. You and your team do good work."

Hunter grinned. "Hey, you're the one who solved the case."

It had been one of the most challenging investigations of Darius' career. Everyone believed the victim's husband had murdered her. Much of the evidence had initially pointed in his direction. Statistically speaking, when a young woman disappeared and turned up dead, her boyfriend or husband was the killer.

But Darius knew only too well how assumptions could bias an investigation, ruining the lives of innocent people while allowing the guilty to go free.

Despite circumstantial evidence and statistics, the killer hadn't been the husband this time around. It had been the meth dealer next door. Hernandez had begun to suspect the bastard was dealing when she'd witnessed a steady stream of vehicles stopping at the house at all hours of the day and night. She'd confronted him rather than calling the police. That had been a fatal mistake.

Chief Irving looked like he hadn't gotten a full night's sleep in the past thirty years. There were heavy bags under his eyes, and his face wore a resigned expression, as if he'd long ago accepted that the bullshit would never end. "I read the case reports from both of you. Good work. Silva, your former boss said you never give up. Like a pit bull, he said. Now I know what he means."

A pit bull?

Darius supposed he *did* have a reputation for persistence. He'd had the highest closure rate of any detective on the Threat Assessment Unit and the second highest at the LAPD. It had cost him a couple of girlfriends, a car, and more than a few nights' sleep.

"Thank you, sir."

They spent the next ten minutes going over details of the raid before Chief Irving changed the subject.

"I have a request for support from the Forest County Sheriff. They've asked for help investigating a hit-and-run that happened yesterday just outside Scarlet Springs. The young woman who was hit is a world-famous climber—the reigning world champion, in fact—and the sheriff wants our help determining whether this was a random act or a personal attack. I've told them you'll arrive tomorrow morning to lend a hand."

It took Darius a moment to sort through that. "You're sending me … *where*?"

Hunter grinned. "Scarlet Springs. It's a small mountain town west of Boulder. I worked with the Forest County Sheriff's Department and the local fire department when they were hit by a wildfire a couple of years ago. They're good people."

"If you've got a good working relationship with them, why don't *you* go?"

"Hunter has a wife and kids, and he lacks your cyber-crime experience."

Hunter shrugged. "I'm good at kicking down doors and pulling triggers, but beyond that…"

Fuck.

The last thing Darius wanted was another celebrity stalking case.

Irving slid a folder across the table, opened it to reveal a publicity photo of a pretty young woman with a bright smile on her face, her golden blond hair in braids. "The victim is Sasha Dillon, age twenty-six, single, no dependents. She's currently in Memorial Hospital with injuries that aren't life-threatening."

Hunter's brow furrowed. "Thank God for that. She's a sweet kid."

Irving went on. "You'll be staying at the Forest Creek Inn on our dime. Take your service vehicle. Also, they don't have the cyber tech that we have, so take whatever you think you'll need—cyber monitor, validator, all of that."

Hunter chuckled. "Listen to you, old man—trying to sound like you know what you're talking about."

Irving shot him a withering glance, but he didn't fool Darius. Irving was fond of Hunter. He turned back to Darius. "Any questions?"

Darius bit back his objections. He respected Irving, and he'd sworn an oath to follow orders. "How long will I be staying there?"

Irving rose. "I'd suggest you pack for a week. If you believe the hit-and-run is the work of a stalker and you need to remain on assignment to direct the investigation, you can always do laundry."

That was *not* what Darius was hoping he'd say. "Yes, sir."

Chuckling, Hunter got to his feet. "Don't look so glum. Be sure to stop by the local brewpub, Knockers. The beer is outstanding. The town owns a ski resort—Ski Scarlet. It's a quirky, fun place to hang out."

"If you say so." Then it hit Darius. He picked up the file and stood. "You already knew about the attack, didn't you? It was *your* idea that they ask Irving for help."

Hunter didn't deny it. "One of their deputies called me to ask my opinion. I gave her a little advice, and she was smart enough to take it."

Darius could appreciate Hunter's wanting to help a friend. "Okay, man. I'll head up, look into it, and let them know what I think."

"Thanks. I owe you a beer."

"Damn straight—and I won't let you forget it."

Hunter looked him over. "You might want to ditch the jacket and tie. You'll stand out like a sore thumb."

Chapter 2

DARIUS DROVE his unmarked service vehicle—a black Chevy Tahoe—through a roundabout, passing a man who looked like an escaped extra from the set of a Jeremiah Johnson biopic, complete with bushy beard and buckskin.

Where the hell had Irving sent him?

Hunter had said Scarlet Springs owned its own ski resort, so Darius had been expecting a smaller version of Aspen—overpriced restaurants, chic boutiques, million-dollar condos. But this wasn't Aspen. It was more like Mayberry.

Instead of sidewalks, Main Street had wooden walkways with log railings. There were no elegant storefronts, no tree lined streets, not even a Starbucks. The town seemed to be a collection of oddball shops, wood cabins, and marijuana dispensaries.

Stoned Mayberry.

He followed his GPS to the Forest Creek Inn and parked in the designated parking area. The inn was the nicest building he'd seen so far—a three-story, yellow

Victorian house with white gingerbread trim. Its grounds were expansive and relatively well-maintained.

He climbed out, the mingled scents of fall leaves and pine taking the edge off his irritation. Scarlet Springs might not be much as towns go, but the scenery surrounding it was stunning—white-capped peaks, dense conifer forests, golden aspen.

That's when Darius saw him. An older man sat barefoot on the back patio, drinking a beer and wearing a pink velour bathrobe that was too small for him.

At nine in the morning?

The man raised his glass. "Mornin'. I'll check you in at the front desk."

That was the owner?

Geezus.

Darius couldn't wait to see his room. He'd be lucky to get more than a stained mattress on the floor and a pot to piss in. He got his duffel and garment bag out of the trunk, made his way to the front entrance, and walked inside, relieved to find that the interior matched the exterior and not the guy on the patio.

From the other side of a door, he heard voices arguing in whispers.

"Get dressed, Bob! You can't check in a guest like that."

"He's already seen me."

"Get dressed. I'll handle it."

The door opened, and a pretty older woman stepped out. "Welcome to the Forest Creek Inn. I'm Kendra, one of the owners."

"I'm—"

"Detective Darius Silva. We've been expecting you. Welcome to Scarlet." She handed him a key card and a small brochure. "Because you're here to help us, I put you in the Matchless Suite. That's our best room. The key card works on the elevator. Our buffet breakfast is available in the dining room upstairs from seven to nine each day. Our WiFi password is in the brochure. If you need anything, just let us know."

He was getting special treatment? "Thank you."

"I hope you can help find the dirty bastards who hurt Sasha."

"I will do my best, ma'am." Darius took the stairs instead of the elevator, swiped his keycard, and stepped into the suite that would be his home for the coming week.

The room was everything he hadn't been expecting. The living area mixed antique wood furniture with modern amenities like a large flat-screen TV. There was a bedroom with a wood fireplace and a king-sized brass bed and, beyond that, a bathroom with modern fixtures, including a towel warmer and a tub big enough for two. A large standing mirror stood off to one side, an ornate antique frame holding silver glass.

Well, you couldn't judge a book by its cover—or a bed-and-breakfast by the day-drinking dude in the woman's bathrobe.

He set his duffel on the bed, hung the garment bag in the antique wardrobe, and glanced at his watch. In ten minutes, he had a meeting with Deputy Julia Marcs, the friend of Hunter's who'd done the initial case report on the hit-and run. The address was already programmed into his vehicle's GPS, so he left the room and made his way down the stairs and back outside.

Across the street, an older woman with long silver hair stood in the open doorway of a small Victorian house, waving to him as if the two of them were friends. Above her hung a sign that read *Rose's New Age Emporium*. He'd made the mistake of looking her way, and she'd taken that as an invitation. She hurried down her front stairs.

Shit.

He'd just opened his driver's side door when she reached him, a white lacy shawl covering her flowy lavender dress. "Welcome to Scarlet Springs. I'm Rose. You must be that detective."

Did everyone in town already know who he was?

"Hi, Rose." He slipped into the driver's seat.

She positioned herself so he couldn't close the door, rested a hand on his arm. "Stop by sometime for a free tarot reading. I also offer past-life therapy, astrology readings, chakra re-alignment, and aura work. I might even be able to help with your investigation. I'm very sensitive to the vibrations around Scarlet."

"Uh…Okay." What the hell was he supposed to say to that?

Her gaze traveled over him. "You've got a lot of third chakra energy—self-control, discipline, warrior strength."

"I've got to get to the sheriff's substation." He started the vehicle, hoping she'd get the point.

She stepped aside. "I'm just across the street if you need anything."

At a loss for words, he closed the door and drove away.

———

SASHA WOKE, every breath agony. She grasped the control pad with her left hand and pushed the call button, hoping Ellie would come quickly. Ellie Moretti was one of the nurses and the wife of fellow Team member Jesse Moretti. That made her family.

As for Sasha's real family…

Her parents had called the hospital several times to

check on her. When they'd heard she was out of surgery and that her life wasn't in danger, they'd decided not to fly out, pleading project deadlines. Not that she'd expected them to come…

The very things she loved about Scarlet Springs were the things they disliked. They thought the town was too small and too far off the map to be good for her career. They wanted her to live in LA instead and use her climbing career as a springboard for film or television, though Sasha wasn't the least bit interested in either.

Her parents also couldn't grasp why she volunteered for the Team. From their perspective, she was a world champion climber and shouldn't waste her time or risk her safety rescuing people. They couldn't see how much satisfaction it gave her to use her climbing ability in a way that served others.

Sasha knew they loved her and only wanted the best for her. She was just the proverbial apple that had somehow fallen far from the tree.

She drew another painful breath. They'd operated to set her broken wrist, and she had bruises all over her body. She also had a mild concussion. But nothing hurt as much as her ribs.

It could have been so much worse.

You're lucky you'll still be able to climb.

She was lucky to be alive.

That's what Austin had said when he'd found her, and she knew it was true. Austin had been the first to arrive on scene, followed by Eric Hawke, the fire chief, who was also a Team member. Other Team members had come after that—Megs and Mitch, Nicole, Creed Herrera, Harrison Conrad, Malachi O'Brien, Chaska Belcourt.

Sasha remembered only bits and pieces. Pain when Eric put in a chest tube to reinflate her lung. Malachi hitting her with an auto-injector of morphine. The worry and rage on her friends' faces. Nicole in tears. Creed shouting that he would find the bastards and kill them. Megs telling Creed to shut the hell up and holding Sasha's hand.

You're going to be okay. We'll make sure of it.

Though Sasha would never tell Megs this, Megs was like a second mother to her.

Ellie walked through the door, syringe in one hand, a bag of IV fluids in the other. "I've got more pain meds, and I want to change out those fluids. Is it still your ribs that are bothering you most?"

Sasha nodded. "It hurts… to breathe."

"Broken ribs are miserable." Ellie held up a glass vial. "I've got a bolus of morphine here. We'll get you feeling more comfortable, and then I'll check your vitals."

"Thanks." Sasha closed her eyes, knife-sharp pain splitting her side every time she inhaled or exhaled.

"Here comes the morphine."

Relief was swift, leaving Sasha floating.

"This room looks like a florist shop. You've gotten so many bouquets that they're all around the nurses station, too."

Sasha opened her eyes, saw that Ellie was right. "Who sent them?"

"After I get your vitals, I'll gather the cards for you."

Sasha drifted off for a moment, her eyes coming open when the blood pressure cuff began to tighten.

"BP is good. No fever." Ellie hooked her stethoscope around her neck. "Let's see who's sending you flowers."

She walked from bouquet to bouquet and gathered the cards, glancing inside at the senders' names. "This one is from Megs and Mitch. This is from your parents. Nicole sent this one. The big one here is from Joe and Rain."

Joe and Rain Moffat ran Knockers, the local brewpub.

Ellie wasn't done. "The florist at Food Mart must be out of flowers by now. These are all from Scarlet Springs residents."

That made sense. The sheriff hadn't yet released the her name to the media. Sheriff Pella felt it was best to keep things quiet for now.

After what happened when Mitch was hurt, I'm afraid we'd have reporters all over Scarlet. We'll keep your identity out of our reports for now, if that's okay with you. I'd appreciate it if you didn't mention the hit-and-run part of this just now.

Sasha wasn't sure what he'd meant by that, so she'd decided to tell people who didn't know better that she'd crashed her bike.

Ellie wrapped the cards in a rubber band and set them on Sasha's overbed table. "You can read through these when you get a chance."

Then Sasha remembered. "I need to call my manager."

Ellie smiled. "You talked to him this morning. I was standing right here."

"Oh. Right." Sasha remembered that now, too. "Sorry."

Scott had wanted to run to the press with the story about her accident. He'd hoped that one of the big sports magazines would pay good money for an exclusive interview with photos. Sasha hadn't had the strength to argue with him, so Ellie had taken the phone, told him Sasha wouldn't be doing interviews for a while, and ended the call.

"No apologies necessary. Between the morphine and your concussion, it's a wonder you remember anything." Ellie took Sasha's good hand. "All you need to worry about now is healing so you can get back to climbing. We've got your back."

This was why Sasha loved Scarlet. The people here weren't fancy, but they took care of their own.

"Thank you, Ellie."

"You try to get some sleep now, okay, sweetie?"

"Okay." Sasha was asleep before Ellie reached the door.

———

DARIUS LEFT his vehicle at the sheriff's substation and rode shotgun in Deputy Marcs' service vehicle to the site of the hit-and-run, listening to her assessment of the situation along the way.

"You'll be able to see where they accelerated. They left a lot of rubber on the road. They weren't pointed down the highway. They were headed straight for Sasha. I don't see how this could be anything but deliberate."

Darius had to agree. "That seems unlikely."

"I've asked Jason Chiago to meet us there. He's a former Shadow Wolf and a Deputy US Marshal. He's Tohono O'odham and an expert at cutting sign. If there's anything I missed, one of the two of you will hopefully find it."

A former Shadow Wolf and a DUSM.

Darius was impressed.

"Here we are. And there's Chiago, waiting for us."

Deputy Marcs pulled into a vehicle turnout. "This is where Sasha said they were waiting when she cycled past them. I already searched the area, but I didn't find anything besides litter here."

"Let's see what the road can tell us." Darius climbed

out of the vehicle, watched for traffic, then made his way to where Chiago stood, his gaze on the asphalt.

Chiago looked up, held out his hand. "Deputy US Marshal Jason Chiago."

Darius shook his hand. "Detective Darius Silva, DPD Major Crimes Unit."

Deputy Marcs joined them. "What do you think, Chiago?"

"I think you're right. They struck Sasha deliberately." Chiago backtracked. "They came out of the vehicle turnout, drove a short distance, and then turned the wheel and accelerated over the centerline, straight toward her."

"That's exactly what she said when I interviewed her."

Darius had a look for himself, saw the thick rubber that crossed the yellow line—and the rubber where they'd slammed on the brakes to keep from crashing into the trees. "I concur. They intended to hit Ms. Dillon. Whether they knew her and targeted her specifically remains to be seen. Did you locate the vehicle?"

Deputy Marcs nodded. "It was found abandoned in the parking area adjacent to Boulder Falls."

"Cams?" Darius was reasonably certain he knew the answer.

Deputy Marcs shook her head. "They might have had another car waiting for them or hiked out or even thumbed a ride into town. People are pretty relaxed about hitchhiking around here. If we could get a description…"

At the sound of an approaching engine, the three of them walked to the shoulder of the highway.

"Did Ms. Dillon see them?" He'd read the report, but sometimes basic details got left out by mistake.

"The man in the passenger seat flipped her off, but she didn't see his face. She heard them laughing before they drove away, and one of them yelled, 'Die, bitch!'"

"What kind of security do you have on Ms. Dillon's room?" Darius was pretty sure he knew the answer to this question, too.

"The hospital has security, and the staff know to watch out for strangers."

Good grief.

Chiago grinned. "It's Scarlet, man."

"I don't suppose she has a bodyguard or private security?"

Deputy Marcs shook her head.

Darius shouldn't have to point this out. "Until we're sure that this wasn't personal, there should be someone outside her hospital room round the clock. If she wants to hire personal protection, that's fine, too."

Chiago got a call and stepped away.

Deputy Marcs nodded. "I'll contact the Scarlet PD and see what Chief Randall can do. Everything within the town limits is his jurisdiction. He's pushing seventy-eight and about as curmudgeonly as an old cop can be. The Town Council keeps pushing him to retire, but he ignores them. He won't be happy about this."

Darius tried to imagine the size of Scarlet Springs PD. How many officers did it take to patrol a single square mile? That's what Scarlet Springs was—one square mile surrounded by reality. They couldn't possibly have the budget or the staff to run a security detail. "If they can't manage it, we'll find another way."

Chiago waved. "I need to go. Good to meet you, Silva."

He jogged to his vehicle, climbed in, and drove away.

Darius walked to the spot where the vehicle had struck Ms. Dillon's bicycle and looked over the edge. Bark was missing from the trunk of the nearest tree, a red reflector lying in the duff, lots of boot prints in the earth. He climbed down, retrieved the reflector, looked up from the area where he believed Ms. Dillon must have landed.

Die, bitch!

That's what the attackers had shouted.

Had they believed they'd killed her? Had it been their intent to kill her?

Regardless, she'd been lucky to survive.

He climbed back up to the road, reflector in hand. "You told me earlier that you've kept this from the media."

"Sasha is a rock star in the climbing world. People all over the world follow her online. I knew that once this news got out, Scarlet would be overrun, and this site would be a tourist spot. I thought it would be good to get a jump on the investigation without a throng of people standing around us taking photos."

Darius hadn't realized rock climbers had that kind of fan base. "Good thinking."

They waited until a truck had passed and then walked back to Deputy Marcs' service vehicle, buckled up, and headed back into town.

Deputy Marcs glanced at him. "Where would you go from here?"

"The vehicle is probably your best lead."

Deputy Marcs slowed at the roundabout. "We're already pursuing that."

"Apart from that, your best bet is to interview her about stalkers and past and present boyfriends. I would also comb through her social media and emails looking for threats."

"It's hard to imagine that anyone would want to hurt Sasha. Everyone loves her."

"Apparently not everyone."

Chapter 3

SASHA ACCEPTED Ellie's help getting out of bed. They wanted her to walk every so often to prevent pneumonia and blood clots. "Can you make sure I'm covered?"

"Sure thing." Ellie leaned over, examined Sasha's rearview. "You're good. You won't be mooning anyone in the hallway."

"Thanks." Holding onto the IV pole with her good hand, Sasha walked slowly toward the door, Ellie's arm around her shoulder.

"Tell me if you start to feel dizzy, okay? I don't want you fainting on me."

Sasha nodded, catching a glimpse of herself in the mirror above her sink as she passed. She stopped, stared. There were scratches and bruises on her right cheek, and she had a black eye and a swollen lip, probably from hitting the ground.

"That's one heck of a shiner." Ellie gave her shoulder a squeeze. "Those scratches and bruises will heal."

Sasha didn't mind. "It makes me look like a badass."

"You *are* a badass."

They left her darkened room and entered the sunny hallway, where dozens of bouquets adorned the countertops that surrounded the nurses station—roses, lilies, delphiniums, chrysanthemums, dahlias, and carnations in a riot of colors.

"Wow!"

Ellie laughed. "I wasn't kidding."

"It smells like roses."

"We'll walk to the end of the hallway and back, okay?"

"Okay."

The hallway seemed terribly long to Sasha. She had climbed El Capitan in under six hours this past summer, almost breaking the women's speed record, but now the end of the hall seemed impossibly far away.

"I feel so weak."

"That's partly the morphine and the anesthesia in your system. You're doing great. One step at a time."

Malachi, one of the ER docs and another Team member, stepped out of the elevator a few feet ahead of them wearing green surgical scrubs, his shoulder-length blond hair tied back in a ponytail. "Hey, Sasha, you're just the person I came to see. I'll take over, Ellie."

Ellie patted Sasha's back. "You're in good hands."

"Hey, Mal." Sasha was happy to see him. "Thank you for your help yesterday."

"I'm glad I was able to be there." His ER schedule meant that he missed a lot of rescues. "How are you feeling?"

"Sore. It hurts to breathe. I keep forgetting stuff."

"I'm not surprised. You suffered some pretty serious trauma."

"I never thought the Team would have to rescue me."

"It gave us all a shock when Megs paged us. 'Sasha hit by car near Caribou turnoff.'" Malachi shook his head.

"Megs is usually all-business on site, but she was pretty shaken up. She let Mitch run the debriefing when we got back to The Cave."

Sasha stopped and gaped at Malachi. "She did?"

"She was too upset to handle it herself. She barely said a word."

The thought put a lump in Sasha's throat. Megs was known for being levelheaded, especially in a crisis. When Mitch had been gravely injured last fall and lay in a coma in ICU, she'd held herself together so well that Sasha thought she must be made of steel.

Then Sasha had to ask. "Have they found them—the guys who did this?"

"Not yet, but they're working on it."

Sasha couldn't help the sick way her pulse picked up at this news.

Malachi motioned toward the chair at the end of the hall. "Sit. Rest for a minute."

Sasha took the last few steps and sat, dread knotting her stomach.

Mal sat beside her, his brown eyes filled with compassion. "I know that's not what you wanted to hear. Deputies found the vehicle abandoned in the parking area across from Boulder Falls. The sheriff brought in some big-city detective to help. He used to hunt down celebrity stalkers in LA or something."

"Really?" Some of Sasha's dread faded.

"People in this town care about you. Hell, Sasha, the whole world cares."

But Sasha knew that wasn't true. Like any woman in the public eye, she had her share of haters, and some of them were scary.

Mal stood. "Let's get you back to bed. How's your pain?"

She gritted her teeth as she got to her feet.

"That bad, huh? Yeah, broken ribs suck."

They slowly walked back to her room, where Mal helped her into bed.

"I'll check with Ellie about your next dose of pain meds. They're hoping to discharge you tomorrow. Megs and Nicole are organizing meals and helping with shopping and housework. I'm afraid the good people of Scarlet are going to drive you crazy once you get out of here. Enjoy the quiet while you can."

That made Sasha laugh—bringing instant regret. "Oh! Ow!"

"I'll ask about those drugs. Rest now." Mal turned toward the door.

"Mal?"

He faced her once again. "Yeah?"

"Can you ask the nurses to give flowers to people who don't have any? There must be people here who are alone. Spread the love. Tell Ellie and the other nurses to take one home, too."

Mal smiled. "You got it."

Sasha sank into her pillows, exhausted. As she drifted into an uneasy sleep, she heard it again—the man's voice.

Die, bitch!

———

DARIUS FOLLOWED Deputy Marcs through the door of Knockers, the brewpub Hunter had mentioned, mouthwatering scents hitting him as he stepped inside.

"Knockers is named after the Tommyknockers," Deputy Marcs told him.

"Who are the Tommyknockers?" They sounded like a rock band.

"The Cornish miners who settled the town believed Tommyknockers were little gnome-like creatures who lived in the mines. One of our local women swears a Tommyknocker saved her life several years back."

Why didn't that surprise Darius?

A woman with long blond hair hurried toward them, tattoos of roses and skulls on her arms and a ring in her nose. "Any news?"

Deputy Marcs shook her head. "Not yet. We're still looking. Detective Silva, this is Rain Moffat. She and her husband, Joe, own this place."

Rain's gaze shifted to Darius, and she picked up a couple of menus. "Thanks for helping with the investigation. We all love Sasha and want these bastards brought to justice."

"I'll do everything I can."

"Can we sit at the Team table?"

"Sure." Rain led them to the back, where a small group of people sat around a long table that was actually four four-tops put together. In the back was a climbing wall like the one at Darius' gym. He'd never seen one in a brewpub before.

Okay, he could admit it. That was cool.

Heads turned as they approached the table.

"Mind if Julia and Detective Silva join you?" Rain asked.

"No. Not at all."

Darius sat across from Deputy Marcs and took a menu from Rain. "Thanks."

Rain put her hands on her hips and gave him and Deputy Marcs a stern look. "Just to be clear, your money isn't good here today. You eat for free."

Darius started to object. He couldn't accept perks or favors while working on an investigation. He would risk opening himself to accusations of partiality. Even the suggestion of impropriety could blow a case in court.

Deputy Marcs leaned over. "Lighten up, Silva. This is Scarlet, not LA."

It was too late, anyway, because Rain had gone.

Shit.

"I don't break the rules."

"Maybe you should try it." Deputy Marcs introduced him. "This is Detective Darius Silva. He's on loan from the DPD, thanks to Marc Hunter. He used to work with the Threat Management Unit in LA, protecting celebrities from crazy stalkers."

An older woman with shoulder-length gray hair stood and reached across the table to shake his hand. "I'm Megs Hill, operations manager of the Rocky Mountain Search and Rescue Team. Thanks so much for helping Julia find these sons of bitches."

Darius had heard of Megs. As the first woman to have free-climbed El Capitan, she was climbing royalty. "Happy to help."

Megs introduced the others.

Darius was pretty good at remembering names and faces. He'd also heard of Mitch Ahearn, Megs' husband, who sat to Megs' right, his hair white. Across from him was Eric Hawke, another Team member and the town's fire chief. Beside Eric sat Nicole Turner, who said she was Sasha's best friend. Next to her sat Creed Herrera, who shook Darius' hand and thanked him.

"What have you found so far?" Herrera asked.

"Let the man read the menu," Megs said. "We can bombard him with questions after Rain takes his order."

Darius needed to nip this in the bud. "I really can't answer questions. This is an ongoing investigation."

"Shit." Megs frowned. Her gaze shifted to Deputy Marcs. "Julia?"

"We don't know anything yet. We found the vehicle, but you probably heard that already. We've impounded it and are doing a thorough search."

Darius lowered his gaze to the menu. He'd have a little talk with Deputy Marcs later. When Rain returned, he ordered the jalapeño burger—and made it clear that he would pay for his meal.

"I understand. Just know how grateful we are." Rain left with their orders.

Darius found the others staring at him. Rather than explaining, he asked questions. "How long have you all known Sasha?"

One by one, they shared how and where they'd met her, with Megs going last.

"I knew who she was before I met her. After she won her first world championship, I read in some climbing magazine that I was her role model. Then we rescued a friend of hers in Eldorado Canyon State Park. She came up here to thank us and to meet me. She stayed and joined the Team. When I look at her, I see myself at her age, except that she's a lot more talented than I was."

Then Nicole spoke. "You need to understand that Sasha could do anything she wants to do. She has a small fortune. Her family is wealthy, too. They're software engineers in Silicon Valley. She's probably the most famous climber in the world right now. But she *chooses* to live in Scarlet because she loves the town and because it makes her happy to use her climbing ability to save lives."

If this was true, Darius was impressed. Still, he couldn't help but be skeptical. He had yet to meet a celebrity who wasn't focused on themselves—their appearance, their wealth, their public image.

Mitch, who'd mostly been silent, spoke. "Her smile lights up the room."

Every head at the table nodded.

Darius would find out for himself this afternoon.

Without warning, Deputy Marcs turned and yelled. "Marcia, Cheyenne, quit staring! Not every hot guy who walks through the doors is looking for a date!"

This made the others laugh.

Darius followed the direction of Deputy Marcs' gaze and saw two young women watching him, one behind the bar and the other in front. When they saw him looking their way, they abruptly became very busy.

"Sorry, Silva. I didn't mean to call you 'hot.' Not that you're *not* hot, I mean. You are, but…" Deputy Marcs' face turned beet red. "Shit."

At this, the others laughed harder.

———

IT MUST HAVE BEEN early afternoon when Ellie woke Sasha again. "Julia Marcs and that detective are here to see you."

Sasha picked up her empty pitcher. "Can I have more water?"

"Let me help you get situated, so you're covered and comfortable." Ellie rearranged the sheet and blanket and adjusted Sasha's pillows. "I'll just raise up the head of your bed a bit more and then get your water."

Ellie walked to the door. "You can come in."

Sasha looked over to see Deputy Marcs. Behind her stood a tall man in a white shirt and dark slacks. Her blinds were closed, so she couldn't see his features. "Hey."

Julia walked over to the bed. "Hey, Sasha. How are you feeling?"

"My ribs hurt a lot."

"I bet they do." Julia turned to the detective, who'd hung back. "This is Detective Darius Silva. He's on loan to us from the Denver Police Department."

Detective Silva stepped forward, gave her a nod. "I'm sorry to meet you under these circumstances, Ms. Dillon. I was hoping—"

The door opened, and Ellie walked in with the pitcher of ice water. "Let me open the blinds so you can see. You're probably going to want to take notes."

Julia took out a pen. "Thanks, Ellie."

Ellie walked to the window and raised the blinds, daylight spilling into the room. "Let me know if you need anything else, Sasha."

But Sasha didn't hear Ellie, her gaze fixed on Detective Silva—or rather his eyes. They were gray like slate with long lashes, his gaze direct and piercing, his brows dark. His face was just as intense—square jaw, hollows beneath high cheekbones, full lips, and a straight nose. Such a handsome face—but so hard.

"I was hoping to ask you some questions."

It took Sasha a moment.

"She's got a concussion." Ellie's voice brought her back. "Call me if you need anything."

"Right. That's fine. Thank you."

Julia motioned to a chair, and Detective Silva sat.

"I know you've already answered a lot of questions, so you'll probably feel like you're repeating yourself. I'd appreciate it if you could tell me what happened from the beginning. Take your time. No detail is too small."

While Detective Silva took notes, Sasha went through her ride moment by moment. Texting Nicole to let her know where she was going. Cycling through town to the highway toward the road to Caribou. Hearing the SUV's engine behind her. The guy on the passenger side flipping her off and yelling at her.

"Who else knew where you were going?"

She had to think. "I posted on my social media that I was going to ride the Caribou loop. My German friend Maritza Braun knew, too, but she's in Slovakia. She's an elite climber, also, and we share details about training with each other all the time. She and I were messaging each other right before I left."

"Did you recognize the men in the vehicle?"

"I couldn't see their faces, just the arm and the hand."

"What did he yell?" Those gray eyes looked into hers.

Sasha cleared her throat. "He shouted, 'Suck my dick.'"

Detective Silva's brows drew together in a frown, his gaze on whatever he was writing. "Did you react in any way—shout back, flip him off, take out your phone?"

"No. I had both hands on my handlebars. I didn't really have time to react because they disappeared around the corner."

Sasha told him how Austin had passed a few minutes later in his patrol vehicle. "I waved, and he waved. I kept riding. Then I went around another curve and saw the SUV sitting in a vehicle turnout. I was sure they'd harass me again, so I crossed to the other side of the highway. The turnoff for Caribou wasn't far ahead."

"Did you shout at them or flip them off or do anything to provoke them when you passed? You might have felt safer then and believed you could fight back."

Did he think she had brought this on herself?

"No. That would only make things worse. I just wanted to ride in peace."

Sasha described what happened next, fighting a growing sense of panic as she recounted the ordeal in detail. "I heard their tires squeal and looked over my shoulder to see them crossing the centerline. They were headed straight toward me. I turned my bike toward the forest, but they were faster. The next thing I knew, they hit the bike, and I went flying over the handlebars."

Sasha drew a breath to steady herself, then another.

"What happened then?"

"I… I felt myself hit the tree and fall, and then I heard one of them shout, 'Die, bitch!' Then they drove …. They drove away."

"Did the person who yelled those words sound angry or amused or drunk? Did you recognize the voice at all?"

"Angry, I think. N-no, not drunk." Sasha's chest felt so tight, her heart thudding, adrenaline making her blood go cold.

Julia leaned down. "Are you okay, honey?"

"It's hard … to breathe."

"She's having a panic attack." That was Detective Silva. "Call the nurse."

A panic attack?

Sasha had never had a panic attack before.

Then Detective Silva was there, sitting on the bed beside her, his voice soft, soothing. "Look at me, Ms. Dillon. Try to slow your breathing."

Sasha looked into his eyes, tried to do what he'd told her to do, the fingers of her good hand instinctively closing around his wrist.

"In through your nose. Out through your mouth. Nice and slow. You're safe. No one is going to let anything happen to you. I promise. In and out. That's it."

The door opened, and Ellie hurried in.

Julia spoke softly. "She's having a panic attack."

"I'll be right back with medication."

Sasha heard them, but she was focused entirely on

those gray eyes and the soothing tone of his voice. By the time Ellie returned with meds, the sharpest edges of her panic had receded, the tightness in her chest lessening.

Ellie pointed toward the door. "Enough questions. Sasha needs rest. Those are nurse's orders."

Julia nodded. "Sorry about this, Sasha."

Detective Silva stood. "I hope you feel better soon, Ms. Dillon. We'll do all we can to find these guys."

Sasha couldn't ask for more than that. "Thank you."

Ellie injected something into her IV. "This is just a little sedative to help you relax. You survived a terrible attack. It wouldn't be a bad idea to talk with Esri."

Esri Tsering was a trauma therapist who volunteered for the Team, helping members deal with the emotionally challenging aspects of search-and-rescue work.

"Yeah." Sasha's worries seemed to melt as the drug took hold, and she drifted off to sleep.

Chapter 4

"WHY DID you ask Sasha stuff that is already covered in my report?"

It took Darius a moment to register Deputy Marcs' question, an image of Ms. Dillon's panicked blue eyes fixed in his mind. She'd grabbed his wrist, her touch giving him an unwelcome jolt. He could still feel the heat of—

"Detective Silva?" Deputy Marcs drove out of the hospital parking lot.

"Sometimes people remember things differently later. Besides, you didn't cover all of it." Darius glanced at his notes. "She says she didn't react in a way that might have provoked a response, so we can rule that out as a motivation—at least for now."

"Are you trying to blame *her* for this?"

"No, of course not." The note of irritation in Deputy Marcs' voice told Darius she was too close to Ms. Dillon to be objective. "I'm trying to understand the attackers' motivation. They passed her once without trying to hit her. If their goal was to harm her, why did they wait to strike?

If she had flipped them off or told them to fuck themselves when she'd passed them, it might explain it."

"Maybe they knew that Austin Taylor wasn't far behind them. His ranger truck looks like any other law enforcement vehicle with overheads and takedown lights. Maybe they waited until he'd passed, and they were sure the coast was clear."

"That's a possibility." Darius made a note to call Taylor later. "The other thing she told us was that the voice sounded angry. If they hadn't meant to hit her—let's say they'd only wanted to harass her—they might have sounded afraid or amused."

"Like, 'Shit, we're in trouble!' or 'Haha, we showed her.'"

"Exactly. Instead, the voice sounded angry."

"What does that mean—that they're a couple of incels?"

"Maybe." Incel scumbags had murdered women using vehicles more than once. "It could also mean that it's personal, that the attackers feel they have a score to settle with Ms. Dillon."

"Who would have a score to settle with Sasha?"

It was time for that little talk.

"I understand that Ms. Dillon is your friend and that Scarlet Springs is a small community where everyone trusts everyone else."

"Well, not everyone. I would never tell Rose anything that I didn't want to be all over town before lunchtime."

She had missed the point.

"This is a *criminal* investigation. None of us can afford to make assumptions. If you let assumptions and biases get the better of you, you risk arresting the wrong people and letting the perps get away. If you leak information, you could alert the bad guys and blow the whole case. You *do* want to solve the case, right?"

"Of course!" Deputy Marcs shot him a fiery glance.

Darius didn't care if he'd made her angry. He knew only too well the cost when law enforcement fucked up. "Good police work demands objectivity, attention to detail —and no leaks. If you want my help with this case, you need to quit making assumptions and sharing information with the entire town. Not a word to anyone outside of law enforcement, or I'll head back to Denver. Understood?"

Deputy Marcs muttered something that sounded like *asshole*. "Got it. But if you expect me to salute, you can kiss my ass."

Darius bit back a grin, certain he'd made his point. "No salute necessary."

Deputy Marcs reached for her handset. "Eight-sixty-five, go ahead."

When she ended the call, she shared the news.

"The vehicle was reported stolen from a driveway in Boulder. Forensics dusted it for prints and found five distinct sets. They're running them through the database, but so far, nothing has popped. The SUV is an older model and isn't equipped with Bluetooth. It couldn't have captured identifying smartphone data."

"Did they check for street cams?"

Deputy Marcs reached for her handset again, called in his question, and quickly got the answer. "There are no cams on the street. They'll send someone from Boulder PD to see whether any of the neighbors have security cams."

Darius mulled over this news. Had the perpetrators known there weren't cameras on the street? Had they stolen the vehicle specifically to commit a crime? A *yes* to either of these questions indicated premeditation, but they just didn't have enough information to know either way.

"Where now?"

"I had more questions for Ms. Dillon, but that will have to wait."

"You wanted to ask her about ex-boyfriends and stalkers, right?"

"Yes. Most of the time, people who commit acts of deliberate violence have some connection to the victim, even if it's only in their heads. That's why motivation is such an important factor. There's usually some kind of trail online—threats, harassment, sexually suggestive comments."

"If someone was harassing Sasha, there are two people in town who would know for sure—Nicole, her best friend, and Megs. She's close to both of them. You just met them at Knockers."

"I remember. Do you have their contact information?"

"They're probably at The Cave."

"The Cave?"

"That's what they call Team headquarters. I'll let them know we're coming."

———

MEGS MET them at one of two large bay doors. "Welcome to The Cave. Nicole is on her way. Let me give you a quick tour."

Darius could understand why Team members called it The Cave. The space was massive, with an enormous vehicle bay that housed two rescue trucks, aptly named Rescue One and Rescue Two. There was more gear upstairs, as well as records of every rescue the Team had ever done.

Darius was impressed. He'd done a little rock climbing, but he had no idea what most of this stuff was or what purpose it served. "This must be a fortune in equipment."

Megs nodded. "It's expensive to run an SAR team. We're funded entirely through donations, so we do what we can to keep costs down. Everyone who works for the Team is a volunteer, even our accountant and web manager."

That surprised him. "No salaries or bonuses?"

"None." Megs motioned to the walls. "As for the gear, we've donated some of it ourselves. One of our volunteers, Chaska Belcourt, is an engineer and has developed specialized equipment for our use."

Megs told him how she and Mitch had started the Team after a friend of theirs had died of hypothermia when a broken ankle had stranded him on a mountainside during a snowstorm. "No one was prepared to undertake a high-risk rescue in the dark, and that included the two of us. After that, we left professional climbing and started the Team, hoping to prevent other needless deaths. We get toned out dozens of times each month during the summer. It tapers off in the fall."

Nicole walked in, her brown hair damp. "Sorry. I was in the shower."

"Nicole has been with the Team for … eight years?"

Nicole nodded, clearly happy that Megs remembered. "Yeah. Eight years."

Megs motioned toward a closed door. "Let's sit in the ops room."

Darius and Deputy Marcs followed Megs and Nicole into what looked like an ordinary conference room, apart from the radio setup on a nearby table and the massive topographic map of Colorado hanging from the far wall. Radio traffic murmured in the background, punctuated by bursts of static.

Megs gestured toward several chairs. "Sit wherever you like. We've got bottled water in the kitchen."

Darius sat. "I'm fine. Thanks."

"I brought my own." Deputy Marcs held up a water bottle and sat beside him.

"How can I help you, detective?"

Darius opened his mouth to answer, but Deputy Marcs beat him to it.

"I told Detective Silva that if Sasha had been getting death threats or had any angry ex-boyfriends or stalkers, she would have told you and Nicole. He wanted to ask Sasha, but she had a panic attack before he got to it. They had to sedate her, and Ellie shooed us out."

Nicole looked distressed. "Poor Sasha. I'm going to visit her after this."

Megs met Darius' gaze. "Sasha is one of the kindest, most genuine people you'll ever meet. She's also attractive, as I'm sure you noticed."

Darius had noticed, but he wasn't about to admit that. Even with a black eye and swollen lip, she was beautiful.

Megs went on. "She gets lots of hate mail. All women athletes do."

"Let's start with past boyfriends or lovers. Has she had any conflict with the people she used to date?"

Nicole shook her head. "She has two ex-boyfriends, but they're still friends. They didn't break up because they hated each other. They just took different paths. It's more the online harassment that worries me."

Megs seemed to agree. "I've seen some of the online comments and emails she gets. It's awful stuff—dick pics, rape threats, death threats, twisted sexual stuff."

"Has she reported any of it to law enforcement?"

Nicole shook her head.

"Not to law enforcement," Megs said, "but she did out

one of them to the climbing community. Last spring, a fellow sports climber started posting explicit images of women from porn videos with Sasha's face on them all over social media using fake accounts. As soon as one of his accounts was taken down, another would pop up."

Darius had seen this before. "He sounds like a winner."

"Yeah, well, he got sloppy." If the look of disgust on her face was any indication, Nicole couldn't stand the guy. "One of the posts said, 'She climbs like a man, but … but she fucks like an animal.' Sorry for the language."

Megs put a hand on Nicole's knee. "I'm sure he's heard much worse."

Nicole smiled. "When she and I read that, we knew right then who it was because he'd recently told her that she climbed like a man."

"Did she confront him?"

Nicole nodded. "You could say that. Sasha ended his professional career."

That sounded like motivation to Darius. "What do you mean?"

"She turned all the information over to her sponsors—who also happened to be his sponsors. They dropped him flat. He's no longer getting paid to climb. Then the International Association of Sports Climbing banned him from competing for a year. He apologized. He said his ego had gotten the better of him. He'd been angry with her for on-sighting a route that he hadn't been able to send."

Darius had been writing all of this down, but that last sentence stopped him. "I'm sorry. On… *what*?"

Megs chuckled. "Speak English, Nicole. I think you've confused this nice man."

Nicole explained. "To 'on-sight' something is to climb it on the first try without having seen it before or having any beta… that is… *information* … about it."

Darius wrote that down. "And *send*?"

Megs answered this time. "Climbers are lazy. Send is short for 'ascend.'"

Nicole nodded. "Yeah. When you climb something, you send it."

"Got it." Darius would have to run all of this by Ms. Dillon, but it at least gave him a start. "What's the name of the guy who harassed her, and where can I find him?"

"His name is Bren Riggs. He's from Utah, but he lives in Boulder." Nicole held up her phone. "I've got his phone number."

———

WHEN SASHA OPENED HER EYES, she found Nicole sitting beside her bed, reading something on her phone. "Hey. What time is it?"

"It's almost five. You've been asleep for a while." Nicole slipped her phone into her pack. "How do you feel?"

"My ribs hurt a lot."

"More than your wrist?" Nicole looked surprised by this.

"I don't have to use my arm, but my ribs move every time I breathe."

"Oh. Right." Then Nicole gave her a teasing smile. "I met that hot detective. He had lunch at Knockers and then came to The Cave. Damn! He's so good-looking it made me nervous to talk to him. Those *eyes*."

"He is good-looking, isn't he?" Sasha remembered the way he'd talked her through her panic attack, those gray eyes fixed on hers, his voice soothing.

"Hell, yes, he is. I told Julia she was lucky to spend her workday in a car with him. She told me he's a bit of a control freak. At lunch, he turned down a free meal because he didn't want to open himself to accusations of favoritism. He made her promise not to share information about the case with anyone."

"I'm sure he has good reasons for that. Why did he come to The Cave?"

"He wanted to ask us about stalkers, ex-boyfriends, hate mail, online harassment—all of that. Julia told him that if you'd had a stalker, Megs and I would know. We told him about Bren."

"You did? Why? Bren apologized. He would never do something like this."

"Wouldn't he? You didn't want to believe he was the one posting those disgusting images, either." Nicole *did* have a point. "You might forgive him, but I can't. I wouldn't leave him alone in a room with Megs, either."

"If the detective goes after him, Bren will think *I* sent him." Sasha no longer counted Bren among her friends, but she didn't want to antagonize him.

"I'm not sure upsetting Bren should be your biggest worry right now. Someone tried to *kill* you, Sasha. Detective Silva has to follow whatever leads he can find."

"I suppose so." Then it hit her, made her stomach knot. "Does Detective Silva think I was a target, that this wasn't random?"

"I'm not sure. He told Julia you needed to have security. They're talking to Chief Randall about putting you under police protection."

A jolt of adrenaline made Sasha's pulse race. "He thinks I'm still in danger."

Nicole frowned, clearly regretting what she'd said. "I'm sure he's just being careful. You need to rest. I shouldn't be talking about all of this with you."

Sasha tried to draw a deep breath to calm herself but

winced at the knife-sharp pain in her ribs. "Don't feel bad, Nic. I'd find out sooner or later anyway."

Nicole reached over, rested her hand on Sasha's arm. "I hope it makes you feel safer to know that you've got a hot big-city detective working on the case."

"It does." Sasha willed herself to smile, not wanting Nicole to feel bad.

Still, she couldn't shake the niggling fear that had closed around her heart.

Nicole changed the subject. "Megs says the surgeon thinks you'll be able to climb again. That's good, at least."

That had been Sasha's first question in the recovery room. "He said it would probably be a couple of months before I can hit the climbing wall again."

"It sucks that you won't be able to compete this year."

"Yeah." It really *did* suck.

"I'm sure it's hard to see a five-year winning streak end like this."

"It's more than that. I was so excited to see everyone again. Maritza already bought the two of us tickets for a sightseeing tour on the Danube. I was hoping to go climbing in the Tatra Mountains, too. I knew I wouldn't be world champion forever. I just never imagined…"

Die, bitch!

Nicole squeezed her hand. "I'm so sorry, Sasha. No one imagined this. I wish I'd been there. Maybe they wouldn't have dared with two of us."

For a moment, there was silence.

Then Nicole smiled. "Marcia and Chey were ogling Detective Silva at lunch today. Julia saw them and yelled at them to stop. She said, 'Not every hot guy who walks through the door is looking for a date.' Then she got all flustered because she'd called him *hot*, and he was sitting right there. She started babbling. 'I didn't mean to call you hot. You are hot, but…' It made everyone laugh."

It *was* funny, but Sasha had so much on her mind. She tried to seem interested. "What did Detective Silva do?"

"Nothing. He didn't even smile." Nicole lowered her voice. "He's *very* serious."

Sasha was fine with that. "I guess he has a serious job."

Right now, that job entailed finding the men who'd almost killed her.

Chapter 5

DARIUS TURNED onto 32nd Street in Boulder's Martin Acres neighborhood. He'd opted to drive the unmarked SUV, concerned that the sight of a Forest County sheriff's vehicle might make Riggs bolt.

Deputy Marcs pointed. "There. It's the white one on the corner."

"I see it." Darius parked two houses down.

Riggs lived in a small ranch-style house of brick and wood, its paint crumbling, its front lawn more bindweed than grass. There were lights on inside, the curtains open. Even with the windows rolled up, he could hear heavy metal blaring.

Deputy Marcs glanced at the house. "At least we know he's home."

While she called dispatch with their location, Darius made sure his body armor was on securely and his bodycam was running. Then he checked his pistol and grabbed his notepad and the manila envelope from the glove compartment. The envelope contained color print-outs of the pornographic images Riggs had posted, as well as photos of the stolen SUV and Ms. Dillon's mangled bicycle.

"I'll go to the front door. You head around back in case he rabbits."

Marcs started her bodycam and checked her firearm. "Got it."

"I'll take the lead in questioning him."

"I knew you'd say that."

They climbed out, and Darius walked up the cracked and crumbling sidewalk, while Deputy Marcs headed around to the back, keeping clear of the windows. Darius waited until she'd had time to get into position before he knocked.

Nothing.

He knocked again, much harder this time.

Someone turned down the music, and the door opened.

Riggs stood there, white powder around his nostrils, his sandy blond hair a ruffled mess, a stupid grin on his face. "We don't want any."

In the center of the room, another man was bent over a coffee table, snorting a line of coke from a mirror.

Riggs laughed at his own joke. Then his gaze dropped to Darius' body armor and his duty badge, and his smile vanished. "You're a cop."

"Cops?" The other guy's head came up. "Shit!"

The door was wide open, so Darius stepped inside.

The other guy—a young man with stringy brown hair wearing a yellow T-shirt and ripped jeans—froze, his body bent over the mirror as if to hide the cocaine, a sandwich bag of white powder clutched in one hand.

Climbing ropes lay in a heap in the middle of the floor. A bong sat in the center of a cluttered dining room table, the air heavy with the reek of weed, beer, and old pizza.

"I'm Detective Darius Silva. I'm not here about the blow, though I'm sure the Boulder cops would love to know about it. Should I call them, Mr. Riggs, or would you like to answer some questions?"

Riggs sniffed, glanced over at his buddy, who stood, wariness on his face.

"Uh… I guess I'll go." His friend tried to slip the bag of coke into his pocket.

Darius shook his head. "Leave the drugs. I'll need your name and ID."

"Right. Okay. I'm Kyle Watts." The kid showed Darius his driver's license then glanced sympathetically at Riggs as he passed. "See you around, man."

As he left, Deputy Marcs entered. "It looks like we interrupted something."

"Yeah. I told Riggs here that I could call Boulder PD about the cocaine, or he could answer some questions."

Deputy Marcs met Riggs' gaze. "That's a pretty good offer. I'd take it. Otherwise, you're looking at six to eighteen months."

Riggs sat, fidgety as hell from the coke. "What do you want to ask me?"

"Where were you yesterday afternoon?"

Riggs' face went pale, and he pretended to be confused. "Yesterday?"

Darius nodded. "Give me a rundown of your entire day."

The kid's face screwed up with feigned concentration. "Well, I … uh… I got up around eleven or so, and my buddy and I grabbed some grub. We came back, smoked some weed, and talked about our next proj. I spotted a sick line near Beethoven's Honeymoon on the Diamond on Longs Peak, and we want to send it before winter sets in. It's got to be a good five-thirteen-C."

Darius pinned Riggs with his gaze. "What did you do after that?"

Riggs shifted, his gaze dropping to the floor. "We went to the rock gym for a workout. Then we came back and ordered pizza."

"Will the security cams and staff at the rock gym be able to confirm this?" Darius had been a detective long enough to know when someone was lying—most of the time. "Maybe you should try telling us the truth."

Riggs was sweating bullets now. "Do I need a lawyer? If you think I did something, man, just be straight and ask me."

"Okay." Darius opened the manila envelope and placed the pornographic images on the coffee table one at a time.

Riggs glanced at the photos, his ears slowly turning red. "I already apologized. She ruined my career. What the fuck does she want now?"

That was apparently too much for Deputy Marcs to hear. "You ruined your own career, genius. She didn't force you to post those images."

Darius changed tack. "Are you angry at Ms. Dillon because she reported the harassment to your sponsors? You must have lost a lot of money."

Riggs' chin came up, his face now as red as his ears. "Yeah, I'm pissed. She could have just come to me and told me she knew I'd done it. Instead, she made a big fucking deal about it. I lost my sponsorships, and I can't compete until next year."

Darius switched the topic again, hoping to keep Riggs off balance. "Did you drive into the mountains yesterday afternoon?"

The kid shifted uncomfortably, averted his gaze. "I don't know. We might have."

Clearly, there was something Riggs didn't want them to know, beads of sweat on his forehead.

"You *might* have?" Deputy Marcs glared at him. "Are you telling us you can't remember? Maybe you need to lay off the weed."

Riggs acted like it had just come to him. "Yeah, I guess we drove up Boulder Canyon. We did some bouldering near Boulder Falls until it started to get dark. Then we came back here and ordered pizza like I said."

"What routes did you boulder?"

"Um… Golden Showers and Bat Bait, I think."

Darius wrote that down and then put the photo of a stolen SUV on the table. "Whose car did the two of you drive? Was it this one?"

Riggs looked at the image, confusion coming over his face. "Nah, man, that's not Kyle's truck. Wait. What the fuck is this all about? If Sasha still has a beef with me, she should call me and talk it over."

Darius took out the photo of Ms. Dillon's mangled bike, set it next to the picture of the SUV, watching Riggs' reaction. "She's in the hospital. Someone stole that SUV and used it to run her down when she was out riding her bike."

"You think I…?" Riggs spluttered, shock on his face.

Or was that fear?

"You were angry with Ms. Dillon, weren't you? You and your buddy stole that SUV then drove it up Boulder Canyon to Scarlet Springs and—"

Riggs' eyes went wide. "That's not true! I didn't—"

Darius kept up the pressure. "Were you hoping to kill her, or did you just want to scare her, maybe shake her up a bit. Was this payback?"

Riggs' eyes got wider, then he shot to his feet, his

expression hardening. "I have rights. I don't have to answer questions. I want a lawyer."

Darius slid the images back into the envelope. "You'll hear from us again. In the meantime, you're under orders not to leave town. Now, about the cocaine."

Darius stood in the bathroom doorway, watching while Riggs flushed the powder down the toilet and rinsed the mirror.

"Do you know how much this cost?" Riggs whined.

Marcs rolled her eyes. "Oh, we feel so bad for you, don't we, Silva?"

"My heart is breaking."

SASHA GLANCED at the list of messages on her phone. There were five from Maritza, three from Scott, one from Daryna, one from her parents, and one from her brother, Sean. She listened to them one by one before deleting them.

She called Scott first, the process made awkward because she was using her left hand. He told her again how sorry he was. Then he pitched his idea of going to the big sports magazines with the story. Instead, she asked him to put out a press release stating that she'd been injured in a bike accident and had no choice but to withdraw from the world championship competition.

"It's fine with me if the public knows I broke some ribs and my wrist. They should also know that I'm going to be fine." When he started to object, she cut him off. "I can't deal with the media right now, Scott. Please just do as I ask. I also need you to cancel my plane tickets and pull me out of the competition. Thanks."

Then she called her parents, who suggested she fly

home and recover there.

"We have to work, of course, but Maria can keep an eye on you during the day, and we'll pamper you in the evenings."

Maria was her parents' housekeeper.

"I can't imagine getting on a plane now. Besides, my friends are watching out for me. They've already planned out a meal schedule and everything. But thanks, Mom."

When she called her brother, she got his voicemail. "Hey, Sean. Thanks for your message. I'm going home tomorrow. Everyone here is taking good care of me."

She'd saved Maritza for last, probably because she was sad that she wouldn't get to see Maritza or join her for sightseeing and climbing adventures. They always had such a great time together. It had never mattered to either of them that they competed against each other in the sports climbing world.

"Hey, Sasha. Are you getting excited?"

Sasha's throat went tight at the sound of Maritza's voice and her familiar German accent. "Sorry it took so long for me to get back to you. I had a bad bicycling accident yesterday, and I'm in the hospital. I won't be coming to Slovakia. I had to withdraw from the competition."

"*What*? Oh, no, Sasha! What happened?"

Sasha hated keeping the full truth from Maritza, but she didn't want to divulge something she shouldn't. She didn't want to make Detective Silva's job harder. "I lost control, went off the road, and broke my wrist and a couple of ribs. The doctors say I'm going to heal and climb again, but it's going to take a couple of months."

"Oh, Sasha, I'm so sorry. That's awful."

Sasha fought not to cry. "The worst part is that I won't be able to join you on the sightseeing tour. I'm sure Daryna would love to take my ticket. I'd hate for your money to go to waste."

"The money isn't important. I was so excited to see you again."

"Likewise."

"How did it happen? Were you going too fast or…?"

Sasha had to make up details on the spot. "I just got too close to the shoulder. Mountain highways are sometimes in pretty rough shape. I must have hit a rock or something. I flew over my handlebars, hit a tree, and landed on the ground."

"Oh, God! You could have been killed."

"Yeah." It could have been so much worse. "I was able to call for help. The Team came and got me to the hospital."

Maritza gave a huff of disapproval. "At least you finally got something from them. I don't know why you waste your time with that when you could be traveling and climbing anywhere in the world."

They'd had this discussion too many times.

"I don't like it when you talk about the Team like that. Climbing to save lives is more important to me than climbing just for myself."

Maritza had never understood that. "I haven't seen news about your accident anywhere. It's not on climbing Twitter or Instagram. I noticed you hadn't replied to any of my posts, but I thought you were off climbing somewhere."

"I had surgery yesterday and was pretty out of it. I haven't posted about it yet. Besides, a biking accident is hardly front-page news."

"Of course, it's news—at least in the climbing universe. You're one of the most famous climbers in the world, and your world championship streak just ended."

Those words hurt, but Sasha let them go. "That was bound to happen sooner or later, right? I'll be cheering for you."

"Thanks, Sasha. That means a lot to me. Is there anything we can do?"

"Thanks for asking, but my friends here are taking good care of me."

The conversation drifted first to Maritza's training program and then to the news about the Russian climbers who'd been caught doping. Maritza had just asked Sasha whether she thought the entire Russian team would be disqualified from the competition when Sasha had to cut her off.

"I'm sorry, but I need to go. I can barely keep my eyes open."

"Oh. Right. Sorry. I really hope you feel better soon."

"Thanks. Talk to you again." Sasha ended the call.

She took a selfie, bruises and all, and posted it on Instagram with an explanation.

```
Yesterday, I had a bad bike accident and
broke my wrist and two ribs. I've withdrawn
from the IASC world championships. I will
miss my friends, but I'll cheer them on
while I recover. #ClimbOn
```

Then she turned off her phone, set it aside, and drifted into a dreamless sleep.

DARIUS PRIDED himself on being able to control his temper, but Deputy Marcs was getting on his last nerve.

"I understand why you didn't call in the cocaine. If you

had, we'd have ended up in a dick fight with Boulder PD. They would have taken him in, processed him, and we'd be lucky if we got to question him before tomorrow."

"So, what's the problem?"

"Why aren't we taking that bastard in?"

"The only evidence we have against him is circumstantial."

Marcs shook her head. "Look at the totality of that evidence. He has motive. The SUV was stolen from a driveway less than two miles from his house. He hangs with a buddy, and there were *two* men in that truck. Sasha said it was blaring heavy metal music, and that's what the two of them were listening to just now. He lied about his whereabouts until you pressed him and was visibly agitated. Then he admitted to being in Boulder Canyon yesterday afternoon. He's hiding something. You *know* he is."

"What does any of that prove?" Darius spelled it out for her. "Boulder is the last stop for anyone heading up the canyon to Scarlet Springs. That's probably why the SUV was stolen here. Riggs and Watts weren't the only duo at Boulder Falls yesterday afternoon. They're also not the only men their age who listen to heavy metal. Yes, he's hiding something, and he was agitated. That's what cocaine does. None of that proves anything."

"Don't forget that he asked for a lawyer. Why would he want a lawyer if he wasn't guilty?"

Darius raised an eyebrow, surprised that she'd said this. "We all have a right to counsel, deputy. Asking for a lawyer doesn't make a person guilty. You know that."

Deputy Marcs glared at him. "You are stone-cold, aren't you?"

"I learned the hard way not to let my emotions cloud my judgment."

"What happened? Did you blow a big case? Is that why you left LA?"

He didn't owe her or anyone else that story. The ordeal had almost ruined his life. "No, I didn't blow a case, and that's not why I left LA. Stay focused."

"Fine. Keep it to yourself. So, what do we do now, Mr. Big City Detective?"

He needed to finish this investigation so he could go back to working with pros like Irving, Detective Wu, Hunter, and Darcangelo. It wasn't that Deputy Marcs was a bad cop or that he disliked her. She had good instincts. But she clearly hadn't worked many big cases, and she talked too damned much.

"Which government agency manages Boulder Falls?"

"That's Boulder County. Why?"

"I'd like to ask them if they have wildlife cams on the trails there. We know when Ms. Dillon was hit. If we can show that Riggs was at Boulder Falls at the time, we can eliminate him as a person of interest. If not, we bring him in."

"I'll contact Boulder County in the morning. What else?"

"I need to talk with Ms. Dillon. She's being discharged tomorrow. I'm hoping to finish my conversation with her. I brought a monitor system that I can hook up to her computer to intercept and trace threatening emails."

"And if you find threats from Riggs?"

He hoped it would be that easy, but in his experience, it rarely was. "Then we have some actual evidence."

They passed the spot where Ms. Dillon had been attacked, yellow crime scene tape still tied to the trees where she'd been hit. Soon, they reached Scarlet Springs and the roundabout at the center of town.

"You heading to Knockers?"

"I hadn't planned on it." He needed space to go over the details of the case, and he wasn't going to find that in a brewpub.

"What are you going to eat? They don't have room service at the Inn."

Shit.

He should have grabbed some take-out in Boulder. "Does anyone deliver?"

"Knockers delivers pizza."

"Pizza it is, then." He stopped beside her service vehicle. "Goodnight, deputy."

She climbed out, grabbed her gear from the backseat. "Where should we meet tomorrow morning?"

"I'll let you know."

With that, he drove back to the Inn, parked, and went up to his room. After a hot shower, he called Knockers and ordered a small pizza. Then he sat down at the desk and let his mind wander through the case. Sometimes, it helped him see things differently as random facts lined up in no particular order.

The SUV passing her and then pulling over, waiting until she'd gone by them to hit her. An angry voice shouting, "Die, bitch!" The man in the passenger seat flipping her off, telling her to suck his dick. Riggs coked up and pretending not to remember where he'd been yesterday.

It's hard … to breathe.

Ms. Dillon's terrified blue eyes.

Darius had felt a strange protectiveness toward her in that moment. She'd seemed so young, so afraid, so vulnerable. But Darius would find the sick fuckers who'd done this to her, and he would put them away.

Chapter 6

IT FELT SO good to be home again.

Sasha walked slowly upstairs to her bedroom, Nicole behind her carrying her bag of belongings from the hospital.

Nicole set the bag on the bench at the foot of Sasha's bed. "I'll toss the clothes into the laundry. Can I make you a cup of tea?"

"I want a shower first."

"I'll help you get set up." Nicole put the bottle of prescription pain pills on Sasha's nightstand and hung a clean towel on the towel warmer in her bathroom. Then she took a box out of the bag she was holding and opened it. "This is a plastic cover for your wrist. I think you just slide it on."

"Thanks."

"Do you need me to stay just in case?"

"No, thanks. I can manage."

"I have to leave for work in half an hour. I'll go down and make tea. Do you want herbal or green?"

"Green." Caffeine might help Sasha feel more like herself. "Thanks, Nic."

Nicole left her bedroom, shutting the door behind her.

Sasha took down her ponytail and undressed, tossing the clothes Nicole had brought her onto her bed. Then she picked up the plastic sleeve, which she carefully slid over her right arm to keep her incision dry.

She walked into her bathroom, flicked on the light, and paused at the sight of her reflection. The swelling on her lip had gone down, the bruises on her face now purple. A dark bruise covered her left side where her ribs had been broken. A dressing covered the place where Eric had put in the chest tube to reinflate her lung. There were nicks and scratches on her left shoulder and thigh.

She removed the dressing, met her gaze in the mirror. "Badass."

That's what she said, but the sight of her body only drove home how very lucky she was to be alive. And it *was* luck. She hadn't had time to do anything to save herself beyond turning her handlebars toward the forest.

She started the water, stepped under the hot spray, and washed her hair and body, every step tricky because she had to use her left hand. Still, the hot water was soothing, the clean scents of lavender and vanilla comforting. When she rinsed the soap and conditioner away, she let out a sigh.

She dried herself, combed her wet hair, and did her best to dry it with a towel without bending over. When she stepped out of the bathroom, she heard voices downstairs. She struggled to dress, slipping into a clean pair of panties, shorts, and a T-shirt before making her way carefully downstairs.

She found Detective Silva, Julia, and Nicole sitting at her kitchen table. "Hey."

Detective Silva stood, his gaze meeting hers from across the room. "Ms. Dillon."

Nicole poured tea into a cup for her and set the pot on the table. "They showed up, so I made a whole pot. I've got to go now, but I'll be back at about eight tonight. You're due for your next dose of pain pills in an hour."

"Thanks, Nic." Sasha lowered herself carefully into a chair. "Have fun."

"Always." Nicole grabbed her jacket and breezed out the door.

"She works at the climbing gym." Sasha tried not to feel embarrassed about the panic attack she'd had last time she'd seen Julia and Detective Silva. "I hope you haven't been waiting this whole time."

Julia shook her head. "We just got here. How are you feeling?"

"Sore. It still hurts to breathe or laugh." She picked up her mug of tea and sipped. "I'm guessing you've got more questions for me."

Julia leaned closer, as if to share a secret. "He wants to ask about your love life."

"My love life?"

Irritation flashed across Detective Silva's face, those gray eyes hard. "When a woman is the victim of a violent crime, the person responsible is often a past or current lover, significant other, or spouse."

Sasha started to laugh at the absurdity of this idea, but pain stopped her. "I don't have a significant other or spouse. I've had a couple of boyfriends, but neither of them could have done this. Elias lives and climbs in Switzerland, and Remy works as a fishing guide in Southeast Alaska. There are no hard feelings between us. Elias is from Switzerland and wanted to live near his family. Remy loves the outdoors and lives off-grid in the wilderness. I chose to stay in Scarlet Springs."

Detective Silva wrote this down. "So, no big arguments? No threats? Did either of them ever act violently?"

Again, Sasha was tempted to laugh. "Not at all. Any man who tried to hit me would find himself on his butt in the street."

"Hell, yeah, he would." Julia gave her an approving smile.

"Describe your relationship with Bren Riggs."

"Oh. Right." Sasha had forgotten that Detective Silva wanted to talk to him. "He's a fellow climber. We've never dated or anything like that."

"Has he asked you out?"

"Yes, but that was a few years ago. He came across as a party boy—not my type."

"How did he take rejection?"

She had to think about it. "At first, he didn't seem to believe I wasn't interested. I turned him down a few times before he quit asking."

"How long ago was this?"

Sasha had to think. "I met him at the climbing gym after my third world title, so that would be almost three years ago now. We mostly see each other at the rock gym in Boulder or out climbing somewhere like Eldorado Canyon."

Detective Silva wrote this down then looked up from his notes. "I understand he posted graphic images on social media with your face on them. Can you tell me how you figured out that he was behind it?"

Sasha had known he'd bring this up. She took a sip of tea and started at the beginning.

MS. DILLON HAD JUST BEGUN to tell Darius about the pornographic images when Deputy Marcs received a call on her radio.

"Eight-sixty-five, go ahead." She stood. "Excuse me."

She walked outside to take the call.

Ms. Dillon went on. "I woke up one morning to a bunch of messages from other climbers and supporters with screenshots of the images. The name on the account…"

Deputy Marcs stuck her head through the door. "Multi-vehicle collision in the Canyon. I've got to go. Are you going to be okay, Sasha?"

"I'll be fine."

Darius and Marcs had driven in separate vehicles today just in case she got called away, so this wasn't a problem. "Good luck."

"The name on the account was fake. I flagged it and reported it. It was removed, and the account was closed. Then the next day, there were more images on another account. They were just like the others—my face on other women's naked bodies. I reported it, and the images were deleted again."

Darius listened as Ms. Dillon told him how she'd realized the problem wasn't going to stop unless she did something about it.

"I looked at other things uploaded to that same account. I recognized the scenery and the routes—the Third Flatiron, Redgarden Wall, Cadaver Crack. When you hang out on high rocks, you get to know the landscape."

"I understand. How did you identify Mr. Riggs?"

"After a couple of weeks of daily images, he slipped.

He posted a sickening photo with the caption, 'She climbs like a man, but she fucks like an animal.' Bren had once told me I climbed like a man."

"Then you confronted him."

"Not right away. I was scrolling through some of the other images he'd uploaded and saw a water bottle in the bottom right corner. The water bottle came from one of our shared sponsors. He'd written his name on it."

"Nice detective work." Darius smiled. "I'm serious."

"Thanks." She smiled back and…

Damn.

Darius had felt that down to his toes.

Knock it the hell off.

"What did you do when you realized it was Mr. Riggs?"

"I was angry. He's supposed to be a friend. He had harassed me in public, so I decided to expose him in public."

Ms. Dillon told Darius how she'd gathered every bit of evidence she had and had passed it to her manager and her corporate sponsors. Then she'd posted the whole story on her website, accusing him publicly.

"What happened then?"

"The sponsors contacted him. He admitted he'd done it, and they pulled his sponsorships. He posted a long apology on his blog. I don't believe he wrote it. It didn't sound like him. I hate to say it, but he's not that articulate or intelligent."

Darius could only agree. "Did the posts stop?"

"Yes. The public response was mostly supportive. My fellow Team members backed me up on social media, especially Megs. She has a huge following. I did get some hateful posts from anonymous people and some email threats. I figured the porn images had drawn in creepers."

"I'd say that's pretty likely."

Darius had glanced through her social media last night, including her climbing and exercise videos. The climbing vids had blown him away, but he'd been impressed with how down-to-earth her public persona was. She gave off a wholesome vibe—the beautiful girl next door who just happened to be the world's foremost female climber. That made her a target for a particular subspecies of male asshole.

While she sipped her tea, Darius moved through his list of questions. Had her online harassment increased after she'd outed Riggs? Had she faced other harassment that seemed to come from the same source? Had anyone accosted her in person? Had anyone followed her here or elsewhere? Had she had any negative interactions with fans or fellow climbers online or in person?

She answered his questions one by one. The harassment had spiked for a time. There were some anonymous posters who'd left negative comments whose avatars she recognized. There'd been a few times when fans had crossed her boundaries and made her uncomfortable, but it was hard now to remember details. She'd had a guy yell at her in a coffee shop once in Moab.

"He told me that men don't want women with careers. He said men only want women who are curvy and who want to stay home and have kids. But that was a couple of years ago."

As she continued to answer, Darius saw that she was growing uncomfortable. "Maybe you should take your next dose of pills."

Her face a mask of pain, she nodded. "Yeah, I'll just get… Damn. They're upstairs on my nightstand. I'll be right—"

"I'll get them." Darius left the table and headed up the stairs.

Sasha's house was a spacious, two-story modern home that resembled a large log cabin on the outside. Tastefully furnished, it was nothing like the villas of the celebrities whose cases he'd taken in LA. There was no swimming pool, no tennis courts, no guest wing, no staff rushing here and there. She had four bedrooms, a kitchen, a few bathrooms, and a living area with windows that faced the high peaks. The only unique feature was the bouldering set-up he'd spotted in the backyard.

He found her bedroom at the end of the upstairs hallway, the scents of lavender and vanilla undeniably feminine. He took the bottle of oxycodone from her nightstand and made his way back to the kitchen, where he found her filling a glass with water.

"Thank you." She took two pills and drank them down. "Can we move into the living room? It's hard to sit here."

"Of course."

She carried her cup of tea into the living room and settled in a leather recliner, the electric footrest rising almost silently. "What was that last question again?"

———

DROWSY FROM PAIN MEDS, Sasha did her best to answer Detective Silva's questions, losing her train of thought. "I ... uh... get along well with my fellow Team members. Megs is really strict. She has to be. Lives are at stake. She doesn't tolerate conflict on the Team. If two people weren't getting along, she'd sideline them."

The questions kept coming. Was there anyone in Scarlet Springs who'd crossed the line with her or made her uncomfortable? How did she typically respond to hateful comments and criticism online? Had she ever gotten into a back-and-forth argument with someone on social media?

After almost two hours, Detective Silva closed his notebook.

"Here's what I'd like to do—with your permission, of course." He told her about technology he wanted to attach to her computer that would enable him to monitor and trace her incoming emails. "This system enables us to collect data that is actionable and admissible as evidence in criminal court."

When he started to explain how it worked, she cut him off. "I won't be able to understand any of that. My parents and brother are software engineers, but it's all technobabble to me."

"I understand." He grinned, his features transforming in an instant, going from hard to oh-so-sexy.

Despite her narcotic haze, Sasha's pulse skipped.

He was still talking about her computer. "Before I start, I need to ask whether there's anything on your computer that you don't want me to see?"

"What do you mean?"

"Sex tapes, illegal pornographic downloads, drug deals, illicit gambling—that sort of thing."

"What?" Now Sasha was awake. "No. Of course, not."

"I had to ask. It's happened more than once."

"Really?" She gaped at him.

For some reason, he seemed to find this funny. "Really."

"I must be pretty boring."

He chuckled. "You're *not* boring."

She listened while he finished explaining what he'd

need from her. Then she had to face getting out of the recliner—a painful process with broken ribs.

Detective Silva, already on his feet, held out a hand. "Let me help."

She took his hand and almost let go, her skin tingling from his touch as he drew her to her feet.

You're imagining things.

"Thanks." She led him to her office at the back of the house, sat at her desk, and turned on her computer. While it booted up, she glanced over at Detective Silva to find him perusing her world championship trophies.

Don't you wish you dusted once in a while?

He caught her watching. "Impressive."

Her computer had booted up, so she wrote down her computer and social media passwords on a Post-It note and stuck them to the screen. "There's a power strip under the desk with a few outlets for your equipment."

"Perfect. I'll get my stuff out of the car and be right back. Don't log into any websites or download any email just yet."

"Okay." Sasha sat in her office recliner to wait for him. She needed to sleep, but she didn't know if he'd need more from her.

Detective Silva returned quickly, carrying a large black case. He unlocked it and started connecting things to her computer, typing in her root password to install software.

"This system will be able to tell if I have a stalker?"

He glanced over at her, smiling again. "I thought you didn't like technobabble."

Her pulse skipped once more.

God, he really was beautiful when he smiled.

"I'm curious." Mostly, she was curious about him.

"It won't be able to pop out a person's name, but it can

identify patterns of behavior and lead us to the computers used by possible stalkers."

"Will they know you're monitoring them?"

"Not at all." He talked for a time about recorders and validators. "All of the evidence is downloaded to a digital forensics lab for analysis, and the chain of evidence is protected. It's new technology. We didn't have anything like this when I first started."

She watched him while he worked. "Why did you become a detective?"

He seemed to hesitate. "I studied Criminal Justice in college and went to work for the LAPD after graduating. I ended up on their Threat Management Unit, which deals with stalkers and threats against celebrities."

"That must have been interesting. Did you meet a lot of cool, famous people?"

"I met a lot of famous people." There was an edge to his voice. "Being famous doesn't make a person cool."

"No, I suppose it doesn't." The pain pills had caught up with Sasha now. "I'm going to go upstairs and lie down. I'm so tired."

But before she could stand up and make her way to her room, she was asleep.

Chapter 7

THINKING Ms. Dillon might need his help getting out of the chair, Darius got to his feet, only to find her asleep. For a moment, he stood there, watching her. Her breathing was slow and even, her bruised face peaceful. He knew she was a world-class athlete, yet she looked small, even fragile.

What the hell is wrong with you?

He made it part of his routine to hold himself accountable for his biases, so he wouldn't lie to himself. He felt drawn to her. There was something about her, something that roused his protective instincts. Hell, yes, she was attractive, but there had to be more to his reaction than that. He'd worked with some of the most beautiful stars in Hollywood and hadn't felt this way about any of them.

Then again, Sasha—Ms. Dillon—was nothing like them. As far as he could tell, there was no pretense about her, no conceit, no guile. She hadn't tried to impress him or get him into her bed or asked him to mix her a drink. She didn't even wear makeup, her small breasts obviously natural, her body slender and strong rather than thin.

Get it together, man.

Surprised by the intensity of his response to her, Darius got back to work, opening programs and logging into her social media. He navigated to her most recent post about her bicycle accident, as she'd called it, and began scrolling through hundreds of comments. Most were positive and supportive, but not all. Some mocked her and gloated over her misfortune, while others were hateful.

```
Must not be that good of a climber if she
falls off her bike. Am I right?

She can still spread her legs. That's all
that matters.

She's overrated. Everyone in climbing knows
that.

It's a shame she chose climbing over
marriage and motherhood. She's wasting her
life. Women aren't meant to be athletes.

She'd feel better if she sucked my cock.

I bet she made this up because she's afraid
she'll lose this year.
```

Darius had never understood the impulse to cut down others on social media. Anonymity seemed to bring out the worst in people, allowing them to hurl obscenities and venom at total strangers without consequences. He began flagging responses so the system could start the long process of pinning down their point of origin. Then he looked for repeated posts from the same account, an indication that someone might have an unhealthy obsession.

A knock came at the front door.

He glanced at Ms. Dillon, who slept on, then rose from the chair, thinking it might be Deputy Marcs back from the MVA in the canyon. He'd never been in the position of answering anyone else's door on a job like this. The celebrities he'd worked with had staff to do it for them.

He left Ms. Dillon's office and walked toward the front door to find Megs and Mitch waiting, their arms full. He let them inside.

"Is she sleeping?" Megs whispered.

Darius nodded. "She fell asleep in the big chair in her office."

"We brought lunch and dinner. You go back to what you were doing. We'll put the food in the refrigerator and let ourselves out. There's enough chili, salad, and cornbread here to feed you, too. Nicole told us you were here."

"Thank you." Darius was touched that they'd thought of him. He didn't say so, but he wasn't going to eat food meant for Sasha.

He left them in the kitchen and walked back to the office, where he began to search once again for people who had commented more than once. It was a painstaking process that he would need to repeat across her social media accounts.

He was still working an hour and a half later when he heard Sasha moan. He glanced over his shoulder to find her awake and clutching her left side, her face contorted by pain. "Are you okay?"

She lowered the footrest. "I must have tried to roll onto my side."

Darius stood, helped her to her feet. "Megs and Mitch

dropped off chili, salad, and cornbread. The food is in the refrigerator."

"Thank you." She ran her good hand through her tangled hair, the mingled scents of lavender and vanilla teasing him. "Are you hungry?"

"I'll keep working and head out a bit later to grab something."

But talking about food made his stomach growl.

She looked up at him, a smile playing on her lips. "Don't be silly. The Internet isn't going anywhere. You need to eat, too, and this will be faster than ordering something from Knockers or going out."

Darius couldn't argue with that, so he followed her into the kitchen.

SASHA OPENED THE FRIDGE, where a red pot sat, its lid on. On the shelf below, she found a plastic container holding a salad and a large square of cornbread wrapped in plastic. She took out the cornbread and the salad one at a time then reached for the pot.

"Let me get that. It looks heavy."

Sasha stepped aside, made room for Detective Silva, who took the pot by both handles and set it on her ceramic cooktop.

"Thanks." She lifted the lid, sniffed. "Mitch's chili. How's the hunt going?"

While Detective Silva gave her an update, Sasha retrieved bowls, spoons, and plates for the salad and cornbread, which she stuck in the microwave for one minute. He helped, taking things from her hand and setting them on the table, grabbing a wooden spoon and stirring the chili as it began to boil.

"How often do you read through comments on your posts?"

She set out butter for the cornbread. "I used to read them all, but as time has gone on, I've begun to avoid them. It's not that I don't care about my followers and fans, but the negative comments can mess with your head. To be kinder to myself, I decided to ignore them—or at least try."

"Smart." Detective Silva took her bowl, filled it with chili, and set it down on the table before her. "Arguing with them only feeds their fire. I'm convinced that the people who attack others online—the trolls, the incels—are just looking for attention. Deny them that, and you disincentivize them."

"I need to remember that next time I'm tempted to reason with someone." She sat, and he joined her. "Thanks for your help with lunch."

"You just got out of the hospital." He dug into his chili, his head nodding when he tasted it. "This is good."

Sasha ate her salad first, the flavors of tomato and Italian dressing bright on her tongue. "Do you have a first name, Detective Silva?"

"It's Darius."

"Darius," she repeated. "That's unusual."

"My father is a history professor. My brother's names are Augustus and Maximillian." The warmth in his eyes told her he loved his brothers. "I call them Gus and Max."

"You're all named after emperors. What do they call you?"

"Dare."

"I like it. That's a great name for a detective." Especially one who seemed to be all edges. "Is this your first time coming to Scarlet Springs?"

He'd just taken a bite of cornbread and answered with a nod.

"What do you think of the town so far?"

He finished chewing. "When I heard there was a ski resort, I was expecting it to be like Aspen or Vail. I had no idea it would be so … small. Why do you choose to live here when you could live anywhere?"

Sasha heard the note of disdain in his voice, as if he, like her family, couldn't understand what she saw in this town. She tried not to get defensive. "I moved here because this is where the Team is headquartered, but I fell in love with the place and the people. I couldn't imagine living anywhere else. I know some of the people can seem a little eccentric."

"A *little* eccentric?" There was a hint of a smile on his lips. "Within ten minutes of pulling into town, I ran into a guy with a long beard dressed in buckskin standing in the roundabout, a man who was drinking beer at nine in the morning wearing his wife's bathrobe and underwear, and a woman who said I had warrior energy and wanted to give me a free tarot reading."

Sasha couldn't help but smile. "The man in the buckskin—that's Bear."

Darius looked like he might laugh. "Bear?"

"His real name is Matthew, but we call him Bear. When he was a little boy, his family had a homestead west of town. His entire family died of scarlet fever except for him. He grew up alone up there until he learned to trust us and began coming into town."

Darius' brow furrowed. "That's rough."

"The fever damaged his brain. He's got the mind of a child—a child who knows his Bible verses by heart. He's probably the gentlest, meekest person I know. A couple of years back, the town pulled together to hire an attorney to ensure that the homestead remained in his hands after the county tried to steal it. That's the thing I love most—people here take care of each other."

"And the guy in the bathrobe—what's his story?"

"That was Bob Jewell, owner of the Inn. His first wife died when his daughters were little, leaving him heartbroken. He remarried, but he drinks too much. I think he likes to antagonize Rose across the street by going out in his underwear. She's the one who offered you the tarot reading. She means well, but she can't keep a secret."

Darius had finished his chili now. "I understand living here to be close to the mountains and Team headquarters. I think it's great that people support each other, but I wouldn't like everyone knowing my business. Don't you find it cloying?"

Sasha shook her head. "No. It's like having a backstop."

"Scarlet Springs is one square mile surrounded by reality." He chuckled at his own joke. "I would find it suffocating."

Some part of Sasha wanted to defend the town, but she knew there was no point. She'd done the same for years with her parents, and they still made fun of Scarlet. Besides, she didn't want to argue with Darius. He was trying to help her.

She looked down at her lunch, realized she'd eaten only a few bites of her chili. "I guess I'm not really hungry. The salad filled me up."

"I'm not surprised. Narcotics suppress a person's appetite." He stood, carried their dishes into the kitchen, rinsed his bowl, and stuck it in the dishwasher. "Where do you keep the plastic wrap?"

"That drawer." She watched as he tore off a piece, covered her bowl, and stuck it and the red pot back into the fridge. "Thanks. I know this isn't part of your job description."

"At least you haven't asked me to make you a martini or give you a massage."

She stared at him. "People have done that?"

"And worse." He met her gaze, his eyes hard as slate once again, any hint of warmth gone. "I should get back to work. Thanks for lunch."

"You're welcome." Sasha watched him walk away, feeling strangely disappointed.

———

DARIUS FILTERED through Ms. Dillon's emails, irritated with himself. He'd known he shouldn't eat lunch with her, but he'd done it anyway. Yes, it had saved time, but at a price. He'd let down his professional barrier, and he'd hurt her. He'd seen it in her eyes.

He'd been honest when he'd said he would find small-town life suffocating. He much preferred the anonymity of the big city. He could get on with his life, surrounded by people, and yet be completely alone. His last girlfriend had called him a misanthrope. But it wasn't that he disliked people. He simply didn't trust them.

And that right there is why you're still single.

It was probably for the best. Darius' job with Major Crimes demanded long hours and came with real risks. It would complicate his life to have a wife and kids at home. His career had come between him and every woman he'd dated. Darcangelo and Hunter had families and somehow made it work. But they'd gotten lucky.

Keep telling yourself that if it makes you feel better.

He shifted his thoughts back to Ms. Dillon's emails. He found a folder labeled *Haters* in her Saved folder and opened it. It was like taking a deep dive through the darkness of the toxic male psyche. A momentary stab of sympathy cut through his concentration. He knew only too well what it was like to be the target of hate.

He found threats of violence and rape, as well as harassment, much of it sexual in nature. He flagged them all for upload into the system for analysis and tracing, then focused on the emails from the past six months. There'd definitely been an uptick in hate mail after she'd exposed Riggs last April. Most of the senders seemed outraged that she'd reported Riggs, accusing her of seeking publicity and trashing his career. Apparently, Riggs couldn't be blamed for his actions because Sasha, as a woman, had asked for it.

```
What do you expect when you flaunt yourself
in tight shorts? Any real man would react.
```

A real *man. Right. Asshole.*

```
Why did you have to ruin his career? It was
just a joke, you fucking bitch. You should
be hanged with your own climbing rope for
ruining his life.
```

Not quite a death threat, but close.

```
If I get my hands on you, my friends and I
will pass you around like the whore you
are. You'll get a cock in every hole until
you can't walk, let alone climb.
```

This was a threat and likely actionable.

```
It's not natural for a stupid girl to climb
```

like that. I'd need to stick my dick in
your pussy to believe you're not a dude.
Lulz!

Geezus.

These weren't the worst emails Darius had seen, but they were bad enough. Sasha's decision to stand up for herself had resulted in a vicious backlash. The hate hadn't come exclusively from men. Darius had seen several online comments from women, fangirls of Riggs who tried to signal their sexiness to Riggs while downplaying what he'd done to Sasha. Other women bashed Sasha for her appearance.

Who would want her? She's flat-chested.

The dumb bitch must be anorexic or bulimic.

She's ugly. My men like curves, not chicks with abs.

But who'd been angry enough to try to kill her?

Die, bitch!

Making a mental note not to exclude women as persons of interest, he continued reading through her emails.

Another knock came at the front door, but this time Sasha answered, her voice drifting back to him. "Esri! Come in."

A moment later, she appeared in the office doorway. "Esri, the Team therapist, is here. I'll be upstairs in my bedroom if you need anything."

"Thanks."

She was wise to get help so soon after the attack. Left untreated, trauma could come back to thrash a person.

He finished flagging emails and began uploading the concerning ones into the system. All new emails, posts, and comments would be uploaded automatically, regardless of who sent them, each embedded with code that would enable Darius to trace their origins. This meant that the most tedious part of this job was done.

He stood, stretched, and was wondering where he might get a good workout in this town when his phone buzzed.

It was Deputy Marcs.

"Silva here. What's up?"

"You'll want to meet me out front and tag along with me to the Boulder County Jail. I just heard from the ranger for Boulder County. They pulled that trail cam footage from Boulder Falls. It shows Riggs and his buddy, Watts, violating a bat closure and smoking pot. When the ranger when to give them a summons, they became abusive and uncooperative. The ranger took them into custody for violating a bat closure, smoking on open space, and obstructing a peace officer."

"Maybe that's what Riggs was hiding."

"Maybe, but there's more. Riggs and Watts were at the Falls that day, but the time stamp shows them on the trail a full hour and eight minutes after Sasha was hit. That means they had more than enough time to run her off the road before they hit the trails. I can be there in ten minutes."

"I'll be ready in five."

Chapter 8

SASHA HEARD Darius leave the house. "I guess he's finished here."

Esri glanced out the window. "He's outside talking with Tommy Squibb."

The Scarlet PD had an officer watching her house.

"Oh, he *is* good-looking—and tall." Esri was about Sasha's height, her dark hair, features, and brown skin showing her mixed Tibetan and Jewish heritage.

"Darius is good-looking, but he's also ... *cold*. He doesn't smile much. He's like a super sexy android or something."

Esri turned back to her. "Most people aren't as open as you are, and most don't smile as often as you do. I bet he's seen a lot of awful things in his line of work. Law enforcement officers often carry a lot of trauma. One way they deal with it is to shut off the negative emotions. The downside is that you can't turn off just *one* emotion. When you turn one off, the others go with it."

"That's sad." Sasha wondered whether that was the case for Darius.

Esri glanced out the window again. "He's leaving with Julia in her squad car."

"I hope this means they've found them."

Esri's gaze was focused on Sasha once more. "So do I. That would give you peace of mind, wouldn't it?"

Sasha nodded. "At least I'd know they can't hurt me again, and I might find out why they did it. I just don't understand why anyone would want to kill me."

Even saying those words made her stomach knot.

Esri's brown eyes were warm with understanding. "We want violence to make sense because that helps us feel safer. It gives us the illusion of control. If we know why someone harmed us, we imagine that we can prepare ourselves and avoid that situation in the future. But often, violence *doesn't* make sense. Sometimes the logic is buried in the mind of the perpetrator. Living with uncertainty after a trauma like this is difficult."

Tears filled Sasha's eyes again, and she reached for another tissue. "I can't let this change me. I can't let this steal my happiness."

"Life *does* change us. Look how being part of the Team has changed who you are in *good* ways. Your priorities and how you view climbing are different now. Traumatic experiences change us, too. The people who are rescued by the Team—that's often the worst day of their lives."

Sasha sniffed. "I hadn't thought about that. I'm always on a high after a rescue. But when the Team rescued me, it *was* the worst day of my life."

Esri took her hand. "Moving forward means processing this experience so that your mind can heal just like your body heals. I can offer EMDR—Eye Movement Desensitization and Reprocessing, but there are many paths to healing trauma. I can also refer you to therapists who use ketamine-assisted psychotherapy for PTSD."

Sasha shook her head. "I'd rather stick with you, if that's okay."

"Of course, it's okay." Esri explained what EMDR was and how it used the eye movement associated with REM sleep to help the brain process traumatic events. "The sooner we start, the better. I would recommend two sessions a week for a few weeks, until you start feeling more settled."

Sasha had never shied away from a challenge. She trained her body to perform at peak efficiency, and that meant getting enough rest, icing sore joints, and pampering herself when her body needed it. Her mind was just another part of her body. While her physical injuries healed, it made sense to heal her mind, too.

"Can we start tomorrow?"

"Tomorrow's Saturday, but I'm happy to see you." Esri drew her phone out of a small handbag, tapped its screen a few times. "How about eleven?"

Sasha didn't have to check her calendar. She'd had nothing planned beyond training and packing for her trip to Slovakia, and now that was canceled. "That's fine."

"We'll meet at my clinic. You know where that is, right?"

Sasha nodded. "I can't drive, but the walk will do me good."

"If you're not feeling up to walking, I'm sure Megs or someone else will be happy to drive you. Maybe Squibb can give you a lift. He'll have to follow you anyway."

Sasha laughed—then moaned. "I can't laugh. It hurts too much."

"Sorry." Esri stood. "You stay where you are. I can find my way out."

Sasha got to her feet. "It's time for another dose of pain meds anyway."

She walked Esri to the door and thanked her for making a house call. "I really appreciate it."

Esri drew a woolen hat over her short, dark hair. "That's what I'm here for."

Sasha waved to Tommy, then shut the door and locked it. Normally, she wouldn't think of locking her door in the middle of the day, but there was nothing normal about any of this.

She found her oxycodone, took two pills, and carried them with a glass of water toward the stairs. She needed sleep. But when she reached the foot of the stairs, she turned toward her office instead.

Inside, she found two pieces of equipment attached to her computer, flashing lights indicating that some kind of program was running. The sight of them ought to have made her feel safer. Instead, these gadgets were an unwelcome reminder that two men had tried to run her down. But Darius, Julia, and so many others were working hard to catch the bastards.

You're safe.

Trying to focus on that, she went upstairs to her bedroom and did her best to make herself comfortable in the recliner. She drew her comforter up to her chin, closed her eyes, and was soon asleep.

DARIUS SIGNED himself into the Boulder County Jail and followed Deputy Marcs through the guarded entrance into Intake, where new arrests were fingerprinted, photographed, and booked into the system. They made their way to the Tank, an area of holding cells furnished only with steel benches.

An officer waved to Marcs, a grin on his face. "What are you doing down here?"

"I've come to chat with some of humanity's finest." Marcs looked over at Darius. "I ran Watts through the system and found nothing. He served a short time in the army but received an other-than-honorable discharge for drug use."

Darius wasn't surprised. "Uncle Sam doesn't want him."

"I asked the jail captain to hold them in separate cells."

"Good thinking." That would deprive them of the chance to sync their stories. "I'll talk to Riggs first, while you question Watts. Then we'll compare notes and switch."

"Sounds good."

Darius found Riggs sitting on the floor of his cell, looking uneasy. His cellmate—a big, bald guy with prison tattoos—was dozing on the bench, arms crossed over his chest. If *this* made the kid uncomfortable, he'd have one hell of a hard time in prison.

A corrections officer unlocked the cell and motioned to Riggs. "Come on, sweetheart. This nice detective wants to have a little chat."

Looking petulant, Riggs got to his feet and walked out of the cell. The CO cuffed him and led him and Darius to a secure interview room, locking the door behind them.

Riggs sat, his gaze on the wooden table.

Darius sat across from him, put his notepad and pen on the table, and waited, watching Riggs closely, allowing his silence and the tension of the situation to put Riggs more on edge than he already was.

Riggs lasted less than a minute. "What the fuck do you want? Are you going to ask me questions or just sit there?"

Still, Darius said nothing, watching Riggs, allowing the tension to build.

"Look, yesterday when you came to my house, I thought you'd come to bust us for violating the closure. That's why I didn't want to admit that we'd been there." Riggs shifted uncomfortably in his chair. "They're threatening me with a thousand-dollar fine and jail time over a bunch of fucking bats."

When Darius said nothing, Riggs went on a rant.

"This is supposed to be a free country, but there are places on *public* land where they won't let us climb. Those routes are closed forever now because of bats. All we did was climb and smoke a joint. We didn't go near the bats. Aren't you going to ask me anything?"

Darius knew it was time. "How stupid are you? You violated a wildlife closure, and, while you were there, you looked straight into a wildlife cam. That's first-rate idiocy, man. Truly top-notch. Congrats."

"I didn't think they checked them." Then comprehension dawned. "You asked them to check, didn't you?"

"Do you think I wouldn't try to confirm your alibi? It turned out not to be much of an alibi, by the way. Violating the wildlife closure and acting like a dick to the ranger are the least of your problems."

Riggs looked confused. "What do you mean?"

"Let me spell it out for you." Darius leaned closer, pinned Riggs with his gaze. "I'm going to need an hour-by-hour account of what you did the day Ms. Dillon was attacked. If you can't provide that, I'm going to believe that you and Watts were in that vehicle and that you tried to kill her. And that big, friendly guy in your holding cell? You'll end up in prison surrounded by men who make him seem like a puppy."

Darius let that sink in. "If I were you, I'd cooperate and save myself some grief. Your buddy is probably spilling his guts to Deputy Marcs right now. Maybe he's cutting a deal, ratting you out to save his own ass."

Riggs' pupils dilated—an adrenaline response. "You can't put me in prison for something I didn't do!"

Darius glared at him. "Convince me! I want to know every damned thing you did on September fifteenth —*everything*. Give it to me hour by hour, and don't bother to lie. When we finish here, I'm getting a warrant to search your phone records—texts, social media, location data. That will give us a good idea of where you were—and when."

Unsurprisingly, Riggs' version of events was different this time. Rather than the two of them returning to his house to get high and talk about future climbing projects, Riggs had returned alone. He'd jerked off to his favorite porno, smoked a bowl of marijuana, and fallen asleep.

"What time did you get home?"

"I don't know—about one-thirty, I think."

"Did anyone see you there? Can anyone back you up?"

"Kyle knows."

"When did Watts get back?"

"It was just after three. We got into his car and drove up to the Falls, where we climbed until it got too dark. Then we came home and ordered pizza, like I said. We were home the rest of the night."

"Where did Watts go?"

Riggs' gaze dropped to the table. "He went to score the coke."

"You didn't go with him?"

Riggs shook his head. "I never go. The dude he buys from doesn't want to work with anyone he doesn't know."

"Do you know who this person is or where he lives—which city?"

"Nah, man. Kyle has never told me his name."

"How long have you known Watts?"

"I don't know—about five years, I guess. Kyle had just gotten out of the army and wanted to learn to climb."

"Where did you meet?"

"We met at a party, I think."

Deputy Marcs tapped on the window.

"One last thing." Darius closed his notepad. "Did you show your face to that trail cam to prove to us that you were at the Falls?"

Riggs looked confused. "No. Why would I do that? I didn't know anyone was going to see it."

The kid was talking, so Darius decided he deserved a reward. "Do you need anything to drink, a trip to the restroom before we go on?"

Riggs shook his head. "We're not finished?"

Darius stood, ready to compare notes with Marcs. "Not yet."

———

IT WAS dark when Sasha awoke. Feeling disoriented after a deep sleep, she carefully got out of her chair and made her way downstairs, turning on the lights as she went. She got a drink of water and closed the blinds in the living room, shutting out the dark. Then she settled on the sofa to check her social media.

She'd been dreading this, some part of her afraid of what she might see online. That's exactly why she needed to do it. She couldn't let fear get the better of her. No matter what anyone had posted, they couldn't hurt her through her phone.

She scrolled through the responses, the overwhelming majority of which were kind and supportive. People from around the world wished her a speedy recovery, some of them fellow climbers and some fans.

```
I'm so sorry to hear about your accident!
You're such a role model for me. I'm
sixteen and just started climbing.
```

```
Feel better, champ! We'll be cheering you
on next year when you clinch that title
once more.
```

```
So sorry! You're the greatest, and you'll
be back. For now, just heal.
```

The tension slowly left Sasha's body as she went from one social media platform to another, soaking in the good wishes and kind words. Yes, there were a handful of hateful posts, too, but most of them were puerile and ridiculous. Spread her legs?

Not for you, scumbag.

A knock at the door made Sasha jump.

Good hand pressed against her ribs, she stood and walked to the door to find Nicole standing there, nose against the glass, Mocha, her six-month-old chocolate lab puppy, on a leash beside her.

Sasha let her inside. "Hey, Nic. You're off early. Hey, Mocha, girl."

Nicole let Mocha off her leash. "The place was pretty slow. Bowen let me go early when I told him I was going to make you supper."

"That was kind of him." Sasha locked the door behind her. "Megs and Mitch brought chili, salad, and cornbread. It's in the fridge if you're hungry. I can help."

"You just rest." Nicole set down her backpack by the

door, tossed her jacket on top of it. "You and Mocha can keep each other company."

Sasha knelt, scratched the puppy behind the ears. "Who's the cutest puppy ever?"

Mocha's entire body wagged.

"That's right, girl. *You* are." Sasha loved animals, but she traveled too much to have a pet. "Come snuggle with me."

Nicole's head was in the fridge. "This smells wonderful. Does this bowl of uneaten chili belong to you—the one wrapped in plastic?"

"Yes. I just wasn't that hungry." Sasha led the puppy to the sofa, sat, and patted the cushion beside her. "Will you keep me company, Mocha?"

The pup jumped up, licked Sasha's face, then flopped down beside her, her head resting on Sasha's thigh, her big brown eyes gazing lovingly up at Sasha.

While Sasha stroked Mocha's silky fur, Nicole got dinner ready and caught her up on happenings at the gym. "Everyone who came through the doors today asked about you. They've got a giant get-well card on the wall for members to sign."

"Aw! How sweet is that?"

"How did it go with the sexy detective today?"

"You mean Darius? That's his name." Sasha told her about her conversation with Darius and how he'd warmed up for a moment when they'd talked about his brothers. "He helped me out of a chair, and he got lunch ready, too."

Nicole stirred the chili. "It sounds like he likes you."

"I doubt it. He and I are nothing alike."

"Hey, opposites attract. Isn't that what they say?"

Sasha dismissed that crazy idea without comment. "He smiled a few times, and when he smiles, he's so damned good-looking he could melt your panties. But most of the time, he was dead serious. Esri said that some people in law enforcement shut off their emotions because they've seen so many terrible things."

"You talked to Esri?" Nicole carried the salad and cornbread to the table.

"I called, and she came over. We had a session in my bedroom and talked for about an hour."

"Did it help?" Nicole set bowls of chili on the table with spoons. "Dinner's ready."

"Thanks! Excuse me, Mocha. I need to get up." Sasha slowly stood and went to sit at the table, Mocha following her and curling up near Nicole's feet. "It did help. You know Esri. She's always so calm. She thinks I should have two sessions a week for a few weeks and then see how I feel."

While they ate, Sasha explained what EMDR was and why it was important to start therapy now.

Nicole dabbed her lips with a paper napkin. "I think you're incredibly brave. You just got home from the hospital, but you're already getting to work."

"Nothing worthwhile is easy. I refuse to let this stop me, Nic."

Nicole reached over, rested a hand on her good arm. "It won't. Trust me. I know you. It won't."

"Thanks. That means a lot to me."

Nicole buttered a piece of cornbread. "Where is that sexy detective now?"

"I'm not sure. He and Julia left in her squad car when Esri was here." And then because it seemed important, Sasha added, "Esri thinks he's hot, too."

Chapter 9

IT HAD TAKEN LESS than thirty minutes for Darius to get a warrant for Riggs' and Watts' phones. They'd driven the phones to the Digital Forensics Lab at the DPD, which would use special software to download all data, including texts, voicemails, contacts, and messages that had been deleted. Then they'd started the long drive back to Scarlet.

"Riggs has motive, opportunity, and no solid alibi." Deputy Marcs' headlights reflected off the rocky canyon walls. "It has to be Riggs."

Darius feared he was beginning to enjoy these arguments with Marcs. "He has motive, opportunity, and no alibi at all—and we have no concrete evidence that ties him or Watts to the crime."

"What more do we need—a text message from Riggs to Watts saying, 'Hey, bruh, want to run over Sasha Dillon after lunch?'"

Darius chuckled. "That would do it. So would fingerprints in the vehicle or cell phone location data that puts them near Scarlet or a credible witness who can ID them as the two men who stole the vehicle."

"We'll have to hope that their prints are a match for those they found in the SUV, because there are no witnesses, no street cams, and cell phone location data is too unreliable to interest the DA. If the prints don't pop…"

"If the prints aren't a match, we work the case. No one said this job was easy."

"What did you think of Watts? He's cagey as hell."

Darius had noticed that, too. "That could be an artifact of his time in the military or maybe addiction. He strikes me as a man who doesn't think far beyond his next high. With any luck, his phone will show us where we can find his dealer."

They lapsed into silence, both of them disappearing into their own thoughts.

Then Marcs slammed on the brakes as an enormous *something* jumped into the road, bounding across the highway in front of them in two giant leaps, the headlights showing tawny fur and a long tail.

"Now you can tell your buddies you've seen a mountain lion."

"That thing was *huge*." Darius stared after it, but the big cat had already disappeared into the trees.

"You hungry?" Marcs drove on. "Knockers is open until midnight on Fridays. They usually have live music— the Timberline Mudbugs, Davey Jane, Gold Dust Creek."

Darius hadn't heard of them but didn't say so. "Just drop me off at Ms. Dillon's place. My vehicle is parked there. I'll head back to the Inn and order something. How late is the climbing gym open?"

He needed some food and a way to burn off tension. He did some of his best thinking while working out. He usually went for a run in the park near his condo after work, but that mountain lion had changed his mind about running at night up here. He would hit the gym instead and then pick up some takeout from Knockers.

"It's Friday night, for God's sake. Don't you ever chill out?"

"The sooner we wrap this up, the sooner Ms. Dillon will be safe, and we'll be free to move on to other things. Exercise helps me think."

"Workaholic." She shook her head. "I think the climbing gym closes at nine, but the rock wall at Knockers is open until just before midnight."

They passed the town limit sign for Scarlet Springs, the canyon opening to reveal a small bowl-shaped valley full of twinkling lights. Marcs drove through the roundabout and then on to Sasha's house.

"Are you sure I can't change your mind?" Marcs drew to a stop, her engine running. "Joe has the best selection of single malt in the area."

"I'll have to check it out some other time." Darius unbuckled his seat belt and climbed out, leaning down to make eye contact. "Thanks for your hard work today. We haven't cracked it yet, but we're getting closer."

"From your mouth to God's ears."

He closed the door and walked toward his vehicle, waving at the police officer on duty outside Sasha's house. Thirty minutes later, he pulled into the climbing gym's parking lot, wearing running shoes, joggers, and an old T-shirt.

Inside, he found a handful of people moving like spiders up the brightly colored holds, ropes trailing behind them like webs. He paid and headed toward the nearest open treadmill, only to stop when he saw it.

A three-foot-high get-well card for Sasha.

Made of newsprint, construction paper hearts, and lots of glitter, it was stuck to the wall just inside the door. A photo of Sasha holding up a world championship trophy was stuck in the center. There must have been at least a hundred signatures and encouraging messages written in a rainbow of colors.

Get better soon, Sasha! You're still the greatest ever!

Can't wait to see you getting vertical again!

Wishing you a speedy recovery! XOXOXO

He glanced at the photo, saw the excitement in Sasha's eyes and the happy flush in her cheeks, and felt an answering hitch in his chest.

Her smile lights up the room.

What the fuck was wrong with him?

More than a little disgusted with himself, Darius made his way to the treadmill, programmed it for interval training, and ran.

"ARE you sure you don't need my help?"

Sasha smiled to reassure Tommy. "I'll be fine. Thanks for the ride, Tommy, and thanks for keeping me safe."

Tommy stood just a little taller, straightened his police baseball-style cap, his dark blond hair ruffled by the wind. "I'm happy to help."

Sasha had spent the past hour with Esri, going over EMDR, learning some relaxation techniques, and giving the eye movement a try to make sure she felt comfortable with it. She'd felt silly watching the lights move back and forth, but it was the first time she'd talked about the hit-and-run without crying. Esri had told her that was likely more a result of distraction than EMDR.

"It takes time. Just trust the process."

"Thanks, Esri."

Sasha slipped out of her coat, let it fall over a chair,

then went to get a drink of water and an oxy. She hadn't taken anything this morning because she'd wanted to be clear-headed for her appointment with Esri. But her ribs and wrist ached unceasingly. She'd just opened the bottle of oxycodone when a knock at the door made her jump out of her skin and sent pills flying everywhere. "Damn it!"

She glanced toward the door, saw Darius waiting there, then looked down at the tablets scattered at her feet. "Come in. It's unlocked—I think."

Darius entered wearing a dark navy business suit and blue striped tie. "I didn't mean to startle you."

She held up her left hand to stop him. "Watch where you step. I spilled my oxycodone everywhere."

She started to kneel to pick them up but made the mistake of bending a little too much. She jerked upright, sucked in a breath at the stabbing pain in her side.

"Are you okay?" Darius helped her stand, his hand holding hers a bit longer than necessary, the warmth of his touch sending sparks of awareness through her.

She nodded, looked into his eyes, and her breath caught in her throat.

For a moment, neither of them moved.

He cleared his throat, let go of her hand. "Go sit down. I'll take care of this."

While Sasha walked to the sofa and sat, Darius knelt and picked up the tablets and dropped them back in the bottle. When he'd finished, he brought the bottle to her, together with her glass of water.

Hoping to wean herself off painkillers sooner rather than later, she took only one oxy this time. "Thank you."

"Sorry again to have startled you."

Sasha couldn't help but feel embarrassed. "Please don't apologize. It's my fault. I totally overreacted. I—"

"No, you didn't." He sat beside her, his gaze soft. "I've

seen trained federal agents come apart when startled after a major incident. Your nervous system is on high alert—and with good reason. Don't be hard on yourself, Sasha."

"Have you ever been through something that shook you up like this—a major incident?" The moment the words were out, she realized she'd been insensitive. She looked away. "Sorry. I shouldn't have asked. I just wondered…"

"It's okay. I don't mind you asking." His gray eyes filled with shadows. "Yes, I have—more than once. It isn't easy, but you'll get through it. I know you will."

For a split second, she thought he was going to take her hand again—or maybe she just hoped he would. But his hand came to rest in his lap, his fingers curled into a fist.

"H-how is the investigation going?"

His expression had become unreadable once again. "I have a couple of questions."

"Okay."

"Do you know Kyle Watts, Riggs' buddy?" He handed her a mugshot.

Her pulse spiked. "You arrested him?"

"Boulder County brought him in for violating the bat closure at Boulder Falls and obstructing a peace officer."

She let out a breath, disappointed. For a second, she'd thought it was over.

She studied the image, tried to remember if she'd seen that face anywhere. "I don't recognize him. Does he climb?"

Darius nodded. "I think so, though not professionally. He was kicked out of the army for drug use."

Sasha handed him the mugshot. "I've seen Riggs out climbing a handful of times in the past few years. There was a guy with him, but we didn't hang out together. I never talked with him."

Darius slipped the mugshot back into his pocket and drew out a folded piece of paper. "Are you familiar with this avatar? This was posted last night."

The paper held the printout of a comment on her tweet about her supposed bike accident. Beside a close-up image of someone's raised middle finger was a comment that made her stare.

```
A bike accident? I heard she was run off
the road in a hit-and-run.
```

"Do you recognize the avatar?" Darius asked again.

"There's something familiar about it. I must have seen it on other comments."

Darius nodded, slipped the paper into his pocket. "Who knows the truth about your little *accident*?"

"Everyone here in Scarlet knows. My family, too. The police in Denver and Boulder. Someone must have said something or posted about it. Why? Do you think the person who posted this is one of the guys in the SUV?"

The thought sent chills down her spine.

"I wouldn't rule out the possibility. This is the only post or comment from that account. There are no other tweets. Just this."

"Can you find them?"

"The poster used a VPN, so we're going to have to request the records from the company. I was hoping you knew the person who used that avatar."

"I don't."

He stood. "I'll head back to your office and make sure everything is running the way it's supposed to."

He turned to go, but Sasha called after him. "Darius?"

He stopped, faced her.

"Thanks."

"You got it."

And then he was gone.

———

DARIUS SAT at the desk and logged into the system, wanting to kick himself squarely in the ass. Had he lost his mind?

In the past eighteen hours, he'd had a physical reaction to a photo of Sasha. Then he'd gone back to his room at the Inn to check her social media and had ended up watching more of her climbing videos instead. He'd had an even stronger physical reaction to those. Now, he'd called her by her first name, held her hand much longer than necessary—and had found himself fighting not to *kiss* her.

What the fuck was wrong with him?

You're attracted to her.

Yeah, no shit. But it was worse than that.

He *liked* her.

He was sexually attracted to her, *and* he liked her.

He'd worked for a decade protecting some of the most beautiful women in Hollywood—models, and actresses whose faces graced magazine covers, stars whose fake tits and asses earned them millions—and he'd felt nothing. Now, here in weird little Scarlet Springs, he'd finally crossed the line and grown attached to the victim in one of his cases.

What. The. Fuck?

Even as he hated himself for it, he understood. Sasha was nothing like any of the women whose cases he'd taken while at the LAPD.

She was warm and genuine, not a conceited bone in her body. Rather than designer gowns, silk bathrobes, and high heels, she wore leggings, T-shirts, and running shoes, no makeup on her face. More than that, she had an air of innocence about her, something pure and kind that life hadn't yet beaten out of her. It showed in her smile, in those blue eyes, in the sweetness of her voice.

And she needed his help.

What she needs is for you to put away the bastards who hurt her.

Darius ought to remove himself from the case. He ought to demand that Irving give this assignment to someone else.

There is no one else.

There was no one else at DPD with his skill set or experience. That meant he needed to get his mind off Sasha and focus on the job.

He glanced through the data the program had captured. Forensics had uploaded its report from yesterday this morning. They had been able to identify a few of the haters, but none of them lived in Colorado. Some came from overseas bots—Russia, China, Belarus—while others came from actual accounts. So far, nothing pointed to Riggs or Watts, but they were just getting started.

Having done what he'd come here to do, Darius left Sasha's office and headed back down the hallway. He'd asked Sheriff Pella for some space at the sheriff's substation so he could set up an office. Since he didn't yet have a keycard to the building, Marcs had agreed to meet him there even though it was her day off. He was used to working with a desk and a whiteboard and felt disorganized without it. The Inn was comfortable and had adequate Internet, but sorting through documents set in piles all over his suite seemed like a great way to miss something. He hoped to get set up today so he could think through the case before Monday.

He opened his mouth to tell Sasha he was leaving, but

the words died on his lips. Sasha had fallen asleep in a recliner, her blond hair spilling over her shoulders, her bruised face peaceful.

Shit.

He didn't want to wake her, but he had no choice.

He knelt beside the chair, touched her arm. "Sasha?"

Her eyes opened, and she smiled, a sweet sleepy smile. "Darius."

"Sorry to wake you. I have to head out now. I didn't want to leave you alone and asleep with the door unlocked."

"Oh. Right." Fully awake now, she took the hand he offered and got carefully to her feet. "Are you coming back today? Just in case I fall asleep again."

So, she wanted him to come back.

"I'll be back Monday—unless something comes up. I'm going to spend the weekend going through the evidence and the forensic data from your social media."

"Okay. Thanks." Was that disappointment on her face?

He opened the door, stepped out into a cold wind. "Stay warm and get some rest."

"I will. Thanks again."

As he walked down her front steps, he heard the door lock behind him.

The sheriff's substation was a short drive away, and he found Deputy Marcs waiting for him, a parka over a pink T-shirt and jeans, her hair out of its ponytail.

The moment Marcs saw him, she burst out laughing. "You're wearing a suit on a Saturday! Oh, my God. This is too good. Wait. I need to get a photo."

Darius reached out to block her phone's camera. "Knock it off."

"Oh, come on!" She snapped a photo. "I won't put it online, but the girls at the bar at Knockers will love this.

They're used to men in plaid, T-shirts, and jeans, and here you are—Mr. GQ in his polyester slacks."

Hand on his hip, he glared at her. "They're a wool blend. You finished?"

"One more. Okay." She drew a keycard out of her pocket and opened the door. "Pella says there's a keycard in your mailbox. I'll show you your office. It's got a whiteboard and a big conference table—everything who wears fancy suits on his day off needs to feel organized."

"Great." Darius followed her inside.

Chapter 10

DARIUS TOOK a drink of lukewarm coffee, his gaze focused on the whiteboard as he mulled over the evidence, starting at the beginning with the undisputed facts.

Sasha Dillon was an attractive, five-time world-champion climber. She got hate mail and hateful comments online from various sources, most of them male. Last April, she had outed Bren Riggs for posting pornographic images with her face on social media. As a result, Riggs had lost his sponsorships and was still angry about it. Some members of the public—most of them Riggs' fanboys—had been angry, too.

This past Wednesday, at approximately one-thirty in the afternoon, two individuals, at least one of them male, had stolen an SUV in Boulder and driven up the canyon to Scarlet Springs. The perpetrators had passed Sasha on the highway at about two-twenty, one flipping her off and yelling obscenities. Then they had pulled into a vehicle turnout and waited for her to pass them.

Sasha, hoping to avoid another confrontation, had crossed the highway. But the perpetrators had been undeterred. They'd accelerated across the centerline, made straight for her, and hit her bike with the SUV, sending her over the embankment and causing her serious injury. A male had angrily shouted, "Die, bitch!" Then they'd driven away and abandoned the SUV at Boulder Falls.

Darius was confident that this hadn't been a random hit-and-run. Sasha had been targeted deliberately. The perpetrators' actions were too personal and vicious to be random or spontaneous. The bastards had passed her and then *waited* for her in the vehicle turnout before striking.

Darius had thought long and hard about this detail. Maybe they'd done it to avoid being seen by the ranger who'd been a short distance behind them, as Deputy Marcs had suggested. Or perhaps they'd passed her to confirm that the blonde on the bicycle was, indeed, Sasha before they hit her. Either way, it meant they'd known they were going to run her down before they'd done it.

All of that was crystal clear.

But when it came to suspects…

Riggs had clear motive and no alibi. By his account, he'd been home alone when the SUV was stolen and Sasha was hit. If he'd stolen the car after Watts had left to buy drugs, he could have made it up the canyon to Scarlet in time to hit Sasha and ditch the vehicle at Boulder Falls— assuming he'd had a wingman and a way to make it back to Boulder before Watts returned.

That raised some questions. Could someone thumb a ride back to Boulder that quickly? Could the perpetrators have hired a car to meet them at Boulder Falls? Did Scarlet Springs have a taxi or bus service? Who would have been Riggs' wingman if Watts was in Denver? And why would Riggs come back to climb at the Falls if he'd just committed a crime nearby?

Darius wrote *transportation* on the board as a reminder to check all of those possibilities. As for Riggs…

He could have done it, but Darius wasn't convinced that he had. The way he'd reacted when they'd discussed the trail cam footage convinced Darius that he hadn't looked into the camera to establish an alibi.

I didn't think they checked them. You told them to check, didn't you?

Riggs might be many things, but clever wasn't one of them.

Then there was the shock in Riggs' eyes when Darius had suggested that Watts was ratting him out. He'd had an adrenaline reaction, and there'd been an edge of desperation in his voice.

You can't put me in prison for something I didn't do!

Had he been afraid because he was guilty? Or had it been the idea of going to prison for a crime he hadn't committed that had made his pupils dilate?

Darius understood that fear only too well.

Watts hadn't been as easy to read as Riggs. Marcs said he'd pretended to be cooperative at first but had dropped that façade the moment she'd asked him for proof that he'd been in Denver buying cocaine that afternoon. After that, he'd grown hostile, insulting Marcs and the police in general, refusing to answer most of her questions.

"If you've got something, arrest me. If not, fuck off."

Darius had taken a turn with Watts, first asking him what he thought of Riggs, trying to get him to relax again. Watts had told him what a great climber Riggs was and how fun it was to hang with him. He'd clammed up again when Darius had asked him about where he'd been and what he'd done on the day Sasha was attacked. Of the two, Watts was definitely the smarter.

So, where did this leave the investigation?

They had two people of interest with motive and opportunity—and no objective evidence to link them to the crime. Darius had an avatar from a suspicious comment he wanted to connect to an ISP address and a name. He also had a long list of haters to identify and investigate. It was a painstaking process, and there were no shortcuts.

He wasn't going to solve the case by standing here and staring at the board. So, he put a cap on the dry erase marker he'd been holding and set it aside. It was late afternoon. He had time to hit the gym before grabbing something for dinner. He might even rope up and try a few of the routes.

He grabbed his notebook, turned off the lights, then locked the door, and left the building.

⸻

IT WAS late afternoon when Megs and Mitch came by. Because Sasha was starting to get restless, they offered to drive her to the climbing gym, where she could at least hang out, watch people climb, and maybe even take an easy stroll on a treadmill. She wasn't used to this much inaction.

Megs helped Sasha into her parka. "If you feel up to it, we can head to Knockers afterward and grab a bite with the gang."

"I probably still have leftover chili."

Mitch opened her front door. "It'll keep until lunch tomorrow."

Megs zipped her parka. "Everyone is asking about you. It will do you good to get out—and it will make people shut up."

"What about Tommy?"

"I'll talk to him. He can follow us if he wants." Mitch went outside and walked over to the squad car parked at the curb.

Megs helped her into their vehicle, waited for Mitch, then drove the short distance to the climbing gym, a cold wind and heavy clouds to the west promising snow. She stopped in front of the gym's door. "I'll let you out here, and then I'll go park."

Sasha removed her seat belt. "I'm not used to needing this kind of help."

"I know how you feel." Mitch opened her door and took her hand, steadying her as she climbed out, a kind smile on his face.

Mitch really *did* know. Almost exactly a year ago, he'd been struck on the helmet by a large piece of falling rock and had spent eight days in a coma. He'd had to re-learn how to talk, walk, and climb.

"Thanks."

While Megs went to park, Mitch opened the door, and Sasha stepped inside.

It was the weekend, so the place was busy, all of the routes on the rock wall taken, the weight room and exercise area busy, too.

"Sasha!" Nicole saw her first. "You're here!"

Heads turned, and a cheer went up.

"She's back!"

"That's Sasha Dillon. She was hurt in a bike accident."

"Sasha's here!"

"Oh, God, girl! Look at you! I didn't think we'd see you for a month." Bowen, one of the owners, hurried around the front counter to meet her. "Oh, sweetie, look at those bruises. Are you sure you should be up and about?"

"I'm not going to climb. I just wanted to get out of the house."

"Of course, you did. You're welcome here. Let's get you a chair so you can watch people climb."

By now, a small crowd had gathered around her.

"Give her space! Let my girl breathe!" Bowen pointed to the wall just to the right of the entrance. "We've got a get-well card for you here."

"How sweet is that?" Sasha walked over to it—a large piece of newsprint covered with paper hearts, glitter, little stickers, and dozens upon dozens of cheering messages. She'd heard about it, of course, but seeing all of the kind words put a lump in her throat. She swallowed. "This is amazing."

She'd begun to read through them, grateful for each one, when a familiar voice cut through the chatter around her.

"Are you sure you should be here?"

Sasha found Darius standing beside her. It was the first time she'd seen him wearing anything but a sports jacket, shirt, tie, and trousers, and *damn…*

"I … um… Tommy's outside." How she got the words out, she couldn't say, her mind all but blank, her gaze moving over him.

There were beads of sweat on his temples, his skin flushed. His gray T-shirt stretched over his pecs and left his biceps and corded forearms exposed. His climbing pants hung low on his hips, emphasizing his narrow waist.

"Who is this?" Bowen's voice left no doubt that he, too, found Darius attractive.

Sasha pulled herself together and made the introductions. "This is Detective Darius Silva. He's working on my case. Darius, this is Bowen. He and his husband, Jake, own the gym."

"Nice place." Darius shook Bowen's hand. Then his gaze shifted back to Sasha. "You said Squibb is outside?"

"And we're here, too," Megs said from somewhere nearby.

Bowen leaned closer to Darius, lowered his voice as if sharing a secret. "I'd like to see anyone get past Megs. She's vicious."

"I heard that," Megs said. "And he's right."

Laughter.

It was fun for Sasha to see Darius on her turf. "Are you working out on the equipment or climbing?"

"I just finished that five-nine route in the middle." He pointed.

"Okay. Let's see it."

In short order, Bowen set Sasha up with bubbly water and a chair several feet back from the base of the route. While Mitch tied in to belay Darius, Megs roped up on the route beside them with Nicole on belay so she could coach him.

"Why don't you try the route marked with the red tape. That's a five-eleven."

Darius looked up at the route, uncertainty on his face. "Are you sure you're not trying to make me look like an idiot?"

"Now, why would I do that?" Megs asked in a voice that left some doubt.

For the next hour, Sasha watched Darius climb, while Megs coached and she and Mitch called up advice.

"Get your center of gravity closer to the wall."

"Left foot. *Left* foot. There you go."

"Lean back and shake your arms out one at a time if you need to."

On his third attempt, he topped out without hangdogging or falling. Sasha and Bowen applauded and cheered as Mitch lowered him to the mat.

Darius shook out his arms and flexed his fingers. "You all make this look so easy, but it isn't. My arms are done."

"It gets easier with practice." Sasha stood, gave one of his forearms a squeeze, and found the muscles hard from exhaustion. "You are pumped."

Megs untied herself. "Time for some food and drink."

Sasha couldn't help herself. Hand still on his arm, she gave him an invitation she was pretty sure he'd refuse. "Come with us to Knockers. Have dinner with us."

His gaze locked with hers. "Thanks. I'd like that."

—

DARIUS WANTED to kick himself in the butt. He knew better than to hang out with Sasha and her friends, but he'd been high on adrenaline when she'd invited him. He hadn't been able to look into those big, blue eyes and say no.

The parking lot at Knockers was full, so he found a spot along the street, parked, and walked to the front entrance. Bluegrass music spilled into the sunset as he opened the door. The place was packed, most of the tables taken, couples crowding onto the dance floor, not an empty seat at the bar.

Sasha stood with Megs and Mitch near the hostess station. She smiled when she saw him, speaking loudly to be heard above the music. "I'm so glad you came."

"You're here? Good. I'll grab you a menu." Megs started toward the back.

People called or waved to Sasha as she passed. She didn't bask in the attention, but acknowledged them with that bright smile of hers, calling them by name, waving back. She was so at ease around people, so open and kind.

She's everything you're not.

"Good to see you, Sasha!"

"Welcome back, champ!"

"So glad you're okay!"

Then the man Darius had seen at the roundabout—the big man with the bushy beard—rose from a meal of fried chicken, mashed potatoes, and a tall glass of milk.

"Sasha Dillon." He was as tall as Darius and still dressed in buckskin. He looked down at Sasha, his expression largely hidden behind his beard. "Heal me, Lord, and I will be healed. Save me, and I will be saved."

Sasha took one of his big, callused hands in hers. "It's good to see you, too, Bear. Thank you for your prayers. This is Darius Silva. He's a detective."

Darius wasn't sure Bear understood what that meant, but it didn't matter. "Nice to meet you, Bear."

Bear ducked his head as if shy. "Darius Silva."

They continued toward the table where Darius had eaten lunch before, but this time it was crowded. He recognized a few of the folks. When the people at the table saw Sasha, they got to their feet to welcome her, big smiles on their faces.

Sasha smiled back. "Everyone, this is Darius Silva."

Creed Herrera and Eric Hawke greeted Darius with a handshake.

"Good to see you again, man." Hawke motioned to the pretty dark-haired woman who sat beside him. "This is my wife Vicki and our kids, Caden and Mollie."

"Nice to meet you."

"I'm Austin Taylor. We talked on the phone." Taylor stood, shook Darius' hand. "Good to meet you in person. This is my wife, Lexi, and our kids, Emily and Kit."

Sasha introduced the others. Harrison Conrad and Kenzie with their boy, Bruce. Jesse with his wife Ellie and twins Daniel and Daisy, and little Dylan.

"Ellie's a nurse," Sasha told him. "She helped take care of me."

"I met her at the hospital."

"Oh." Sasha seemed not to remember. "On the other end of the table are Chaska and Naomi and Chaska's sister, Winona, with her husband Jason and their baby boy, Chayton. I think you've already met everyone else."

Darius tried to make eye contact with everyone, did his best to memorize names with faces. "Good to meet you all."

He took a seat at the end of the table, leaving room for Sasha, Megs, and Mitch to sit close to their friends.

Megs sat beside him, handed him a menu, then looked down the length of the table. "Darius just topped out on that new five-eleven route at the gym."

"Way to go!"

"He's new to Scarlet, and he's already crushing five-eleven?"

"A detective who climbs. I like this guy."

Darius wasn't *new* to Scarlet. He was just visiting. And he couldn't take credit for *crushing* the route. "I had a lot of very expert coaching, and it took me a few tries to make it without falling."

Rain and a server who said her name was Cheyenne arrived with drinks, then took their orders. By the time they'd gone, the conversation had moved on, leaving him free to talk with Sasha.

"You did a great job today." There was a soft smile on her lips.

"If that's true at all, it's only because I had so much help." It struck him as crazy that he'd had two of the most famous women climbers in history—both world champions —coaching him.

"You move well. You could easily master that level of difficulty on your own."

He wasn't so sure. "I've watched a few of your climbing videos. I've seen how you move up the rock. You seem immune to gravity. You make it look effortless."

"Thanks, but I've had years of practice. I lived at the rock gym as a teen. I didn't want to do anything else. When my friends got into boys, I just wanted to climb."

"I feel sorry for the boys in your high school. It must have been painful when they realized you'd rather hang with a rock than go out with them."

Was he flirting with her?

Hell, yeah, he was.

Sasha laughed—then grabbed her side, pain contorting her face. "Ow!"

"Sorry about that. I shouldn't have made you laugh."

Just then, a server brought their meals—a jalapeño burger with fries for Darius and a taco salad for Sasha.

"Can I get you anything else?"

"No, thanks." Then Sasha looked up. "What are you doing out from behind the bar, Marcia?"

The woman shrugged. "Just helping."

Still holding her side, Sasha watched Marcia walk away, an amused look on her face. "She wasn't helping. She brought the food so she could check you out."

But Darius was more concerned about Sasha. "Are you okay?"

"I only took one pill when you were there today, and I haven't had anything since. And that was before noon."

That was almost eight hours ago.

"What do you say we get boxes and take the food back to your place?" Darius knew he was treading on dangerous ground, but he couldn't stop himself. "You can take your meds and get some relief."

She nodded. "Okay."

"I'll be right back." Darius got to his feet and went to get boxes.

He knew he was close to crossing a line, but right now, he didn't care.

Chapter 11

BY THE TIME they'd finished eating, the oxy Sasha had taken was starting to kick in, the pain in her ribs and wrist fading.

Darius stood. "I'll clean up. You make yourself comfortable."

"Thanks." She settled on one end of the sofa, picking up the conversation where they'd left off. "So, your family moved to Arizona when you were ten?"

Darius cleared the table and sorted the recycling from the trash. "It was a big change from upstate New York. No snow. No trees in our yard. Hot, dry summers. My brothers and I played outside more often in the winter."

Sasha could believe that. "With a history professor for a father and a music teacher for a mother, you and your brothers must be smart."

"Oh, we are." He chuckled. "Just ask us. We certainly had interesting conversations around the dinner table. By the time I started kindergarten, I probably knew more about the fall of Rome than most adults."

Sasha tried to imagine a precocious five-year-old Darius talking about ancient Rome and found herself smiling. "Were your parents supportive of your desire to become a police detective?"

Darius washed and dried his hands and sat on the other end of the sofa, seeming to dominate the space. "I majored in bio-chem at Tempe my first year, then switched to criminal justice and information technology at the University of Northern Colorado in my sophomore year. Law enforcement wasn't what they'd wanted for me, but they understood."

"Bio-chem was my major, too. Cornell. How did you end up in LA?"

"Cornell? Fancy. A position came open, and I had the skills they—"

A loud *thunk* came from outside on her deck.

Darius was on his feet in a blink. He moved quickly toward her sliding glass door and peeked through the blinds.

But Sasha knew that sound. "The wind is really picking up. I bet that was just my wooden bear that got blown over again."

"You're right. It was the bear. It's starting to snow. You've got wood on your deck. Mind if I start a fire?"

"I'd like that. Thanks."

Sasha watched him work, some part of her purring to see the big stack of wood in his arms, his butt doing amazing things for his climbing pants, his biceps shifting as he piled firewood and kindling next to the stove and built the fire.

Why did he affect her like this? She'd spent her life around strong men, and no one had made her feel this way —as if her senses were heightened and her heart was beating a little too fast. "Why did you leave LA?"

With the fire now crackling, he closed the stove's iron door and returned to his seat on the sofa. "It wasn't any one thing. It was everything. Traffic. Potholes. The cost of living. Plastic people. Celebrity culture. One day I realized I didn't want to be there any longer, so I started looking for something in Colorado. I missed the mountains, the change of seasons, skiing, the laid-back attitude."

Sasha had never seen Darius so relaxed, his gaze warm, his features not quite as hard. "You told me the other day that one of the celebrities you'd worked with had asked you to mix her a martini and give her a massage. Is that the craziest thing that happened?"

"God, no." He shook his head, a grin on his face. "There was an up-and-coming actress who had her personal assistant lead me to her bedroom for an intake interview. The actress was wearing nothing but a silk robe, which *accidentally* fell open a time or two. I was trying to work, but she kept interrupting me, asking me whether I found her beautiful or sexually attractive and wanted to touch her."

Sasha's mouth fell open with surprise. "What did you say? I mean, I suppose she *was* beautiful."

In one motion, Darius leaned closer, bringing his face even with hers, his gaze seeming to pierce her, his lips curving in a lopsided grin that Sasha felt to her core. "Not to me. I prefer *real* beauty, not the synthetic kind."

Sasha's pulse skipped, warmth rushing into her cheeks. She stared into his gray eyes, and for a moment, she thought he might kiss her. "Wh-what did you do?"

He slowly sat back. "I told her that when she was dressed, we could continue talking in her living room. Then I walked out. But enough about that. How did you get into climbing?"

"Every summer, my parents sent my brother and me to

a summer camp in Yosemite. As you know, they're software engineers. They worked long hours and didn't really have much time off. I think I was eight when the camp brought in one of those big, portable rock walls. Each of us got a turn. Some of the kids were scared, but I fell in love with it then and there. I kept getting back in line."

She told him how her parents took her to a rock gym when they'd heard this. "One of the instructors told them he thought I had talent, so they signed me up for lessons. They didn't imagine it would become my career. They just wanted to make sure I had a sport—a way to stay fit."

"What do they think now?"

"They're proud of me, I know, but they also don't like that I live in Scarlet. They don't understand why I won't move back to San Jose or LA and try to parlay my climbing success into a film career or something."

"Is that what you want?"

"Not at all." She was starting to feel drowsy but fought not to show it. She didn't want this time with Darius to end. "If I stop climbing competitively, I would want to teach climbing and focus on rescue work. I'm also interested in wildlife photography."

"Are your parents coming to help you?"

"No. They've got deadlines." The excuse sounded hollow to her ears, and she found herself rushing to make it better somehow. "If I'd been seriously hurt, they'd have come. They *did* send flowers."

He frowned. "I'm glad you've got so much support here in Scarlet."

"Th-thanks." Sasha yawned. "Sorry."

Darius glanced at his watch. "It's late. I should go and let you get some rest. I'll stoke this fire, make sure you're settled, and get back to the Inn."

She didn't want him to go, but she was afraid of

seeming like she was coming onto him like one of those Hollywood stars. Ten minutes later, she stood by her open front door, saying goodnight, snow swirling in the darkness. "Thanks for your company tonight—and your help."

Oh, how she wished he would kiss her.

"Thank you." He gave her a warm smile, reached up, brushed a strand of hair off her cheek, his touch scorching. "Get some rest."

Then he turned and walked to his vehicle.

DARIUS TOSSED and turned all night, endless thoughts of Sasha drifting through his mind, mixing with restless dreams. He gave up pretending to sleep at seven when the scent of freshly baked croissants roused him. Feeling strangely on edge, he got up, showered, dressed in jeans and a dark blue Henley, and went down to the dining room.

He had to give Bob and Kendra Jewell credit. Their French pastry chef, Sandrine, put together a breakfast no sane person would want to miss. He piled his plate high with scrambled eggs, bacon, and freshly sliced fruit, grabbed a couple of warm croissants, and settled at a table near the window.

"A latte this morning, Mr. Silva?" Sandrine had the effortless grace of the French, her dark hair streaked with gray and piled in a twist, her accent pleasing. "Orange juice?"

"Both, please. Thank you."

Outside, fat flakes still fell, the landscape covered in white, evergreen branches drooping with the weight of the snow. As beautiful as the sight was, the sense of unease that had gnawed at him all night didn't let up. He knew damned good and well why.

Sasha.

He'd enjoyed yesterday more than he could say. Getting pro climbing lessons had been a trip. Watching the townsfolk shower love on Sasha had touched him. They'd even opened their arms to him. But those hours alone with Sasha...

He'd been on a handful of dates this past year with women he'd met through dating apps or on the job. One had been a prosecutor. Another had worked for an investment firm. Another had worked in public relations. They'd all been beautiful, interesting, successful women. But none of them had gotten inside him the way that Sasha had.

What was it about her that made her different?

Yes, she was beautiful, intelligent, and kind, but it was more than that.

He'd watched her making her way through Knockers to the Team table yesterday, and he'd seen how easily she connected with others. Her smile was as genuine as her concern for the people around her, and they loved her. She was open and trusting, her big heart worn where everyone could see it.

But she was also the victim of a violent crime and emotionally vulnerable. As the detective assigned to her case, he had no business getting involved with her.

Even so, there'd been a part of him that had wanted to stay—not to sleep with her necessarily, though he would've had a hard time turning her down, but just to be close to her, to hear her voice, to see the sparkle in those blue eyes, to be on the receiving end of that smile.

He understood now why she chose to live in Scarlet Springs. If her parents couldn't be bothered to show up even when she was in the hospital, he doubted they'd given her all the love and nurturance she'd needed growing up. But here in Scarlet, she'd found a way to fill the emotional gaps. The Team was like a family for her, and she had friends here who loved her and would bend over backward to help her.

It floored him that she was still single.

And you're hoping to do something about that, are you?

He couldn't, not now anyway, not as long as he was working on her case.

Darius should go back to Denver and tell Chief Irving that he'd crossed a line. Irving could send someone else, while Darius assisted from Denver. Except that Darius didn't want anyone else on the case.

It doesn't matter what you want, does it?

He finished his breakfast and thanked Sandrine, who was wiping tables. "The croissants are delicious."

"I'm so glad you've enjoyed them. Are you staying with us longer?"

"I'm not sure."

If he *was* staying, he needed to do laundry. Darius had packed for a week—work clothes, exercise clothes for running or climbing, and the clothes he had on his back today. "Is there a washer or dryer here I can use?"

Sandrine began to clear away his dishes. "No, but Bob and Kendra might let you use their washer and dryer. I can ask for you if you'd like. We know you're working hard to help Sasha."

"No, thanks. I was just checking. Thanks for breakfast."

"You're welcome."

He went back to his suite, shoved his dirty laundry into his duffel, and carried it down to his vehicle, the cold sucking the breath from his lungs.

Austin Taylor was busy shoveling snow, woolen hat on

his head, sunglasses hiding his eyes. He stopped when he saw Darius. "How's it going?"

"Do rangers shovel sidewalks here?"

Austin grinned. "It's my day off. The Inn belongs to my father-in-law. I try to help him out, mostly to keep him from doing something stupid."

"That sounds like a big job."

Taylor laughed. "You have no idea."

"Any luck with the dashcam footage?"

"They pulled it Thursday, and I know they're looking through it. I'm hoping they'll have an answer for you tomorrow. I wish I could remember more, but—"

A pager went off in Taylor's pocket.

He fished it out. "The Team is being toned out. We've got a car off the road in the canyon. Children inside. The driver has injuries."

In the distance, Darius heard sirens.

Taylor jammed the pager back into his pocket, carried the shovel to the back porch. "Want to come see the Team in action? You can toss your bag in the back."

That was one invitation Darius couldn't resist.

Taylor jogged back to the truck, opened the liftgate, and yanked a yellow T-shirt out of a bag of gear. "I keep everything ready."

"Smart." Darius tossed his duffel inside.

Austin pulled the T-shirt, which read *Rocky Mountain Search & Rescue*, over his parka. "Let's roll."

SASHA RODE with Nicole to the scene of the accident. She couldn't help with the rescue, but she hated being sidelined. Sheriff Pella stood in the middle of the road ahead of them, directing traffic, the highway closed to all vehicles apart from rescuers.

Nicole slowed down, rolled down her window. "Hey, Sheriff."

"Hey, Nicole, Sasha." He waved them through.

Sasha saw that Eric had brought one of his rescue trucks. There were also two ambulances, lights flashing.

"I hate it when rescues involve little children."

"I hate it when a rescue involves my best friend." Nicole squeezed Sasha's hand. "You were our last rescue."

Sasha hadn't realized that.

Nicole pulled up behind Rescue One and parked. "I'll leave the door unlocked. If you get cold, I've got a blanket and hand warmers in the backseat."

"Thanks, Nic."

While Sasha unbuckled her seat belt, Nicole walked around to the rear of her SUV and opened the liftgate. "Stay away from the edge. It's slippery as hell out here."

"I'll be careful." Sasha climbed out into the cold wind.

A white Honda Accord lay on its roof in the creek twenty feet below them. Fortunately, the creek was shallow this time of year, the water a mere trickle. A long string of vehicles sat parked along the edge, most of them belonging to Team members, who were already hard at work, yellow Team T-shirts over their parkas.

Nicole joined them, first checking in with Megs, who stood near Rescue One directing the operation, a man in a hooded blue parka beside her.

"Sasha!" Megs motioned her over.

Huddled against the wind, Sasha walked toward Megs, pulse spiking when she recognized the man next to her. "Darius! What are you doing here?"

His cheeks were red from the wind and the cold.

"Taylor and I were talking when his pager went off, and he invited me to come along."

"Why don't you explain to Darius what's going on? I'm Incident Command at the moment." Megs stepped away, then responded to a call on her radio. "Canyon Command. Affirm. We do have EMS on scene."

"You'll be out of the wind over here." Darius motioned her toward the front end of Eric's rescue truck. "I just asked Megs whether you have specialized jobs."

"We don't. We're an all-volunteer organization, so we can never be sure who will show up. Everyone has to learn how to do everything. All of us are certified as EMTs or paramedics, and we're all expert climbers. Most of us are trained in search and rescue, too. We've all worked together for years, so we know what to do. As we arrive at the scene, we just fall in and get the job done."

"It must take a lot of training."

"It does. Eric is inside the vehicle giving first aid to the driver. He'll decide the safest way to get her out. But before we can move her or the kids, we need an anchor. That's what Chaska is constructing."

"An anchor?"

Sasha explained. "There's no way to carry a person up this rocky slope without ropes. If the rescuers were to trip and fall, we'd dump the poor person onto the rocks or into the creek. That means we have to create an anchor. Think of it as a kind of top rope like you have at the climbing gym. It has to be strong enough to support the weight of the victim, the litter, the rescuers, and all of their gear. That's kind of Chaska's specialty. He's a math geek—a mechanical engineer."

"So, he'll be on belay for everyone more or less."

Sasha nodded. "You could say that. Nicole is putting on her climbing harness. Creed and Austin, too. They'll be part of the crew that helps bring up the litter. Jesse is helping Eric, probably keeping the kids calm. We try to have six people on a litter, but we can do it with four or five. Oh, there's Harrison. That's six."

"Harrison Conrad? He's the guy who climbed Mount Everest, Lhotse, and Nuptse by himself a few years back, isn't he?"

"That's him. He's a total badass."

Darius smiled down at her. "From where I stand, you're all badasses."

Chaska stood, breathed onto his cold fingers, and took hold of his handset. "Canyon Command, sixteen seventy-two. The anchor is ready."

Sasha explained what was happening, as Nicole, Austin, Harrison, and Creed tied into the ropes and used the anchor to rappel themselves down the steep, rocky embankment. "Harrison has the litter strapped to his back in two pieces. He'll snap it together when he gets to the bottom."

Five minutes later, the crash victim was loaded into the litter, Eric staying behind to be with her children as the others slowly brought the litter up to the road.

"Mama!" a little girl in a pink snowsuit wailed.

Eric bounced her on his hip, while holding the older child's hand.

"Poor little thing." Sasha huddled closer to Darius, the wind cutting through her layers. "When the mother in the ambulance, they'll go back down for the kids. Eric will come up with them."

"I'm impressed." Darius glanced at his watch. "We got here fifteen minutes ago, and the woman is out of the wreckage and inside the ambulance."

"This was an easy rescue." Sasha shivered. "When you're bringing someone with severe injuries down a fourteener or a thousand-foot rockface, it can take hours. Sometimes we're called out to retrieve a body, and sometimes the person we're trying to save dies before we can complete the rescue. It's not always happy endings."

Darius frowned. "Let's get you out of the cold."

Chapter 12

DARIUS FOLLOWED Sasha down the hall to her laundry room, duffel bag hanging over his shoulder. "Thanks for this."

"I'm happy to help." She pointed to shelves next to the washing machine. "The detergent and fabric softener are there. Can you figure out how to use the machine, or should I start it for you?"

He chuckled. "I think I can handle it."

"I'll leave you to it."

Nicole had offered them a ride home from the rescue site before heading back to work, and when Darius had mentioned grabbing his laundry from Taylor's vehicle, Sasha had invited him to wash his clothes at her place.

He hadn't been able to refuse her—not that he'd tried. He wasn't really here for his laundry, though that was a convenient excuse. He was here for Sasha.

Darius had only two small loads—one light and one dark. He sorted them, dropped the first load in the washer, and got it running. With that done, he walked back to the kitchen, where he found Sasha stirring something on the stove.

"I'm making hot cocoa. Want some?"

Darius couldn't remember the last time he'd had hot cocoa. "Sure. Thanks."

Snow was starting to fall again. While she finished making hot cocoa, he brought in more wood and built another fire. Soon, they sat together on the sofa, the fire crackling, steaming mugs in hand.

Darius took a sip, the rich taste of chocolate warming him. There was something else. He looked in the mug. "Marshmallows?"

She smiled at him over the rim of her cup. "You strike me as a man who hasn't had enough marshmallows in his life."

Taken aback, he stared at the marshmallows, little pillows of white bobbing in the chocolate. He hadn't enjoyed marshmallows since he was a child. "I guess not."

"Sometimes, it's the little things that make the day brighter."

When was the last time he'd thought about small pleasures or worried whether his day was bright? Hell, he wasn't even sure what that meant. For him, a good day was making progress on a case and getting a solid workout. There was nothing else.

You know how to live, man.

Sasha looked worried now. "I can get a spoon if you want to take them out."

"No. No, they're good." He took another sip.

She seemed to relax. "You've seen the Team in action now. What did you think?"

"Watching you all reminded me of seeing our SWAT team in action. It's not the same thing, of course, but it's not all that different, either."

She tilted her head to the side, curiosity on her face. "How so?"

He took another sip. "You all have a high level of expertise. You have to work together like a well-oiled machine. You risk your safety for the greater good with no margin for error. Lives depend on your doing the job right."

Her brow furrowed at those last words. "We do everything we can, but sometimes it isn't enough."

While Darius listened, Sasha told him about times the Team had returned with a body and not a living person, her gaze shifting to the world outside the window, her face shadowed by sadness.

"The worst one happened not long after I joined the Team. Some jerk had crossed a double yellow line to pass a slow driver and struck a mother and her kids in a little car. The car rolled into the creek and landed upside down, just like today. It was late May, so the water was running high. A little girl took off her seat belt and got washed out of the window."

"Jesus."

"Jesse Moretti broke all of the rules and jumped into the water before ropes were in place. He did his best to reach her, risking his own life, but the water was too fast. He tried to grab her arm, but he missed her by inches. We pulled her from the water miles downstream, but it was too late. Everyone was devastated. I still remember the terror on her little face as she washed away. I thought of her today."

Darius rested his hand on her shoulder. "I can see why. But those kids today—they're safe right now, and they still have a mother, thanks to the Team."

She smiled—a sad smile—and nodded. "Megs tells us to focus on the lives we've saved and not the ones we couldn't. Otherwise, we wouldn't be able to do this—not for long, anyway. But you know more about that than I do, given your job."

It was an invitation to talk about his work, but he let it go. That was the last thing on his mind at this moment.

"You're amazing. You know that, right?"

She gave him a puzzled look, as if she didn't understand.

"You're beautiful. You're kind. You're a world-champion athlete who turned aside from other, more profitable options to save lives. That's incredible."

Nicole had told him as much on his first day in Scarlet, but he hadn't believed her.

Sasha's next words took him by surprise. "Have you ever been in love?"

God, how could he answer that? Why was she asking?

He didn't want to open old wounds, but he didn't want to lie to Sasha, either. She was so open and honest. And she was too … important to him.

He nodded. "I was once—a long time ago."

"What happened?"

"She … was murdered."

─────

SASHA STARED AT DARIUS, saw the flicker of desolation in his eyes. "I'm so, so sorry, Darius. I shouldn't have asked. It's not my business."

"It's not something I talk about."

"Right. That's okay. I mean… I'm so sorry."

"Don't worry about it." He watched her, an amused gleam in his eyes. "I'd rather talk about why you asked me."

She was so focused on the word *murdered* that it took her

a moment. Heat rushed into her cheeks. "Um… well, no reason, really. Curiosity, I guess."

"Right." The humor in his eyes told her he wasn't buying it. "I interrogate people for a living, you know."

"I guess I find you interesting."

"You guess?"

Her cheeks burned hotter. "Okay. I definitely find you interesting—and alluring."

"Alluring?"

"Yeah. You know. *Hot*." Did he have to make her come right out and say it? "You're not like any man I've ever met."

He turned the tables on her. "Have *you* ever been in love?"

Sasha thought about it for a moment, sipped her hot cocoa, remembering Elias and Remy. "No, not really. I've dated a couple of guys, but I've never been in love."

But she could play at this game, too. "Now, Mr. Detective, why did you ask?"

His lips curled in a slow smile. "Curiosity, I guess."

She shook her head, laughing. "If I can't get away with that, you can't either."

"You want honesty? Okay." His expression grew serious. "It's everything I said earlier. You're beautiful—truly. You're good to people. You're also an elite athlete who saves lives when there are so many other things you could do. You intrigue me."

"No one has ever said that before."

He frowned. "I don't understand that."

"I get a lot of male attention, but most of the time, it's from guys who want to sleep with me—or who want to prove that they can climb better than I can."

"I'm guessing they fail?"

"On both counts."

They both laughed.

"I started winning competitions when I was still a kid, and everyone treated me like their little sister. But when I turned sixteen or so, boys' attitudes toward me changed. They started to get angry if they couldn't outclimb me. That's when the sexual attention started, too—from grown men and boys."

She told him how she'd gone to her first regional championship and overheard two male climbers talking about her in the hallway of their hostel. "Then one of them said, 'That's what I love about these competitions. It's the perfect place to bump uglies with super-fit chicks.'"

Darius' face took on a look of disgust. "Classy."

"I'm really glad I overheard them. When he hit on me later, I threw his words in his face. I told him I'd come to climb, not to hook up with creeps."

"Was he ashamed of himself, or did he get angry with you?"

"I'm not sure. Both? He walked off, red in the face. The next time I saw him, he seemed embarrassed and barely spoke to me. He died in a BASE jumping accident a few years later."

"Sorry to hear that. Did you tell your parents what happened? I'm sure they tried their best to protect you."

"I was afraid they'd pull me out of competitions if they knew, but I told my brother. He said I was a girl in a man's sport and that I should expect things like that to happen. Then he told me to be careful."

"I'm not sure I like his response. A man's sport? Women climbers should *expect* that sort of thing? That sounds like victim-blaming."

Sasha hadn't thought of it that way, but then she'd been much younger. "He was right that I needed to be careful. I didn't realize it then, but that confrontation forced me to think through my reasons for competing. I was successful at such a young age that I could have gotten swept away by it. But that experience forced me to think hard about what was important to me."

"And what is important?"

"Friends. Pursuing the sport I love. Working with people I admire. Being a part of something bigger than my own ambition. Giving back to my community. Finding happiness outside of climbing."

Two dark eyebrows rose. "You really don't know how uncommon your attitude is. Living in Hollywood, working in Beverly Hills, I met so many young women who measured their self-worth in fancy cars, big bank balances, movie roles, and the men they were sleeping with."

She couldn't stop herself from asking. "Were you one of those men?"

"I had my share of offers." He took her empty mug, set it with his on the coffee table, his gaze pinning her to the spot. Then he took her good hand, caressed it with his thumb, making her skin tingle. "But, no, I wasn't. I wasn't even tempted. But you, Sasha…"

He leaned forward and brushed her lips with his.

Sasha sucked in a breath, contact making her lips burn, sending delicious shivers down her spine. When he started to pull back, she grabbed the front of his T-shirt with her good hand, and held fast. "Kiss me."

DARIUS IGNORED the voice inside his head, warning him not to do this. He'd had just a taste of Sasha, and, *damn*. She'd felt it, too—the shock, like sparks. He could see it in her eyes and feel it by the way her hand was fisting in his T-shirt.

He leaned forward, brushed his lips over hers again and again, until his blood ran hot and both of them were breathing fast. Then, careful not to hurt her, he cupped her face to hold her steady and claimed her mouth with his.

His brain went blank. There were no objecting voices now, only Sasha and the thrum of his pulse. She whimpered, yielding to him, her lips pliant.

Soft skin. A hint of spearmint. The scents of lavender and vanilla.

He teased her with his tongue, outlining the curve of her lower lip before sucking it into his mouth, thrilled by her quick intake of breath. When his mouth closed over hers again, she parted her lips for him, her tongue meeting his.

But it wasn't enough.

He took the kiss deeper, slid the fingers of his free hand into the silk of her hair, lost in the feel of her. She arched against him—then gasped and jerked back, her hand letting go of his shirt to press against her ribs.

"Sorry." Her voice was tight. "That was my fault."

Heart thrumming, Darius saw the pain on her face, regret jagged in his chest. "No, *I'm* sorry. I shouldn't have—"

"You didn't hurt me. I did." Her lips, wet from kissing him, curved in a little smile, some of the heat of their kiss lingering in her eyes. "I wanted to get closer to you."

Her words took some of the sting out of his anger at himself, because, yeah, he'd felt the same way. "Can I get you anything? Is it time for an oxy?"

She shook her head. "If I take oxy, I'll just fall asleep, and then you'll leave."

Unable to stop himself, he ran a finger down her bruised cheek. "Rest is probably what you need."

"I'd rather keep kissing."

Yeah, well, Darius heard that. "Do you have an ice pack around?"

"I have *so* many ice packs. I am the queen of ice packs."

Darius got to his feet, checked her freezer, saw a dozen or so neatly stacked ice packs in different shapes and sizes. "You're not kidding."

"They go with the job."

He grabbed a long rectangular one, found a linen dish towel, and wrapped it around the ice pack. When he returned, he found her, face pale, still holding her side. He sat next to her, held out the wrapped ice pack. "Here."

"Thanks." She moved to the recliner and accepted his help getting situated with the ice pack against her side, wincing at the contact.

"I'm getting that oxy."

This time, she didn't argue.

He found her prescription, took out a pill, and brought it to her with a glass of water. "I hope this helps."

"Thanks." She took the pill, swallowed, set the glass on the end table beside her. "Stop looking at me like that. It really isn't your fault."

Her injuries weren't his fault. The men who had attacked her, the men he was supposed to track down and bring to justice, were to blame. But what had happened between them just now…

"I'll get some more wood for the fire." Needing distance, he stepped outside onto her deck, a cold wind hitting him in the face, taking some of the heat out of his blood.

He loaded his arms with firewood, the voice he'd ignored earlier coming back in full force. Sasha had been home from the hospital for only two days, for God's sake.

She was still healing. But he just hadn't been able to stop himself, had he?

What the hell was wrong with him? He knew the rules. He shouldn't have kissed her. He should never even have touched her. She was a victim in a case he was supposed to solve, not a woman he'd met through a dating app.

Get a grip on your damned self.

Arms full, he drew a deep breath and walked back inside, piling the wood beside her woodstove. Avoiding eye contact, he stoked the fire, then closed the cast iron door, fighting to keep his voice casual. "That ought to keep you warm for a while."

"You're leaving."

It wasn't a question.

"I wish I could stay, Sasha, but I just crossed a line with you. Police officers, detectives—we aren't supposed to get involved with the victims in our cases. I broke the rules. I'm sorry for that."

"I'm not sorry, and I really wish you would stay. Besides, your laundry is still in the machine. I think the washer just finished."

Shit.

"Right." He'd forgotten about that. He really had no choice but to stay, at least for a while. "I'll get the next load going and put the first in the dryer."

He made his way to her laundry room, furious with himself now, and moved his shirts into the dryer, then started another load in the washer.

I hope you're proud of yourself.

It wasn't just that he'd kissed her. He *cared* about her. In just a handful of days, he'd developed feelings for her, and he knew she had feelings for him, too.

What the fuck was wrong with him?

He'd be lucky if Irving didn't take his balls with his badge.

He walked back to the living room, hating himself for the vulnerability he saw in her eyes. Fighting to keep his emotions off his face, he sat on the sofa. "Are you hungry?"

"A little. Rain dropped off a pan of lasagna this morning on her way to Knockers. I think all we have to do is reheat it."

"I'm on it." He found the lasagna in the fridge, turned on the oven, waited for it to preheat, searching for some way to salvage this situation and pass the next couple of hours. "Do you have any DVDs of your favorite climbs or competitions?"

"Climbing DVDs? You want to watch climbing DVDs?"

He'd rather go back to kissing her, but he didn't say that. "Yeah. You can tell me all about it, what it was like."

Chapter 13

"HE KISSED YOU?" Nicole dropped her fork and gaped at Sasha, Mocha curled up at her feet. "Well?"

"Well, what?" Sasha dabbed her lips with her napkin.

"How was it?"

Sasha wasn't sure how to answer. "It was… *perfect*. Until I forgot about my ribs. I guess I kind of arched toward him."

"Understandable. Who wouldn't?"

"It hurt—a lot. I jerked away, and he stopped. He apologized and told me that he'd broken the rules. He said he couldn't get involved with a victim from one of his cases. Then he went out to get wood."

Nicole gave Sasha a knowing smile. "He probably had to cool off."

"When he came back in, he was in control again."

"How romantic is that? He knew he couldn't kiss you or get involved when he walked through your door, but he did it anyway. He couldn't help himself."

Still reeling from disappointment, Sasha didn't see the upside. "Romantic?"

"Yes, romantic. His attraction to you made him break the rules. What happened then?"

"Before we kissed, I thought I was truly getting to know him. But afterward, it was like a door had closed. He was kind. He was polite. He got me an oxy and water. He kept the fire going. He even asked to watch climbing videos."

"He asked to watch climbing videos?" Nicole's eyes got wider. "No guy I've dated has ever asked to watch climbing videos."

"We're not dating."

"You know what I mean."

"We watched my climb of El Cap, and then that one of you and me bouldering in Bishop. He had lots of questions. I'd taken an oxy and got really drowsy. When his second load of laundry came out of the dryer, he thanked me, stoked the fire, asked me if I needed anything, and then he left. I fell asleep until just before you got here."

"Hang on." Nicole jumped up from the table where they'd just eaten dinner and ran down the hallway, Mocha at her heels. She returned a few minutes later, holding the excited puppy, a disappointed look on her face. "I was hoping he'd left a sock behind. You know how socks are."

That made Sasha smile. "Devious. I like it. Except that he is still working on my case. I'll see him again. I'm just not sure he'll open up the way he did yesterday."

"That sucks."

"Yeah."

"But tell me more about the kiss. It was perfect?"

Sasha could still feel the heat of his lips against hers, smell the scent of his skin, her pulse responding to the memory. "It was the best first kiss I've ever had. We just connected, you know? Like electricity or something. He got the balance just right—forceful but not sloppy or clumsy, gentle but not boring or too sweet. He knows what to do with his tongue. I'll say that much."

Nicole got a pained expression on her face. "Damn. A guy who knows how to use his tongue…"

"Yeah."

"So, what else?"

"What do you mean?"

"What did he say? You said you got to know him a little."

Sasha wanted to tell Nicole that Darius' girlfriend had been murdered, but he hadn't wanted to talk about that. She was sure he wouldn't want her to share that information with anyone. Besides, she didn't really know anything beyond what he'd told her. It didn't seem right to talk about it behind his back.

Sasha thought for a moment. "His nickname growing up was Dare."

"I like it."

"I put marshmallows in his hot chocolate, and he stared at them like he'd never seen a marshmallow before. He told me he hadn't had them since he was a boy."

"Aww. Sounds like you'd be good for him. He's *way* too serious."

Sasha recounted much of the conversation—his observations about the Team and SWAT, the way he tried to comfort her when she'd told him about rescues that had gone wrong, what he'd said about her.

"He told you that you're beautiful?" Nicole was starry-eyed now. "I think he really likes you. A man like him wouldn't say that unless he really meant it."

"You think so?"

"I know so." Nicole stood and began clearing dishes off the table. "I'll clean up and take Mocha for a potty break and then make cookies. Why don't you go get into your jammies and make yourself comfortable?"

Nicole had a day off tomorrow, and she and Mocha had come to stay the night.

"Thanks, Nic. I really appreciate it."

Sasha made her way upstairs, where she washed her face and brushed her teeth, her gaze fixing on her lips, the memory of that kiss flooding her—the heat, the caress of his tongue, the hungry way his fingers had slid into her hair.

It had been perfect, until she'd brought it to an end.

But she would see him tomorrow, wouldn't she?

She carefully undressed, the bruises on her ribs a dark, angry purple. She found her favorite fleece lounger hanging in her closet and pulled it gently over her head, catching sight of herself in the mirror again.

Why didn't she own anything feminine?

Pretty much everything she wore was some form of activewear. She didn't have anything made of silk. It was all fleece, Spandex, and polypropylene. Leggings. Sports bras. Tank tops. Sweatpants. As for shoes… She wouldn't even go there.

Stop it. Don't do this to yourself.

Darius hadn't stopped kissing her because she wasn't wearing silk or a lacy bra. He'd stopped because she'd been in pain—and because he'd felt he'd done something wrong. After all, he'd kissed *her* and not that movie star who'd given him a peep show through the folds of her silk bathrobe.

But was their first kiss also going to be their last?

God, she hoped not.

She turned away from the mirror and walked back downstairs, where Nicole and Mocha were waiting for her.

DARIUS DROVE down the canyon to Denver early Monday morning. Rush hour traffic had I-25 backed up in both directions as he neared downtown. Why was this highway constantly under construction?

Such a pain in the ass.

What had happened with Sasha yesterday had been out of line—and entirely out of character for Darius. He'd called early this morning and left a message telling Chief Irving, asking for a brief meeting. He had no idea how Irving would react. But that's not what mattered. In Darius' book, doing the right thing meant facing the consequences of one's actions. He just hoped it didn't cost him his badge.

Knowing that Irving would have no choice now but to assign someone else to the case, he'd checked out of the Inn after breakfast, surprised to find himself reluctant to leave Scarlet Springs. He hadn't wanted to be there in the first place, so why should it bother him to go?

You didn't tell her goodbye.

No, he hadn't. What the hell would he have said to her?

It was wrong for me to kiss you. I'm not sure I can do my job because you turn me on, so I'm going back to Denver. Someone else will take over.

Lame.

Arriving thirty minutes later than he'd intended, he parked in the secured underground garage. He made his way upstairs, straightening his tie before he knocked on Irving's office door, his shirt smelling like Sasha's fabric softener.

"Come!"

"Good morning, sir."

"Morning." Irving studied him. "Your message sounded urgent. Sit and tell me what's on your mind."

Darius took a seat. He'd rehearsed this conversation in his head, but it was different when he was sitting face to face with his boss. He came right out with it. "You need to assign someone else to the Dillon case. I have compromised myself and the department and will accept whatever discipline you see fit."

Irving leaned forward, a frown on his face. "What the hell did you do?"

"I'm attracted to Ms. Dillon. Yesterday, I … I did laundry at her house. We spent time talking, and I kissed her, sir. She's the victim in this case, and I crossed a line."

Irving leaned back in his chair, his expression unreadable. "Was it consensual?"

"Yes, sir. It was. She asked me to kiss her."

"So she's attracted to you, too."

"It would seem so, sir."

"It would seem so?" Irving raised a bushy white eyebrow then punched a button on his intercom. "Darcangelo, get your ass in my office."

Darius wasn't sure what this had to do with Darcangelo. He worked in Vice, not Major Crimes. "You're assigning him to the case, sir?"

He supposed that made sense. Darcangelo had come to the DPD from the FBI, where he'd investigated sex trafficking. He had solid cybercrime experience.

"No, I'm not assigning him to the case. It's still yours."

"Mine?" Darius couldn't understand this. "But, sir—"

Darcangelo appeared in the doorway, a maroon button-up shirt hanging over the waistband of well-worn jeans, dark hair pulled back in a ponytail. "What's up, old man?"

"Come in and shut the door behind you." He

141

motioned to the chair beside Darius. "Silva has some concerns about his ability to manage this case. It seems he feels attracted to Ms. Dillon. He did laundry at her house yesterday, and they kissed."

Darcangelo didn't seem fazed by this news. Instead, he grinned. "Laundry, huh? Is that what the kids are calling it these days?"

Heat rushed into Darius' face. He hadn't expected Chief Irving to humiliate him by sharing his situation with anyone else in the department.

"Not to put you on the spot, but please tell Silva how you met your wife."

Darcangelo's brows rose in surprise. "You want me to tell him…?"

"I believe that's what I just said."

Darcangelo gave Darius a glance, clearly not comfortable with this request. "I was on loan to DPD from the FBI, working undercover to catch Alexi Burien, a notorious Russian mobster who trafficked in children—a ruthless killer. Tessa witnessed the murder of a teenage girl who was one of his victims. She got caught in his web and became a target. I tried to protect her."

Darius had heard of Burien and how Darcangelo had eventually taken him down. He hadn't known that Darcangelo had met his wife on that case.

Irving chuckled. "What Darcangelo isn't saying is that he and Tessa got involved *while* he was working on this case. He made it his personal mission to keep her safe, breaking lots of rules in the process. He even moved her into his FBI safe house. You can imagine where that led. I hired him anyway."

Darcangelo seemed to understand what this was about now. "You asked Irving to take you off Sasha's case because you kissed her?"

"We have a code of conduct, and I violated that code."

"Not by much. You seriously need to lighten up, man." Darcangelo stood, pushed a button on Irving's phone. "Hunter, we need you in Irving's office—now."

Darius soon found himself listening to Hunter tell how he'd taken Sophie hostage to break out of prison and had later gone on the run with her. He'd known that Hunter had once been wrongly convicted, but he'd had no idea that he'd gotten together with his wife by putting a gun to her head.

"*And* he got her pregnant while evading capture," Darcangelo added. "He could have landed her in prison, too."

Hunter crossed his arms over his chest, glared at his buddy. "Thanks for spelling that out for us, Dickangelo."

Darcangelo shrugged. "Just keeping it real."

"Geezus." Darius didn't know what to say to that, so he pointed out the obvious. "You weren't SWAT captain at the time."

"True, but, as you can see, I hired him anyway." Irving pointed toward the door. "You two clowns can go now."

Chuckling, Darcangelo and Hunter left the office, closing the door behind them.

"One of the many things I respect about you, Silva, is your strict adherence to the code of conduct. But you can't stop yourself from having feelings. You're not just a cop. You're also a man. And you're the best detective for this job. No one has your combination of experience and skills. I trust you to use your best judgment where your interaction with Ms. Dillon is concerned. Get back up to Scarlet, and get the job done."

Confused but strangely relieved, Darius stood. "Yes, sir."

———

"YOUR LUNGS SOUND CLEAR. There's no sign of infection in your incision. Your X-rays look great." Dr. Renshaw, the town's orthopedic surgeon, turned away from his computer screen. "Can you wiggle your fingers for me?"

Sasha winced at the pain in her wrist as she did what Dr. Renshaw asked.

"Great job, Sasha." Nicole had driven Sasha to her appointment and stayed with her to offer moral support.

"Good." Dr. Renshaw examined her stitches. "You'll have swelling in your fingers for a while, but everything seems to be healing well. Come back on Wednesday, and Amy will remove those stitches and put you in a cast for the next four or five weeks. When that comes off, you can start aggressive PT. I assume you're going with a physical therapist from out of town?"

"I'm going to the Mountain's Edge clinic in Boulder. They work with a lot of climbers. They helped me before with a strained hamstring."

Dr. Renshaw nodded. "I hear good things about them. How about your pain?"

"My ribs hurt a lot more than my wrist."

Dr. Renshaw didn't seem surprised. "Broken ribs are miserable."

"How much longer before I don't need oxycodone?"

"You can try some kind of non-steroidal anti-inflammatory if you want. Make sure to take it with food. That might get you through the day, but you'll probably need oxycodone at night for another four weeks or so."

Nicole met Sasha's gaze. "Oh, she's not happy about that."

Dr. Renshaw gave Sasha a sympathetic look. "I know it's hard, but this will pass."

"Thanks, Doc."

Amy, the RN, carefully rebandaged Sasha's wrist, first washing her skin with a sterile wipe and applying a clean dressing. "Just hold it steady. There you go. I'll print Dr. Renshaw's instructions and have them waiting at the front desk."

"Thanks." Sasha accepted Nicole's support climbing down from the exam table.

Nicole held up Sasha's parka. "That went as well as it could have."

"All good news." Sasha tried to focus on the positive and not the fact that she still had five weeks of basic recovery ahead of her.

While Sasha paid and booked her next appointment, Nicole drove her vehicle to the front door so that Sasha wouldn't have to cross the icy parking lot. She helped Sasha climb in and closed the door behind her.

"Thanks, Nic."

"Are you kidding? What are best friends for?"

It was a cloudless day, the trees garlanded in white, the high peaks gleaming against the bright blue sky.

Nicole drove first to Food Mart to pick up a few things, including kibble for Mocha. "You just wait here. Can I grab anything for you?"

"More extra-strength Tylenol?"

"You've got it."

Sasha let her mind drift, knowing where it would go.

Darius. The kiss.

She hadn't heard from him yet today. She knew she shouldn't read anything into that. He had a case to solve, and he couldn't do that in her living room. But still…

A white crossover pulled into the empty space beside her.

Rose.

She climbed out, spotted Sasha, and motioned for her to roll down her window.

Not wanting to be rude, Sasha did as she asked.

"How are you feeling, sweetie? Oh, look at those bruises. Your pretty face! Well, they won't last, will they?"

Sasha knew Rose meant well, but sometimes she was annoying. "I kind of like them, but they will heal."

"So, they must have found out who did it, right? I saw that sexy detective pack up his vehicle and leave this morning. Kendra says he checked out."

"He… he checked out?" Sasha's heart sank.

"Oh, you didn't know?" Rose smiled from behind her mirrored sunglasses, no doubt thrilled to be the bearer of news. "He left bright and early. I saw him drive away."

This was news to Sasha—and it hurt.

He'd come to her house to do laundry only yesterday. Why would he do that if he'd planned to return home to Denver?

Sasha knew the answer. He hadn't originally planned to go back to Denver. He'd left town because of the kiss.

She did her best not to let her emotions show. "I haven't heard that he solved the case. He must think he's done what he can here in Scarlet for now."

"I guess that makes sense. The police have a lot more technology in Denver, right? You take care of yourself. Give me a call when you'd like to start chakra work."

That would be never, but Sasha didn't say so. "Thanks, Rose."

Rose went inside to do her shopping, leaving Sasha to deal with her emotions.

Why hadn't Darius at least told her he was leaving

town? Why hadn't he said goodbye? Had he felt no connection to her at all?

Then again, why should he? They'd only known each other for five days. What right did she have to put expectations on him? If he thought kissing her had been such a terrible thing, why did she care that he was gone?

Except that she *did* care, because it hadn't been terrible. It had been wonderful, and not just for Sasha. She knew he'd felt it, too—the connection.

Nicole hurried out, bags in her hands. She put the groceries in the back then climbed into the driver's seat. She gave Sasha one glance. "What's wrong? What happened?"

"Darius checked out of the Inn this morning. He left town."

"What?" Nicole stared at Sasha. "Are you sure?"

"That's what Rose just told me."

Nicole looked less than impressed. "Rose has been wrong before."

"Kendra told her he'd checked out. I'm sure he left because of what happened last night. He said he'd crossed a line with me."

Nicole put on her seat belt and started the engine. "If he left town because of one little kiss, that makes him a coward. But Darius doesn't strike me as a coward."

Chapter 14

DARIUS WAS A COWARD.

He'd spent the past hour in traffic, struggling to make sense of his meeting with Chief Irving and raging against what felt like a blatant disregard for the police code of conduct. He'd tried to hold himself accountable, and they hadn't taken him seriously. But that wasn't the problem—or not the whole problem, anyway.

This wasn't about rules. Not really. It was about Sasha.

Darius had kissed her, and what he'd felt for her had scared the hell out of him. He shouldn't feel anything for her. He'd known Ms. Dillon for less than a week, for God's sake. He had no business having feelings of any kind for her.

But he did.

And the moment he'd realized that, he'd run.

Damn it.

What the hell was wrong with him?

And what the hell was wrong with Irving?

One of the many things I respect about you, Silva, is your strict adherence to the code of conduct. But you can't stop yourself from having feelings. You're not just a cop. You're also a man.

That was true, but that didn't mean he wasn't responsible for his actions. Wasn't the entire point of having a professional code of conduct to prevent officers from acting on their emotions and impulses? What good were rules and regulations if they were abandoned when they became inconvenient? If the line moved every time someone crossed it, what was the point of having any boundaries at all?

Where other cops might see shades of gray, Darius saw a slippery slope. One day, it's a detective kissing the victim in one of his cases. The next, it's an officer arresting someone based on prejudice or using too much physical force or accepting favors in exchange for turning a blind eye.

The code of conduct existed to protect everyone.

I trust you to use your best judgment where Ms. Dillon is concerned.

What the hell did that mean? Had that been Irving's way of telling Darius that he wouldn't fire him for sleeping with Sasha, provided it was consensual?

Insane.

As for Darcangelo and Hunter, they'd seemed to find the whole thing entertaining. Darius had a deep respect for both men. He would trust either of them with his life. And yet, Darcangelo had clearly bent the rules to the breaking point, while Hunter had committed a list of serious felonies. He'd eventually been pardoned by the governor, but he'd still broken the law.

Yet Irving had hired them both.

Shit.

Darius was going in circles again, his thoughts spinning.

He slowed as he entered a hairpin turn and braked hard for a cyclist who took up most of the lane as she struggled up the steep grade. A few seconds of watching the woman pedal hard told Darius it would be difficult to ID a cyclist from behind unless you already knew them and recognized their helmet or bike. This was an effective enough demonstration to convince Darius that the bastards who'd hit Sasha had passed her to be sure of her identity before they attacked.

He was still musing on this when he passed Bear in the roundabout.

"Darius Silva!" Bear called out.

Darius couldn't explain it, but the man's greeting touched him.

What was it about this town, about these people that had him feeling sentimental because someone recognized him and said hello?

He parked at the Inn and checked in again.

"Boss decided you weren't done here, huh?" This time Bob was wearing jeans and a Led Zeppelin T-shirt.

"Something like that." Darius rode the elevator up to the third floor, let himself into the room, and dropped his duffel on the bed.

He'd stopped at his condo before leaving Denver to check his mail and change his suit for a turtleneck and jeans. He'd decided to ditch his work suits for warmer, more casual clothes—jeans, Henleys, flannel, boots. He told himself he wasn't lowering his standards. He was adapting to his environment.

When in Rome…

He'd just gotten his laptop set up when his phone buzzed.

Austin Taylor.

"Silva here."

"Hey, it's Taylor. I got the footage back from my dashcam. I'm sorry to say there's nothing. The stolen SUV must have been far enough ahead of me that the cam missed it."

Damn.

Darius had hoped the footage would give them a clear view of the assailants. "How much of the footage did they review?"

"They scanned it starting with my check-in call when I drove up the canyon."

"Where were you before that?"

"I was near the roundabout at Frank's filling station. I stopped, filled the tank, took a leak, got some coffee. When I got back into the truck, I put myself back into service, called in my destination, and then headed up the highway."

Struck by a sudden thought, Darius had to ask. "Do you have to turn off the camera manually, or does it shut off automatically?"

"It's manual." Taylor swore, clearly understanding. "It's my day off. I'll head into the office and ask them to scroll back."

Darius closed his laptop. "Text me the address. I'll meet you there."

━━

SASHA SAT ON THE SOFA, feeling awkward at the sight of Nicole, Megs, and Lexi cleaning her house, Mocha curled up, asleep beside her.

They'd started her laundry, Nicole cleaning the bathrooms, while Megs handled the kitchen and Lexi dusted and vacuumed floors.

"I can probably manage that."

Lexi lugged the vacuum out of the broom closet. "Like hell you can."

"I'm guessing you don't know what 'rest' and 'take it easy' mean," Megs said from the kitchen. "Remember when you and I went to clean Hawke's cabin because he didn't want Vicki to see what a pig he truly was?"

Sasha couldn't help but smile. "How could I forget?"

"You stepped up to help rescue a fellow Team member from the embarrassment of his own filth, enabling him to win a wife and reproduce." Megs wiped down a granite countertop. "This is karma paying you back. No feeling guilty."

Nicole appeared at the bottom of the stairs. "She's just cranky. Rose told her that Darius checked out and left Scarlet this morning. She's been down ever since."

Megs looked at Sasha with deepened interest. "So, that long face is about our handsome detective?"

"What long face?" Sasha glared at Nicole. "I'm not cranky."

Nicole laughed. "See what I mean?"

"I believe I do."

Lexi plugged in the vacuum. "Detective Silva isn't gone. I got a text from Austin just before I came here, saying that they were at the ranger station going over his dashcam footage together."

Sasha hated the way those words gave her mood a lift. "That doesn't mean he's still staying in town. They probably have a lot more technology in Denver. That's where their cyber forensics lab is—or whatever they call it."

The conversation lapsed as Lexi started the vacuum, the sound scaring Mocha.

"It's okay, sweetie." Sasha stroked the puppy's silky head.

It took less than an hour for the three women to get Sasha's house clean from top to bottom. Then Megs put the leftover lasagna in the oven to reheat and threw together a salad. The four of them sat down for lunch, with Sasha deliberately steering the conversation away from Darius.

"I would be flying out for Bratislava tomorrow."

Megs reached across the table, squeezed her good hand. "I'm sorry. This sucks."

"What do you want to do about the championships?" Nicole shook the bottle of Italian dressing, sprinkled it over her salad. "We can't just be sad about it. Maybe we should have a party. You can cheer on Maritza and your other friends."

"I had planned to watch, but a party would be nice." Sasha didn't want to spend the day feeling sorry for herself.

Megs poked at her salad. "I'm sure we can persuade Joe to move one of those big TVs close to the Team table. We can make sure you're comfortable and turn it into a celebration."

"I'd like that."

"Then I'll give Joe a call, and we'll make it happen."

"Thanks." Sasha couldn't feel sad about missing the championships, not when so many people cared. "And thanks for cleaning my house."

The conversation had moved on to which climbers had the best chance of winning in each category of competition—speed climbing, free climbing, and bouldering—when a knock came at the door.

Sasha turned, saw Darius standing with Julia, and her pulse skipped. He stood there in jeans, a black turtleneck, and a fleece-lined denim jacket, a small laptop in hand.

"I've got it." Nicole was on her feet in a heartbeat, an

excited Mocha on her heels as she walked to the door. "Hello, Detective Silva. Come on in."

"I'm here, too," Julia said.

Sasha waved. "Hi, Julia."

Darius stomped the snow off his boots and stepped inside, bending to pet the puppy. "Sorry to interrupt your lunch."

"No problem," Nicole and Lexi said almost in unison, their transparent enthusiasm somehow amusing and irritating at the same time.

"Ms. Dillon, I was hoping you might have a moment to look at some footage." He held up the laptop.

"Of course." Sasha motioned to him and Julia to join them. "Have you had lunch yet?"

"No, but we can't stay."

Whether Darius saw through this overly friendly welcome, Sasha couldn't say, but Megs was fighting to keep a smile off her face.

Lexi dabbed her lips with a napkin. "We were just talking about you, Detective."

"Oh?" Julia looked interested. "Do tell."

Nicole explained, while Sasha tried not to look worried about what her friends might say next. "Rose said you must be done with the case because you'd checked out of the Inn and left town."

Darius seemed confused. "Well, I'm right here and still working on the case."

Sasha felt her friends watching her and had to fight not to let her emotions show—except, of course, she was no good at pretending.

She changed the subject. "What did you need to show me?"

Darius sat beside Sasha and set the laptop on the table, but he didn't open it. His gaze met Sasha's, his gray eyes soft with concern. "This is footage of the SUV that hit you. Are you sure you'll be okay seeing it?"

Sasha nodded. "Thanks for asking."

He opened the laptop, turned it toward her. "We recognize the man in the passenger seat, the one who flipped you off, but not the driver. I was hoping you might be able to tell us who it is."

Then he clicked play, Megs, Lexi, and Nicole crowding around behind Sasha.

Sasha saw herself, riding through the roundabout. And there was the SUV, sitting on the side of the road across from the gas station. It waited until she'd ridden out of sight, then pulled into the street and followed her.

Chills skittered down her spine. "They were waiting for me."

"Lying in wait is more like it," Julia interjected.

Darius enlarged the image and slowed the playback. "Watch here. Do you recognize the driver? We've put out a BOLO and sent the image out to the CBI and FBI databases, but I thought maybe you'd know him."

Sasha studied the man's face. He had dark hair and a goatee, his eyes hidden behind sunglasses. "I'm sorry. I don't. Do any of you know who he is?"

Megs, Lexi, and Nicole shook their heads.

Sasha pointed to the screen. "Who's the other man?"

"That's Kyle Watts, Riggs' buddy. We put out a warrant for their arrest twenty minutes ago."

———

DARIUS STOOD, service weapon drawn, waiting for a signal from Boulder's SWAT captain that the property was surrounded.

A whisper sounded in his earpiece. "Go!"

A SWAT officer hit the front door with a battering ram, wood splintering, what was left of the door swinging on its hinges.

"We're in!"

SWAT officers went first, Darius and Julia following them inside.

"Get down on the ground! Get on the ground now! Hands behind your head!"

But Riggs wasn't listening. Instead, he was doing his best to evade them, dodging the officer trying to apprehend him and typing a text message on a new phone as fast as he could with shaking hands. "I'm not resisting! I'm just sending a text! I'm—"

He hit the floor with an *oof*, a little burner phone flying.

While a SWAT officer held Riggs down with a knee to the back, Darius stopped the phone with his foot, picked it up, saw that the message had already been sent.

Cops here with guns. It's bad. Think
they're going to arrest me.

It was a burner phone, and there was no identifying information about the message's recipient, apart from a phone number.

Darius knelt beside Riggs. "Who did you warn?"

The SWAT officer holding Riggs down barked at him. "Answer him, or I'll start asking the questions!"

"I-I sent it to Kyle."

"Kyle Watts?"

"Yeah, man."

Darius sheathed his firearm, drew flex cuffs out of his pocket. Resembling plastic zip ties, they were much lighter than handcuffs and easier to manage.

Darius Riggs' his wrists, restrained him. "Brennan

Michael Riggs, you're under arrest for conspiracy to commit assault resulting in grave bodily injury."

"I had nothing to do with it!"

"Bullshit!"

Then Captain Skalbeck walked over to Darius. "We've cleared the place. There's no one else here."

Darius stood, held up the phone. "He used this burner phone to send a text to Watts, warning him. Where is he, Riggs?"

"I swear I don't know! I-I just have that number. You took our phones, so w-we had to get new ones."

Captain Skalbeck turned to his men. "Let's turn this place over, find out what this shitweasel is hiding. You found drugs here before?"

Darius nodded. "Cocaine."

While SWAT tore the place apart, Darius and Deputy Marcs hauled a handcuffed Riggs out to Marcs' service vehicle and shoved him in the back.

"Aren't you going to read me my rights or call an attorney or let me make a phone call or something?"

"Eventually." Marcs laughed. "You watch too many TV shows, Riggs."

Darius sat in the front and turned to face Riggs. "You've got one chance, *one chance* to make this easier on yourself. I won't ask again. Where is Watts?"

Riggs was sweating now, his gaze darting between his house and Darius. "He…"

"Out with it!" Darius shouted, letting his rage show.

"H-he said he had shit to do. I don't know exactly where. Denver."

"Another coke run?"

"Probably. I-I don't know. H-he just said he had some shit to do in Denver. Am I really under arrest? I didn't do anything."

"Didn't do anything? You just tipped off a suspect in an active investigation that we were coming for him!"

Marcs shrugged. "That's aiding and abetting a fugitive, for starters."

"What?" Riggs gaped at them.

"Aiding and abetting. Conspiracy to evade prosecution. Criminal stupidity." Darius let that sink in for a moment, but he had to ask. "When did Watts leave?"

"About twenty minutes ago. I don't know."

If the bastard had left twenty minutes ago, he was probably still on Highway 36.

Darius climbed out of the car, waited for radio traffic to clear, then called that information into dispatch, giving them the year, color, and make of Watts' vehicle.

Captain Skalbeck saw Darius and made his way over. "Did the shitweasel give you anything helpful?"

"Only that his buddy was on his way to Denver."

Skalbeck nodded. "I heard the call go out. We found a small amount of powder that field-tested positive for cocaine. We've got a couple of computers and some flash drives. Where do you want us to take this shit?"

It was a good question. The assault on Sasha had happened in Forest County. The suspects lived in Boulder. And Darius worked for the City of Denver, while the victim lived in Scarlet Springs.

"Their phones are with DPD's forensics lab, so that's probably where the computers and flash drives should go. You can keep the coke."

"Got it. What about the shitweasel?"

"Forest County issued the warrants."

"He's all yours. We'll book him on drug charges later."

Darius waited until SWAT cleared them to leave, signed for Riggs, and was crossing the street on his way back to Marcs' service vehicle, when the sudden roar of an engine made him look. Watts' truck was tearing down the road, heading straight for him.

Darius leaped back, drew his weapon, but he was too late.

BAM! BAM! BAM!

Pain exploded against his chest, forcing the breath from his lungs, and driving him to his knees in the vehicle's path.

"Officer down! Officer down!" Marcs' called.

Someone dragged him out of the street, the world around him exploding in gunfire. As he fought to stay conscious, there was only one thought in Darius' mind.

Sasha.

Chapter 15

SASHA WAS desperate for fresh air, sunshine, and movement. She was used to lots of physical activity, and being sedentary for so long left her restless. So, after lunch, Sasha and Nicole went for a short walk with Mocha along the edge of the reservoir, throwing a rubber chew toy for Mocha to fetch.

It was warmer today than it had been, the snow beginning to melt, the high peaks still gleaming white. Sasha spotted a bald eagle soaring over the water, wings outstretched. She snapped a photo with her phone to share later on social media. Still, she couldn't shake a sense of uneasiness.

It's probably just a trauma reaction.

Esri had said that might happen.

Sasha couldn't get her mind off the footage Darius had shown her. She'd never met those men or done anything to harm them, but they had almost killed her. It was also strange to think that Darius had gone to arrest them.

Why had Riggs let it come to this?

Back home, Nicole started a fire and made tea, setting

their mugs on the end tables. "You've been quiet all afternoon. Are you okay?"

"I guess seeing that footage bothered me more than I realized."

Nicole sat beside her, took her left hand. "Darius and Julia will find them."

Sasha knew Nicole was right. "I just can't believe Riggs was behind this. I don't even know his roommate. Why would he try to kill me?"

"Riggs must have talked him into it. He knew you'd recognize him if you saw him, so he had his buddies do it. But it's not your job to worry about this stuff." Nicole picked up the TV remote. "What do we want to watch?"

They ended up streaming a documentary about the first all-woman team to summit K2. As riveting as the footage was, Sasha found herself checking her phone for new emails and local news updates—something that would tell her whether Riggs and his buddies were now behind bars and her life could return to normal.

Afternoon stretched into evening. While Nicole took Mocha out to go potty and then made a run to Food Mart for a rotisserie chicken, Sasha checked her social media, sure that Riggs' arrest would be news in the climbing community.

Then she saw it—a breaking story.

Her heart raced.

Officer shot during suspect arrest. Shooter dead. Police seeking information.

She clicked on the story and watched a live report from outside the Boulder Justice Center.

"… had just arrested one man when another suspect in the case tried to run an officer down with his vehicle and opened fire, hitting the officer twice in the chest."

The camera cut to a man in a SWAT uniform, other

uniformed officers milling around in the background.

"At approximately sixteen-hundred hours today, Boulder SWAT, in cooperation with the Denver Police Department and the Forest County Sheriff's Department, exercised an arrest warrant in the City of Boulder. We had one suspect in custody when another approached at high speed in his vehicle and opened fire on a Denver police officer. The officer, who was wearing body armor, was struck in the chest by two rounds and injured. SWAT returned fire, and the suspect in the vehicle was killed. The officer was transferred by ambulance to the hospital, and his injuries are being treated at this time. One suspect remains at large."

On Sasha's screen, the SWAT captain was still speaking, but Sasha couldn't hear his words over the pounding of her own pulse.

Denver police officer shot.
Transported by ambulance.
One suspect at large.

If Forest County and DPD were involved, it must be Darius. It had to be Darius.

Sasha tried to send Nicole a text but was all fumbling fingers. No sooner had she hit send than Nicole walked through the door, groceries in her arms.

"I think Darius has been shot. I just saw a news clip about a Denver police officer who was shot while arresting someone with Boulder SWAT and the Forest County Sheriff's Department. That could only mean—"

"Sasha, slow down." Nicole set the groceries on the counter. "You think Darius was shot?"

Sasha showed Nicole the news segment. "Who else could it be?"

Nicole looked worried. She drew out her mobile phone, found Sasha's text. "I'm going to call Julia."

Why hadn't Sasha thought of that?

Sasha listened while Nicole spoke with Julia, the phone on speaker.

"Sasha's worried that Darius is the officer who was shot."

"He's okay, but, yes, he took two forty-five rounds to the vest. His body armor held—but only just. He's got some bruised muscles and two huge impact marks. They transported him to the hospital to make sure there weren't any broken bones or internal bleeding. Bullets can still do damage when they don't penetrate."

Nicole, who'd been watching Sasha this entire time, seemed to read Sasha's mind. "But he's going to be okay?"

"Yeah. I just finished booking Riggs into the county lockup. Some buddies of Silva's are picking him up at the ER and driving him back to Scarlet."

"Are *you* okay?" Nicole asked Julia.

"I think this took a good five years off my life and gave me a few more gray hairs, but, yeah, I'm okay. I'm looking forward to a hot bath and a glass of wine."

"Thanks, Julia. Sasha was kind of freaking out when she heard the news."

"Tell her not to worry. Her hot detective is safe—and so am I."

"We're glad to know you're okay, too." Nicole ended the call. "So, he's okay, and he'll be back soon."

Sasha sank into a chair, shaky with relief. "Thank God."

———

ICE PACK HELD against his chest by bandages, Darius sat on the gurney in the ER, growing more impatient by the minute. How long did it take to discharge someone? He didn't have time for this. Riggs was sitting in the Forest County jail, and Darius had questions that needed answers.

What a fucking mess today had become. One minute, they'd been wrapping up, and the next…

Darius hadn't anticipated that Watts would try to rescue Riggs, especially not with an overwhelming police presence at the scene. He'd imagined the bastard would run as far and fast as he could. But Watts had tried to kill Sasha out of a misguided sense of loyalty to Riggs. It made a kind of twisted sense that he would throw his life away trying to free his friend. But now he was dead.

What a waste.

Darius glanced at his watch. What was taking so long? He'd been waiting to leave for more than an hour. The X-rays had shown no broken ribs, and there'd been no internal injuries. Then again, he couldn't go anywhere without transportation.

He heard familiar voices, exhaled in relief. At least his ride was finally here.

"We're with DPD. Is Detective Silva here?"

"Yes. He's in the last room on the left. I've got his discharge paperwork. He should be ready to go in a few minutes."

The curtain moved aside to reveal Darcangelo and Hunter.

"Hey, guys. It's about time."

Darcangelo's gaze dropped to the bandages that held the ice pack in place. "How do you feel, man?"

"Like someone took a baseball bat to my chest." He unwrapped the bandages to reveal two dark, overlapping bruises, each with an angry, red bullseye. "X-rays showed no cracked ribs or fractured sternum, so I guess I'm good to go."

"Damn." Hunter frowned. "Thank God the plates held."

"Just barely." Darcangelo picked up the two ballistic plates that had stopped the bullets, both pitted where the rounds had struck, one cracked. "Either one of these shots would have been fatal."

That thought had occurred to Darius, too. "I guess it wasn't my time."

Hunter took the cracked plate, turned it over in his hands. "You are one lucky son of a bitch. What the fuck happened?"

Darius shared the highlights, giving Marcs props for getting him out of the path of the truck. "If she hadn't dragged me out of the street, I'd be roadkill."

"Sounds like you owe her a beer."

Darius couldn't disagree with this. "At least one."

"The son of a bitch who did this is dead, right?" Hunter set the damaged plates back on the overbed table.

"Very."

"What about that piece of shit you arrested?"

"He's chilling at the Forest County Jail—which is where I should be, too."

Darcangelo rested a hand against Darius' bare shoulder. "You need to take care of yourself first. The little fucker isn't going anywhere. Given that he warned his buddy, the DA will charge him in the shooting."

Darius' phone buzzed with a text from Marcs.

Sasha is worried about you. Might want to let her know you're okay. Just FYI…

"Bad news?"

Darius shook his head. "Ms. Dillon heard I'd been shot and is worried."

Darcangelo crossed his arms over his chest and exchanged a knowing look with Hunter, but Darius cut them off before either of them could speak.

"*Don't* make me kick your asses. Not a word."

Hunter bit back a grin. "I'd like to see you try."

Darcangelo's gaze narrowed. "Listen to you. I kicked your ass when—"

Darius was saved by the timely arrival of his nurse, who went over his discharge papers and removed the IV they'd started in the ambulance. And then, at long last, he was free to leave.

He got to his feet, wincing at the sharp pain on the left side of his chest.

"I'll carry your gear." Darcangelo handed him his shirt, picked up Darius' vest and service weapon. "I once took five rounds to the vest. Sorry to say, but it's going to hurt for a while, man."

"Something to look forward to." Darius pulled on his turtleneck, reached for his jacket, and followed the two men out of the ER.

They piled into Hunter's SUV and started the drive up to Scarlet, Darius' thoughts drifting back to the case, while Hunter and Darcangelo got into an argument about Hatch versus Pueblo chiles and who made the better salsa.

"Something about this doesn't click for me." Darius hadn't meant to speak aloud.

Hunter and Darcangelo stopped bickering.

Darius tried to explain. "Riggs is dumb as a rock, and he's not a good liar. He still maintains his innocence. He claims he had nothing to do with the attack on Sasha. Based on his reactions, his body language, some part of me believes him."

Was that a true hunch, or was it Darius' past speaking?

"You think his buddy might have done it without him

knowing?" Hunter asked.

"It's a possibility."

"What about the other guy—the one who was driving the stolen SUV?"

"He's still in the wind." But Darius would find him.

Thirty minutes later, they made their way through the roundabout, Hunter and Darcangelo talking about a wildfire that had come close to wiping Scarlet off the map a couple of years ago. Darius hadn't realized how connected they were to the community.

"I will never forget the sight of that jumbo jet roaring up the canyon and dropping its load on the flaming front." Then Hunter met Darius' gaze in the rearview mirror. "Want us to drop you off at the Inn, or do you want to grab some food and a beer at Knockers? Darcangelo is buying."

"Thanks, but not tonight." Darius had other plans. "Take the next right."

Hunter chuckled. "Silva is looking for trouble tonight."

AFTER SUPPER, Sasha took a hot shower, blew her hair dry, and slipped into her favorite sleep camisole and shorts. She put on her fluffy bathrobe, brushed her teeth, and made her way downstairs to where Nicole was playing with Mocha in front of the fire.

Nicole looked up. "Feel better?"

Sasha nodded. "A little."

Nicole got to her feet. She was opening the climbing gym tomorrow morning and needed to get up early. "Are you going to be okay tonight?"

"I'll be fine. I'll just curl up on my recliner with a cup of tea and stream something until I get sleepy."

While Sasha looked through her assortment of herbal teas, Nicole got her things together, set them by the front door, and then leashed Mocha. "I get off tomorrow at two. I'll check on you then."

Sasha set her box of chamomile tea on the counter and walked over to give Nicole a careful hug. "Thanks, Nic. You're the best."

"Try not to worry about him, okay? Julia said he was okay... Oh. He's *here*."

Sasha's heart missed a beat. She looked outside, saw Darius walking up the path to her front door.

"I'll get out of your way." Nicole picked up her bag, opened the door, and led Mocha outside. "Hey, Detective Silva. We heard what happened. Sasha has been worried sick about you."

Darius' gaze met Sasha's. "I'm okay, really."

Sasha held the door open for him. "Thanks, Nicole. Have a good night."

"See you tomorrow." Nicole made her way down the steps, Mocha darting about on her leash. "Mocha! You're going to get us tangled, girl."

Sasha closed the door, locked it, and for a few heartbeats, she stood there face to face with Darius, their gazes locked. She wasn't sure who took the first step, but in the next moment, she was in his arms, holding him as tightly as she was able.

He sucked in a breath, stiffened. "Easy."

Sasha stepped back, saw lines of pain on his face. "You're hurt."

"My body armor held, but the rounds left big bruises."

"Go sit on the sofa and take off your shirt. I'll get an ice pack."

Sasha half expected him to object, but he didn't. While she grabbed an ice pack from the freezer, he took off his jacket and boots and pulled his T-shirt over his head, his back turned toward her as he walked barefoot to the sofa.

She wrapped the ice pack in a linen dish towel and walked over to him. What she saw stopped her, made her stomach knot. "Oh, my God."

The left side of his chest had two angry bruises, each the size of her palm with a raw, red center.

"It's not as bad as it looks. No cracked ribs."

Sasha sat beside him, pressed the ice bag gently against the bruises. "Not as bad as it looks? You could have been killed, and it would have been my fault."

To her surprise, Darius laughed. "I'm pretty sure you didn't pull the trigger."

"No, but you were there to arrest them on my behalf."

"This isn't on you, Sasha."

"If I hadn't outed Riggs in public—"

Darius caught her chin, lifted her gaze to his. "It's *not* your fault."

Sasha looked into his stormy gray eyes, and this time she heard him. "I'm so glad you're okay."

"Yeah, me, too. I wasn't sure for a moment whether my vest had held."

"What happened?"

As he recounted his afternoon, Sasha noticed what she hadn't before. The muscular curve of his shoulders. Strong biceps. The dusting of dark curls on well-defined pecs. Flat, brown nipples. His abs. The trail of dark hair that disappeared beneath the waistband of his jeans.

She was so taken by him that she lost track of what he was telling her. "Wait… You're saying that Riggs warned his friend?"

Darius nodded. "Riggs sent him a text. Watts apparently decided to take matters into his own hands and rescue Riggs."

Sasha listened as Darius told her how he'd been crossing the street when Watts had shown up in his truck, heading straight toward him.

"I drew my weapon, but he got off a few shots. I went down. Marcs dragged me out of the path of the truck, saved my life. SWAT returned fire. It took me a minute to realize the rounds hadn't penetrated my vest."

"That must have been scary and so painful."

"It's not on my list of things to do again."

"Bren is in jail?"

"In jail—and facing serious charges now."

"What about his friend—this Watts guy?"

"Dead. SWAT took him out." Darius seemed to study her. "Are you okay hearing all of this? I know it must be a lot after what you've been through."

"I …" Sasha wasn't sure what to say. "I can't believe this happened. I can't believe that Bren would have his friend try to kill me. I'm sorry that this Watts person did what he did and died as a result. But I'm so, so grateful that you're safe and here with me tonight."

He touched a hand to the ice bag. "I certainly have a better understanding of what you've been going through."

"We're twins." Sasha untied her bathrobe and carefully lifted her cami to show him her bruises. "Our injuries came from the same jerk."

His brow furrowed. "God. I'm so sorry."

He reached out, ran his fingers gently over her skin, his touch leaving a trail of heat, making her gasp. His gaze met hers once again. "I want you, Sasha. I'm working your case. I shouldn't want you. But I do."

Sasha's breath caught in her throat.

Then he leaned closer, let the ice bag fall away—and kissed her.

Chapter 16

HEART SLAMMING IN HIS CHEST, Darius held himself back, brushing Sasha's lips with his, her minty taste and the clean scent of her skin filling his head. He teased her lips with teeth and tongue, his senses focused entirely on her response—the way she tensed, that little intake of breath, the hand that slid hungrily up his arm. When she parted her lips, he took what she offered, seeking her tongue with his.

God, yes.

He knew he shouldn't be doing this, but he didn't give a damn. For a few short moments today, he'd thought his life was over. In the confusion of pain, gunshots, and sirens that had followed, Darius had thought only of Sasha.

He was damned lucky to be alive—and so was she.

Mindful of her injuries, he cupped her cheek to hold her in place, at last claiming her mouth in a full-on kiss.

She moaned, the sound igniting a backdraft inside him, years of restraint going up in flames in the span of a single heartbeat.

It had been so long since he'd let himself go, so long since he'd felt this way for a woman, so long since he'd ached like this. His head was spinning, his body shaking, need for her thrumming in his chest. Fighting to restrain himself, he drew back, looked into her eyes, both of them breathing hard.

She stood, took his hand. "Come."

He knew where she was leading him. He knew where this would go. And still, he followed her.

When they reached her bedroom, she turned to face him and let her bathrobe fall to the floor, standing there in a pink pajama camisole and matching shorts.

She started to pull her camisole over her head, but he stopped her.

"Let me." He took hold of the soft fabric, lifted it over her head, and let it fall to the floor, then drew down the shorts and tossed them, too.

The breath left his lungs in a rush. "You are … *beautiful*."

Darius took his time, drank in the sight of her. Those beautiful eyes. Long, golden hair. Her small, perfect breasts with their rosy nipples. The triangle of dark blond curls between her thighs. Her slim, athletic legs and little toes. He reached out, cupped one delicate breast, caressed its velvety tip with his thumb, saw her body tense, his cock going rock hard as her nipple drew tight.

But she wasn't about to be left out.

She reached for his fly, unzipped his jeans, and slipped her hand inside his boxers to stroke him, her dilated pupils and the naked hunger on her face telling him she liked what she saw.

He knew she couldn't easily bend, so he pushed his jeans and boxers over his hips and stepped out of them, hiding nothing from her. It took some effort just to stand there and let her look her fill, her good hand exploring him from his abs to his bruised chest and back down to his cock again.

She lifted her gaze to his, stepped backward, and sat on the edge of her bed. "I'm on the pill."

And that *right there* only proved how out of his mind he was right now. The guy who'd never gone on a date without a condom hadn't given a thought to protection.

"Oh," he said stupidly.

Still looking into his eyes, she smiled, took hold of his cock, drew him nearer—and took him into the heat of her mouth.

"Mmm." He willed himself to hold still, his fingers sliding into her hair as she explored him, caressing his length with her hand, swirling her tongue over the aching head. "*Geezus.*"

It felt so fucking good, the sight of his cock disappearing into her mouth intensely erotic. But Darius knew where this would end.

He caught her face between his hands. "Stop."

Lust a jackhammer in his chest, he dropped to his knees, ignoring his own discomfort. With Sasha still sitting upright, he scooted her bottom to the very edge of the bed and pushed her knees wide apart, opening her to his view and his touch.

Darius had always found every inch of women's bodies beautiful—all those delicate folds, that sweet, sensitive flesh. To her credit, Sasha didn't seem to be self-conscious the way so many women were. "You are perfect—good enough to eat."

He parted her with his fingers and tasted her with a long stroke of his tongue.

"Oh!" Her hips gave an involuntary jerk, her eyes going wide.

"Hang on, angel. I'm just getting started."

He explored her with tongue and fingers, testing, tasting, teasing, getting the measure of her, seeking the best ways to pleasure her. Then he covered her with his mouth and suckled her.

She cried out, her body jerking, her fingers sliding into his hair. "Oh, Dare."

Darius built up a rhythm, sucking her, stroking her clit with his tongue, and before he knew it, he was lost in her, drunk on her. Like a starving man, he feasted on her, her erotic taste and scent making him moan, his blood burning for her.

Her breath was uneven now, every exhale ragged, her fingers fisting in his hair, her thighs tensing.

He slid a finger inside her wet heat and was gratified at her throaty moan. She was close, so close. He thrust deep, caressing her inside and out.

Her body went rigid, her head fell back, and she shattered, coming with a cry.

He rode it out with her, keeping up the pace until her climax had passed and she sagged against him. He kissed her inner thighs then rocked back on his heels, holding her so that she wouldn't slide off the bed.

Her head was tilted to the side, blond strands covering one cheek, her eyes closed, a blissed-out expression on her face. She raised her head, opened her eyes, and gave him a smile that he felt to his balls. "You are freaking *incredible*."

"It's not over yet."

SASHA'S HEART skipped a beat at those words. Weak from pleasure, her mind blissfully blank, she looked into Darius' smokey eyes, saw his need for her still burning. But she was still healing, and he'd been hurt today.

She asked the obvious question. "How are we going to do this?"

Sasha talked about it for a moment, working through the possibilities. As a climber, she was all about finding creative ways to move her body. "You could sit on the edge of the bed, and I could straddle your lap."

Darius' brow furrowed. "Yeah."

"Or you could lie down on your back, and I could ride you, though you'd have to help me get on top."

Those furrows grew deeper. "Right."

"Or maybe I could sit in the recliner and drape my legs over the arms, and you could—"

"Geezus, Sasha." A look of pain on his face, Darius took hold of his cock as if he thought it might otherwise explode. "I get the idea."

Sasha couldn't help but laugh. She ran a hand up the uninjured side of his chest, felt his heartbeat beneath her palm. "Am I torturing you?"

"Yeah—but don't apologize. You've given me ideas."

She liked that.

Then he went all serious. "Do you trust me?"

"Of course."

"Then just relax into my arms." He pressed his forehead to hers, wrapped his arms around her. "Relax, Sasha."

Slowly, carefully, he bore her back onto the bed, his arms supporting her torso, his eyes looking into hers as they moved together.

When she lay flat, he stood upright once again, towering over her, his cock looking huge and hard against his belly. "Does that hurt?"

"No. Was it painful for you?"

"Not really." He grinned. "You just relax. I'll take care of everything."

Damn.

She brought her feet to rest on the bed's edge and let her legs fall open, gratified by the way his gaze moved there—and stayed.

"Sasha." He said her name with such reverence that it put an ache in her chest. Then he reached between her thighs, his fingers working magic, rekindling the fire he'd just slaked. "You are *so* wet."

"That's your fault." She'd expected him to enter her, but he didn't.

Instead, he supported his weight with one arm, lowered his head to her breast, and sucked her nipple into the heat of his mouth, his tongue and lips sending little jolts of pleasure through her.

Sasha slid the fingers of her good hand into his hair, stretching her injured arm over her head—a position of total surrender as she gave herself to him. "*Yes.*"

But he was in no hurry, his mouth moving from one breast to the other, lavishing both with the same sweet attention, his hand still busy between her thighs. Oh, it felt so good, so good, her hips now moving on their own, her body instinctively seeking release.

Breathless, she raised his head from her breast. "I want you inside me."

His gaze met hers. "Are you sure?"

"Yes!"

Keeping his weight off her with one arm, he took hold of his erection with his other hand, his gaze locked with hers as he slowly nudged himself inside her.

It was the most intimate erotic experience she'd ever had—seeing her pleasure mirrored in his eyes, being emotionally connected while their bodies came together, his gaze penetrating her while his body did the same.

He gave her a moment to get used to the delicious feel of him inside her. Then, without breaking eye contact, he began to move, slowly withdrawing from her, only to bury himself inside her again.

"Oh!" She couldn't help but moan, the hard feel of his cock almost unbearably sweet as he thrust into her, stretched her, filled her completely.

He seemed to find his stride, falling into a rhythm, withdrawing almost completely before driving deep. Then he lowered his mouth to one of her breasts once more, suckling her, her womb clenching with every strong tug of his mouth.

She slid her left hand up his arm, held onto the strong curve of his shoulder, her hips rising to meet each thrust, the precious ache inside her already promising bliss.

He raised himself up again, holding his weight with one hand while the other toyed with her breasts, his jaw set, an expression of sexual pleasure-pain on his face.

She wrapped her legs around his waist, urging him on.

His response was immediate. He picked up the pace, thrusting into her faster, harder—and, *oh, my God*, it was heaven. The hard, silky feel of him. The sweet stretch as he pounded into her. Then he reached down between her legs to stroke her clit—and Sasha was lost.

She called out his name again and again, beyond thought, the ache inside her drawing itself into a tight, shimmering knot, the pleasure carrying her higher and higher... until it exploded. She cried out as climax blazed through her, a firestorm of ecstasy.

But Darius wasn't far behind her. He drove into her, hard and fast, letting himself go at last. He came with her

PAMELA CLARE

name on his lips, finishing with a few deep thrusts, his body shaking apart as orgasm claimed him. "*Sasha.*"

He collapsed onto the bed beside her, breathing hard.

She took his hand. "You… are… *incredible.*"

———

DARIUS KISSED the top of Sasha's head, rested his cheek against her hair, one hand lazily fondling her breast. "Comfortable?"

"Yeah. You?"

"I'm good." He was—mostly. Yes, his chest was sore, but he wanted Sasha in his arms. The discomfort was worth it.

Figuring out how to hold Sasha in the post-orgasmic glow hadn't been easy. They'd tried lying on their sides facing each other, but that had been too painful for her even with his help. It hadn't been that comfortable for him, either. So, while she'd gone into the bathroom, he'd come up with a plan.

Darius now sat on Sasha's bed in his boxers, his back resting against a stack of pillows, while Sasha, now wearing only her bathrobe, sat between his thighs, her back against his chest.

This was new territory for him. He'd mostly given up dating apps, but back when Friday night had been swipe night, he'd rarely stayed long after sex. For some reason, sitting and talking with a woman he'd just fucked felt much more awkward and intimate than having sex with her, the rush of orgasm fading into sharp loneliness.

But Sasha was different. *He* was different. He felt none of the emptiness he was accustomed to after sex. Instead, he felt only … contentment.

"Where did you learn to use your tongue like that?"

Darius couldn't help but feel gratified. "That's my secret."

"Oh, come on!"

Darius chuckled. "I read a lot of sex-ed books in high school—not the typical stuff, but more adult books. My teenage self believed that the secret to holding onto a woman was knowing how to make her come."

"What a smart boy you were. I mean, you weren't wrong. What I cannot understand is why a man with your good looks and special *talents* is single."

"Being a detective means working long hours—late nights, weekends, holidays. I lost a couple of girlfriends because they weren't comfortable with that."

There's more to it than that, and you know it.

"But that's just the nature of your job. Mine involves lots of travel. Yours involves working hard to catch bad guys."

He loved that she saw it so simply. "I guess they didn't think I was really home when I came home. They said I wasn't emotionally available—and they weren't wrong."

Why he'd shared that, he couldn't say.

"Is that because of what happened?"

"Becca's murder? Yeah. Probably."

"Becca was her name?"

"Rebecca."

For a moment, neither of them spoke, and Darius was sure that Sasha was trying to decide whether she should ask him more about it. It wasn't something he talked about freely. He'd never told anyone, outside of job interviews, not even his ex-girlfriends. But some part of him wanted Sasha to know.

"I met Becca my first year at college. I was studying bio-chem, and she took biology as a science requirement. She had trouble with it, so I helped her."

"Of course, you did."

"She and I were friends at first, but there was something about her. We got together that spring. First love is one helluva drug."

"So you loved her?"

"I did—or I thought I did." Darius told her how they'd gotten an apartment together their sophomore year over their parents objections. "My mom and dad wanted me to focus on my education, but when you're young…"

He told her how Becca had decided mid-semester that she wanted a kitten, even though their lease didn't allow pets. "I like cats. Don't get me wrong. But we were both nineteen-year-old college students. We had no idea where we'd be living next year, no money for vet bills, and we had signed a lease agreeing not to have pets."

"I understand. I love animals, but I don't have a cat or a dog because I travel so much. It would be irresponsible and unfair to the animal."

"Exactly." Darius told Sasha how he and Becca had gotten into an argument about it, steeling himself for what came next. "I went for a walk to cool off. That was the last time I saw her alive. She was so angry with me."

Darius closed his eyes as unwanted images filled his head, an all-too-familiar sense of dread settling in his stomach. "When I … When I got back, the door to our apartment was ajar. I went inside and found her half-naked and lying in her own blood. Someone had stabbed her repeatedly and cut her throat. It was the most terrifying, awful thing I'd ever seen."

"Oh, Darius. I can't imagine."

Darius told Sasha how he'd rushed in and tried to save Becca's life, not realizing at first that it was too late. "I shouted for help, yelled for someone to call an ambulance. One of our neighbors stuck her head through the door, saw me bent over Becca, and screamed. I didn't imagine for one minute she'd think I'd done it."

"She thought *you* were the killer?"

"So did the police. I had Becca's blood on my clothes, my hands, my face, the soles of my shoes. The neighbor said she'd heard Becca and me arguing shortly before I called for help. They took me in."

Chapter 17

"THEY ARRESTED YOU?" Sasha was so taken aback by what Darius had just said that she turned to face him— only to be brought up short by knife-sharp pain.

She gasped, pressed her hand against her side, moaned through gritted teeth.

A big hand came to rest on her shoulder. "Easy. Are you okay?"

"I just … forgot."

"Right. Let's go downstairs. We'll get you settled in your recliner with an ice pack and an oxy."

"But I want to be able to touch you and be close to you."

"I want that, too, but I don't want you to be in pain. Let me get up first, and then I'll help you."

It wasn't a painless process for him, either, judging by the way his breath caught as he got to his feet and then helped her to stand.

In short order, she was cocooned in her recliner, ice pack on her ribs, oxy on the end table beside her for later, a warm blanket tucked around her, the fire in the woodstove blazing.

"I'm sorry. You were telling me something important, and I cut you off."

"It's okay." Darius sat on the end of the sofa closest to her.

"Please tell me this is the worst thing that ever happened to you."

"Without a doubt." He took her hand and picked up the story where he'd left off. "They cuffed me and took me in. They questioned me for hours. They didn't even let me wash her blood off my hands. I could smell it. I can still smell it."

Sasha squeezed his fingers. "I'm so sorry. I can't imagine how horrible that must have been. To find Becca dead like that and then to be blamed for it…"

"As a detective myself, I understand why they thought I'd done it. No one else had been seen entering or leaving the apartment. The neighbor overheard us arguing. Statistically speaking, when a woman is murdered, you want to look at the men in her life, past and present. I was found over her body, covered in her blood. There was only one problem. Despite all that, I wasn't the killer."

Sasha listened, her heart breaking, as Darius described what had followed.

"I didn't get to see my parents for almost forty-eight hours. The police twisted everything I said." Darius drew a breath, exhaled, and Sasha could see that sharing this with her came at a price for him. "When I told them I'd gone for a walk to cool off and that Becca had been dead when I returned, they made up a story about how I'd left to hide the knife I'd used to kill her."

"But your parents got you a lawyer, right?"

Darius nodded. "They did, though I could tell my

mother doubted me. It's a horrible feeling to have the two people you trust most in the world look at you and wonder —even if just for a second—whether you're a killer."

"Oh, Dare. I'm so sorry."

"The lawyer was a piece of work." Darius laughed, but there was no humor in it. "When I told him I hadn't killed Becca, he said, 'Of course, you didn't.' But I knew by the way he said it that he'd have said the same thing to a serial killer."

"Did anyone support you?"

Darius nodded. "My father and my brothers. When I got a few minutes alone with my dad, he asked me point-blank whether I'd killed her. I swore to him I hadn't. He promised to stand by me, but it wasn't easy for him. He was a professor at the university, and his son had just been accused of murder."

Sasha blinked back tears as Darius told her how the press and strangers on social media had hounded his family and the university.

"I was suspended pending the outcome of the case. Friends I could once count on dropped me. I felt like a pariah. For six months, the local papers covered the story every day, putting my face on the front page. Social media was even worse. I got death threats, and so did my brothers. People posted the worst things."

Sasha could easily imagine. "That's terrible."

"When my parents retained an attorney, some took that as proof of guilt. When my attorney asked the judge to release me to house arrest because I'd gotten beaten up twice and threatened with rape while in jail, people laughed about how the rich boy didn't like the pokey. Or they said I deserved everything I got. It was nothing but hate twenty-four hours a day."

"Inmates threatened to *rape* you?" Sasha couldn't

imagine a big man like Darius facing a threat like that, but he'd been much younger then.

"Oh, yeah. I was fresh meat in their eyes." He caressed her hand with his thumb. "When the judge transferred me to in-home detention, assholes vandalized our house— spray-painted 'murderer' on our garage door, even threw rocks through the window. My father took a leave of absence, and my brothers left high school for homeschooling. My mother quit giving piano lessons. For six months, we lived under siege."

"That's terrible. What happened to innocent until proven guilty?"

"It died with the advent of social media."

Furious on his behalf, Sasha didn't hold back. "That's fucked up."

"The DA kept pushing me to make a plea bargain, but I refused because I hadn't done it. They threatened me with the death penalty. They made up a story about how I'd raped her and stabbed her to death in a rage." Darius met Sasha's gaze, and she saw utter desolation. "I've never felt so completely helpless. When you tell the truth, and no one believes you…"

It probably wouldn't make one bit of difference to Darius so many years after the fact, but Sasha said it anyway. "I believe you."

SASHA'S WORDS meant more to Darius than she could know. He fought to hold it together, his soul lacerated, his mind spinning with unwanted memories. "Forensics found my DNA all over her. My semen was inside her."

"But there were reasons for that. You were her lover. You'd tried to revive her."

Darius nodded. "Believe me, my attorney and I made that argument. No one listened—until six months later, when another young woman was raped and stabbed to death in the same apartment complex."

"Oh, God."

"A part of me was relieved at the news. I wanted to shout, 'See? It wasn't me!' But a young woman had died. I felt guilty for being happy when I heard."

"No one could blame you for that."

"This time, they couldn't pin the murder on me. I was confined to my home and made to wear an ankle bracelet, so they knew I hadn't done it. I hated that damned thing, but in the end, it saved me."

"I'm so glad it did."

"A different detective took that case. He was careful, precise, meticulous with details. He asked questions I'd already answered, but he saw different possibilities. Maybe I had just taken a walk. Maybe the killer had known that. Maybe that's why he'd acted when he had. And if I'd hidden the knife, where the hell was it?"

"He's why you became a detective, isn't he?"

Darius nodded. "Because he followed the evidence, it took him only a month—one damned month—to tie both killings to an unregistered sex offender living in our building. The guy had been busted on DNA evidence before and was careful to use condoms on his later victims. He killed them so they couldn't ID him."

"I hope he's in prison."

"He's dead—killed by inmates. It felt like justice to me, though I know it wasn't."

"In the end, you were exonerated."

"I was, but the damage was done. The ordeal ended friendships, dragged my family through the mud, laid so much stress on my father's shoulders that he had a heart attack a few weeks after I was cleared. My mother apologized for doubting me, something she still regrets. Strangers still recognized me, and some hadn't followed the story long enough to know I was innocent. Newspapers run your face on the front page when you're arrested, but they don't run big front-page pieces when you're released because you were innocent all along."

"You ran into people who still thought you were guilty."

He nodded. "I couldn't stay in Tempe. Too many bad memories. I couldn't stand the way people looked at me. So, I transferred to UNC and moved to Colorado."

"And your girlfriend. You never got to mourn Becca, did you?"

The question sent an unexpected shard of pain lancing through Darius, and his throat went tight. "No, I never got to mourn her. Even remembering her brought all of it back. I pushed her out of my mind—or tried to. If I had stayed that day, if I'd tried to work it out rather than going for that walk…"

His words trailed off as Sasha lowered her footrest, pushed aside her blanket and ice pack, and struggled to her feet, hand against her side.

"Are you okay?" Darius started to get up to help her.

"Stay. I'm fine." She took the few steps from her chair to the sofa, and he saw tears on her face. "I'm so sorry, Darius."

She straddled his legs and sat on his lap. "You're shaking."

Get it fucking together, man.

Embarrassed, he fought to rein in his emotions. But then she drew his head down to her breast and stroked his hair like a mother comforting a child.

Something in him snapped.

The corners of his eyes stung, his throat too tight to speak.

Was he fucking crying?

He coughed, swallowed, fought to make it stop, but Sasha was there, whispering reassurances in his ear, holding him as if he were precious, comforting him the way no one ever had. For the first time since he was a kid, he wept.

"I'm sorry," she whispered, again and again. "I'm so, so sorry."

And Darius realized she was crying, too.

He raised his head, looked into her beautiful eyes, kissed salty tears from her cheeks. "I'm the one who should be sorry. I dumped all of this on you when—"

She pressed her fingers to his lips. "Shh."

Then her mouth claimed his.

He let her shape the kiss, the tumult inside him giving way to a different emotion, a different need. Relentless. Insistent. Demanding. She slid one hand up his bare chest, thumbed his nipple, her lips never leaving his. Then she reached down between them, took hold of his already rigid cock, and stroked him.

Burning for her, Darius cupped one breast, teased its nipple, felt her heartbeat beneath his palm. It was racing, just like his.

At last, she broke the kiss. "I want you inside me."

She rose up a few inches, guided him to her entrance. Then with a moan, she slowly sank onto him, her body taking him inch by inch.

She was tight and wet and hot.

She started to move, then winced. "I think you're going to have to take over."

"I can do that." She was so small that he could grasp her hips and bring his thumbs together on that sensitive spot just above her clit. "Just enjoy the ride."

He flexed his abs and bucked into her, fucking her from beneath.

Sasha's head fell back on a moan, her nails digging into his shoulder.

At some kind of emotional edge, Darius held nothing back but drove into her hard and fast, gratified by the way each thrust made her moan. God, he wanted her, needed her, needed everything she could give him, her touch offering him consolation, absolution, salvation.

His mouth took off without his brain, moaning nonsense. "Sasha, God, I … I want… You … are… Need… you… are *too much*."

It felt so good, so good, nothing in his head now but Sasha and the feral pleasure of sex, orgasm already uncoiling at the base of his spine.

Her every exhale was a moan now, her body going stiff. "Darius!"

She came apart in his arms, bliss shining golden on her beautiful face.

He let himself go, climax scorching through him as he spilled everything he was inside her.

SASHA WOKE up to a kiss from Darius, who stood beside her, already dressed.

"Good morning."

She smiled. "Good morning."

"I thought you might want to wake up before any of your friends come over, given what you're wearing—or not wearing."

She looked down, saw her bare breasts. "Oh. Right."

He helped her out of the recliner. "I got a text this

morning from the forensics lab about the contents of Riggs' and Watts' phones. I'm going back to the Inn to grab a shower and have a virtual meeting with them."

Sasha must have been sleepy—or maybe she was confused. "But the case is closed, isn't it?"

Darius shook his head. "It won't be closed until we find the bastard who was behind the wheel of that SUV."

Sasha had forgotten about him. "Will I see you tonight?"

He kissed her forehead. "I would like that, but I can't be sure what time I'll be finished. I need to interrogate Riggs, and I've got an online meeting with a friend at the FBI who might be able to help me."

Sasha couldn't help but feel a little disappointed, but this was his job. "I've got a session with Esri, the trauma therapist, but other than that, I'll be here."

He frowned, his gaze dropping to the floor. "About last night…"

"If you tell me you regret last night—"

"No! No. Not at all. Are you kidding? It's just…" His gaze dropped again. "It wasn't easy to share that. I … I haven't cried since I was a little boy."

She ought to have known. He'd been utterly vulnerable with her last night, and it had left him feeling shaken and exposed.

She cupped his cheek with her good hand. "Your secret is safe with me. Besides, those tears belonged to a nineteen-year-old boy who never got the chance to shed them. Thank you for trusting me with that side of yourself."

He looked at her like he'd never seen her before. "You are too good to be real."

"Oh, I'm real." She stood on tiptoe, kissed him. "You have my number, right?"

"I do. I'll shoot you a text so you'll have mine."

"Stay in touch, okay? And no getting shot today."

"No getting shot." He grinned. "Yes, ma'am."

They walked together to the door, where Darius took her carefully into his arms and kissed her. "Stay safe."

She watched him go, already missing him. Then she locked the door behind him and went upstairs to take a shower. She caught her reflection in the mirror, saw the telling smile on her face. "You lucky girl."

But as she showered, his story came back to her. Finding Becca dead. Being arrested. Facing interrogation alone.

He must have been so afraid.

And then, being beaten in jail, for God's sake! Living under siege. All of the hatred directed at him and his family.

Sasha found herself in tears again. No wonder he was emotionally closed off and so serious all the time. She understood, too, why correct procedure was so important to him. If not for that detective, he might have gone to prison or been sentenced to death for a crime he hadn't committed.

She dried off, dressed, made herself breakfast. On a whim, she googled his name. There they were—all those newspaper articles about Becca's murder with Darius' mugshot on the cover. He looked so young and terrified.

She became so preoccupied with reading the articles that she almost forgot her therapy appointment and arrived one minute late to find Esri waiting for her.

"How are you feeling?"

Sasha knew she was here to talk about her own situation, but she hadn't been able to stop thinking about what Darius had told her, the details running through her mind again and again. "I got together with Detective Silva last night."

"Got together? You mean you became intimate with him?"

Sasha nodded. "I can't share what he told me, though if you googled his name you'd find it. But my heart breaks for him. He opened up completely, and… I think I'm in love with him."

And that wasn't at *all* what she'd come here to talk about.

Esri looked genuinely surprised. "How long have you known him?"

"I guess it will be a week tomorrow."

"You're in a vulnerable state right now. Do you think that might have an impact on your feelings toward him? He's working to keep you safe, after all."

"It could be, but he's vulnerable, too. You were right about him. You said many law enforcement officers have seen awful things and that they shut off their emotions to cope. That's exactly what happened to him. But last night, he opened up and shared a side of himself that I don't think anyone has seen."

"Sexual intimacy can make it easier for some men to share their feelings. But how are *you* doing? Any nightmares? Anxiety?"

Sasha told her about the anxiety that had troubled her yesterday and how the news that Darius had been shot had given her another panic attack.

Esri gaped at her. "Darius was shot? I saw the news report last night, but they didn't ID the officer. How is he?"

Sasha told Esri what had happened and how she'd had trouble breathing again when she'd gotten the news. "Is that something I'm going to deal with all the time now?"

"I don't know. I'm also not sure that we can blame your response yesterday on the attack. It's hard to say. Hearing that someone you care about has been shot is its own trauma. The two are related, right? The same attacker?"

Sasha nodded. "Yes."

"I think we should devote some time to that at your next session."

They decided to do more EMDR focused on the hit-and-run and see how Sasha felt on Thursday.

Esri turned on the EMDR lights. "Are you comfortable?"

"Yes."

"Just relax."

Chapter 18

DARIUS FINISHED his meeting with Forensics and took his laptop and his folder of printouts to the Forest County Jail, where he was meeting Marcs. Doing his best to put last night out of his mind, he went over his notes with Marcs, bringing her up to speed.

"They found angry messages from Riggs to his friends after Sasha outed him, but within a month or so, she drops out of his conversations."

"That doesn't mean he wasn't plotting something."

"No, of course, it doesn't." Darius set the printout of Riggs' phone activity aside and put Watts' phone records in front of her. "Watts, on the other hand, never let up. He posted online about her and left harassing comments on her social media right up to the day of the attack."

"ClimbrBro? That's Watts?"

"Yeah." Darius pointed to a few of the posts. "On more than one occasion, he threatened her with sexual violence."

Head shaking, Marcs read through his texts and online

comments. "I'm having a hard time feeling bad about his being dead right now."

"Oh, just wait." He took the pages and turned to the relevant printout. "Shortly after Riggs lost his sponsorships, Watts began having conversations with someone using a VPN to conceal their location. The person, who calls himself Tiger889, openly talks about harming Sasha."

"Are we sure that's not just Riggs using a burner or something?"

Darius nodded. "They talk about Riggs in the third person. Watts calls him his 'bro-man' and 'bruh' and shit like that. He really talks Riggs up. It's clear that Watts thought Riggs was some kind of a hero."

"Can you track down this Tiger bastard?"

"I'm working on it, but my guess is that this is the man we're looking for—the one who was in the driver's seat."

"Oh, look, they're trying to speak in code."

"Yes, cute, isn't it? They started referring to 'the project' over and over again. That's climber slang, but I'm also certain it refers to the attack on Sasha. Here, Tiger tells Watts that he'll arrive that weekend. Then, the Saturday before the attack, he tells Watts he's in Denver. They set up an in-person meeting, and that's the last message."

"So, they meet in person to work out the details, and the following Wednesday, they steal the SUV, wait for Sasha to take her bike ride, and strike."

"That's my guess."

"But how did they know Sasha would be going for a bike ride at that time?"

"Social media." Darius called up Sasha's accounts on his laptop, pointed to the screen. "She told them herself."

Darius would have to talk with Sasha about that.

"Shit." Marcs handed the printouts back to Darius.

"It's clear Watts was guilty. He was in the truck. We have a trail of messages to this Tiger guy. We're still looking for him. What do we know about him?"

"He's more tech-savvy than Watts. He's smarter. He doesn't live around here. He must have driven or flown in from elsewhere. And we have a photo of him, taken from Taylor's dashcam."

"What about Riggs?"

"There's a possibility he might not have known about their plans. Unfortunately, he complicated his situation when he sent that text message, warning Watts. I'm going to have a little chat with him now. Want to sit in?"

They walked together to the guard station, turned over their firearms, and asked for Riggs to be brought to one of the secure interview rooms.

Riggs shuffled in, wearing four-piece restraints and an orange jail uniform.

"You look like hell." Darius wasn't kidding.

Riggs clearly hadn't slept worth a damn, his hair rumpled, his jaw dark with stubble. He was probably going through some kind of withdrawal, too, judging from the sweat on his forehead, the chemical scent emanating from his skin, and his pallor.

He glared at Darius. "You again. I thought you'd been shot."

"Me again." Darius sat across from him. "I *was* shot, but I was wearing body armor, so the rounds didn't penetrate. Unfortunately, Kyle Watts didn't make it. He died at the scene from gunshot wounds."

Riggs was clearly shaken by this news, his eyes filling with tears. "I didn't know he was going to shoot at people, or I wouldn't have texted him. I just wanted him to come bail me out. I didn't even know you wanted to arrest him."

Darius wasn't here to talk about that. He started with a welfare check. "Have you been getting meals?"

"If you can call the shit they serve here food."

Darius wouldn't argue. "Do you feel safe? Has anyone harassed you?"

"I'm fine. Why do you care?"

"He cares. Isn't that enough?" Marcs interjected.

Riggs watched Darius, as if trying to decide whether he could trust him. "I've been mostly alone, but the guards aren't very friendly."

"It's not their job to be friendly, but they do need to keep you safe." Darius set a print of the image of Watts and the other man before Riggs. "Who is the man at the wheel?"

Riggs looked at the image but showed no sign of recognition. "No idea."

"Are you sure?"

"If I knew who he was, I would fucking tell you, all right? Then he could back me up and tell you that I had nothing to do with it."

Darius left the print on the table, then set the chat with Tiger889 and ClimbrBro in front of Riggs. "Do you know who these two are?"

Riggs read through the chat, shook his head. "I didn't know about this. I had no idea. I didn't know anything."

"That's not what he asked you." Marcs repeated Darius' question. "Do you know who those two people are?"

Clearly distressed, Riggs pointed. "I know one of them. ClimbrBro—that's Watts. But I don't know the other one."

"Are you certain you've never heard that name before or encountered that person online yourself?"

"Not that I remember." Riggs looked pleadingly at Darius. "Look, man—"

Marcs interrupted. "*Detective*. Call him detective or sir."

Riggs' face turned red, his gaze shifting to Marcs and back. "Detective, I didn't know about this. If I had known, I would have tried to stop him. As much as I think Sasha was a bitch to wreck my career over some stupid photos, I wouldn't try to *kill* her."

"You know what, Riggs?" Darius leaned in, lowered his voice. "I believe you."

Riggs looked like he might cry again. "You… you do?"

Darius nodded. "I believe that you didn't orchestrate this attack or participate in it. But I need you to help me find the bastard who talked Watts into attacking Ms. Dillon. It's *his* fault that your buddy is dead. If you help me, I'll talk to the DA on your behalf."

Riggs nodded. "Okay. What do you need me to do?"

―――

WHEN SHE GOT HOME from her appointment, Sasha fell asleep in her chair, only waking when her mobile buzzed.

Megs.

"Hey!"

"How are you feeling?"

"Sleepy. I just woke from a nap."

"There's a Team meeting this afternoon at one. If you'd like to join us, I'll swing by and pick you up. We can stop at Juana's on the way and eat at The Cave."

Sasha glanced at the time on her phone and was surprised to see it was already twenty past noon. "That sounds great. I'll be ready."

She ended the call, got slowly to her feet, and went in search of her Team notebook. By the time her coat and boots were on and her front door locked, Megs was waiting at the curb, talking with Tommy.

"Hey, Megs. Hey, Tommy." Sasha climbed carefully into the front seat.

"I thought you might like to get a taste of your normal routine. I know everyone will be glad to see you. Besides, who can resist Juana's?"

"Not I." Sasha was just being honest.

"I love Juana's."

"You can follow along, and I'll buy you lunch, too, Tommy."

"Thank you, ma'am." He jogged back to his squad car.

They stopped at Juana's taco truck, the words *Tacos Sabrosos* painted in bright red on the side. She and Megs walked up to the window.

Juana smiled when she saw Sasha. "You're looking good! I'm so happy to see you out and about. Order whatever you want—my treat."

"Thank you, Juana."

"When I heard what had happened..." Juana shook her head, a fallen expression on her face. "Some of the guys out there—they're just loco."

"Some of them *are* loco, Juana. Thank you." Sasha ordered her usual assortment of street tacos—the carne asada, the carnitas, and grilled chicken.

Megs ordered next, and the two of them stood to the side to wait for their food. "I heard the sexy detective had been shot, but I don't know the details."

Sasha shared what she knew, leaving out anything personal.

Megs shook her head in disgust. "I saw Riggs with that asshole Watts a few times out climbing. I never liked either of them."

Everyone knew that Megs was an excellent judge of character.

"It all feels surreal to me. Kyle Watts tried to kill me, and now he's dead. I never met him. He almost killed Darius, too. Darius has huge bruises on his chest...."

The moment the words were out, Sasha knew she was in trouble.

Megs raised an eyebrow. "So you've seen them, these bruises?"

Sasha's face burned. "I gave him an ice pack."

"I see." The smile on Megs' face told Sasha she *did* see.

Megs carried Tommy's order to his vehicle. Then she drove with Sasha to The Cave, where Tommy parked out front. Inside, they found Mitch finishing an inspection of ropes. He stopped when he saw the paper bag in Megs' hands.

"Tacos?"

"Damned straight."

They sat in the Ops Room to eat.

"Don't you think Sasha has a glow about her?" Megs handed Mitch a packet of hot sauce and a napkin.

Mitch looked carefully at Sasha's reddening face. "I suppose she does."

"She's been keeping company with that very handsome detective."

Mitch's eyebrows shot upward as understanding dawned. "Oh."

"It's not like that at all," Sasha lied. "Okay, it's *exactly* like that. But, I really care about him."

That stopped Megs in mid-bite. "I've known you for six years, and during that time, you've dated just a couple of guys. This is the first time you've said that."

Sasha couldn't help but smile. "I know. He's different."

Team members began drifting in, filling seats. One by

one, they checked on her, then milled about, talking. Last to arrive was Nicole.

She rushed through the door just as Megs started roll call, a big smile on her face when she saw Sasha. "I got someone to come in an hour early so I could be here."

"Hey, Nic."

Nicole sat beside Sasha, lowered her voice to a whisper. "So? What happened?"

"Later," Sasha whispered back.

Megs neared the bottom of the attendance sheet. "Austin Taylor is here. And Nicole Turner is here … and pestering Sasha for details about her love life."

"Love life?" Eric cracked open a bottle of water. "Is it the detective?"

All eyes turned her way, and Sasha blushed again. "Stop looking at me."

Megs started the meeting. "We are looking at a slight budget shortfall for this fiscal year—about fifteen grand. It's been a busy year, and a couple of our rescues were hard on the equipment. We need to make major purchases —ropes, trauma kits, new tires for both rescue vehicles. Rather than doing a fundraiser at Knockers, I wanted to share with you all an opportunity that has come our way."

Megs explained that one of the climbing gear stores in Boulder was happy to use their auditorium for presentations by Team members. "They'll charge for tickets, retain the cost, and give us the proceeds."

"Cool!"

"That's great."

Megs held up her hand to quiet the noise. "They say we ought to anticipate a haul of about five grand per night. They say that big-ticket speakers often bring in more."

"Send Sasha." Creed grinned. "She'll fill the coffers."

"Thank you for volunteering your injured teammate, Herrera."

Sasha raised her hand. "I'm happy to do it as soon as this investigation is finished. I don't think I'd feel comfortable being in public before that."

"I wouldn't want you to do it until this is all behind you. It's not worth the risk. The last thing any of us wants is to see you on a stretcher again."

"Amen to that."

"Yeah, no kidding."

Megs looked over at Harrison. "Conrad, your name came up specifically."

"I'll do it. Sign me up."

"Hawke, they asked about you, too. Your role in saving this town didn't go unnoticed outside Scarlet. The program director at the store wonders what it's like to be both the town's fire chief and a Team volunteer."

Hawke looked surprised. "I'll do it, but I can't guarantee anyone will show up."

Taylor laughed. "Seriously, dude? You think 'Hunky firefighter who almost died saving an entire town' won't sell tickets?"

Eric stuck out his chest. "I had no idea you thought I was a hunk, Taylor."

Laughter.

Megs ignored all of this and turned to Chaska. "Belcourt, the store owner asked about you, too. The gear you've designed for us has had a big impact in search-and-rescue circles. He wants to know how you do it and why you won't patent it."

Everyone laughed at the astonishment on Chaska's face.

"I'd be happy to do it, but are they even going to

understand what I'm talking about when I get into the engineering part of it?"

"I have no idea. But they'll pay regardless, so that's all that matters."

More laughter.

Megs looked up from her notepad. "There's our fifteen grand. Sasha, if you're up for it when this case is closed, I'm certain the owner will kiss your feet."

"I'd love to."

"Great. Now, on to other matters. As you know, we normally gather at our place to watch Sasha compete at the world championships. This year is different. Friday, we're having a party at Knockers to support Sasha and cheer on the less-deserving people who will leave with trophies that would have been hers."

Laughter.

———

"YOU MUST BE GOING out of your mind. What's the population of that place?" Brian Kelso grinned at Darius through his computer screen.

"Around fifteen hundred. But, really, it's fine." A part of Darius couldn't believe he'd just said that. "There are some quirky people here, for sure, but at least they're genuine. Most of them are solid—good people who just love the mountains."

"If you say so." Kelso glanced at his watch. "You keep working this from your end, and we'll work it from ours."

"Thanks."

Darius closed his laptop, stood, and stretched, satisfied with the day's progress. With the FBI's access to better tech, he hoped Kelso would be able to track down Tiger889's VPN in a matter of days. In the meantime, he needed to speak to the prosecutor on Riggs' behalf, as he'd promised.

He'd spent the afternoon at the jail, trying not to think about Sasha and searching through climbing-related pages on social media with Riggs. Perhaps because Darius had told Riggs that he believed him, Riggs had been free with his speech, sharing more than he'd realized. Among the details that Darius had found interesting was the fact that Watts had more or less once been Riggs' stalker. Watts had manipulated his way into Riggs' life with flattery and illicit drugs, and then he'd used Riggs and his money, while pretending to be his friend.

More importantly, Darius had found the avatar of the middle finger he'd been searching for on a few climbing subreddits, as well as the comments on Dark Web climbing sites and the comments sections of some climbing webzines. All of this person's comments had focused on Sasha and had been posted in the past six months.

Someone out there hated her with a passion.

Yeah, well, the joke's on you, buddy.

Darius would find him and take him down.

He drew his phone out of his pocket to send Sasha a text but hesitated. What could she still see in him after last night? They'd had mind-blowing sex, and then he'd poured out all of the broken parts of himself. He'd told her the entire story, and then he'd fallen the fuck apart. But rather than judging him or showing disgust, she'd offered him compassion. She'd even *thanked* him.

Those tears belonged to a nineteen-year-old boy who never got the chance to shed them. Thank you for trusting me with that side of yourself.

Darius had never shared his past with anyone, probably because some part of him was still afraid people wouldn't believe him. But Sasha believed him, and she'd made a point of telling him so.

What the hell does she see in you?

Darius pushed the thought aside, sent her a text message to tell her he was done for the day, and asking if she wanted him to stop by, giving her a chance to tell him to fuck off. Her reply was quick and to the point.

`Are you kidding? Can't wait to see you.`

Her words unleashed a rush of pheromones. He'd spent all day pushing aside thoughts of last night, sure he'd be too fucking turned-on and distracted to do his job. But he didn't have to worry about that now.

He packed a few personal items in his duffel— toiletries, razor, a change of clothes, his bathrobe. Then he locked up and took the stairs two at a time down to the Inn's front entrance. In two minutes flat, he stood at Sasha's front door, a list of potential sex positions that wouldn't hurt either of them percolating through his mind.

Yeah, well, he'd better get those out of his head, or he'd walk through the door with a boner.

He knocked, and Sasha answered, wearing a short little black dress that made his jaw drop, her arms, legs, and feet bare, her long blond hair hanging loose. "*Damn.*"

She looked up at him, confused. "Damn?"

Had he said that aloud?

He tried to get a grip. "You look… *hot.*"

He stepped inside, closed the door, dropped his bag on the floor—and kissed her. Maybe it was the fact that he'd tried to block her from his mind all day, but he wanted her—now.

"The table." His voice sounded gruff—a measure of his need for her.

"*Yes*." She walked backward to the dining table and, without him to steady her, stepped onto a chair, and then sat on the edge of the table.

She pulled that little dress above her hips to expose her panties then spread her legs. "You're all I could think about all day."

Geezus!

He pushed the crotch of her panties aside. "You're everything I tried *not* to think about all day."

Then he dropped to his knees and claimed her with his mouth. He'd learned a lot about her last night, and he put all that sexual knowledge to use now, lavishing attention on her clit, sliding a finger inside her to stroke her.

She threaded her fingers through his hair, spread her legs wider, her toes curling, her breath going ragged.

God, yes.

She tasted so good—like desire and woman.

He willed himself to be patient, to give her enough time to get close to the edge. He knew he wasn't going to last long this time, his cock aching. When her hips started moving, thrusting toward his face, he lost it.

He stood, positioned himself between her thighs, and slowly buried himself inside her wet heat, carefully encircling her waist to support her. "*Sasha*. God, you feel good."

She felt even better than he remembered. But any notion he'd had about going slowly went up in flames when she wrapped those athletic legs around him and held him close. He thrust into her, driving deep and fast, her heels digging into his ass, the pressure somehow adding to his pleasure.

They both moaned with every thrust, her head falling back, her eyes squeezed shut, her lips parted. He kissed her throat, inhaled her scent, tried to focus on her pleasure. Oh, but he was losing this battle.

Panting. Sweating. Heat rising. His self-control melting.

She cried out as she came, pleasure lighting up her face, the sight of her driving Darius over the edge, the two of them falling together through fire into paradise.

Chapter 19

THE NEXT FEW days were magical for Sasha. She was still healing and slept more than usual during the day. But at night...

No man had ever made Sasha feel the way Darius did —giddy, breathless, as if she were out of her mind in the best possible way. She was crazy in love with him. She hadn't told him. It had all gone so quickly. It made no sense.

Still, Sasha was in love with him.

It wasn't just the sex that blew her mind. It was Darius. His stiff suits and seriousness had concealed a sensitive man with a big heart. Every day, he seemed to laugh a little easier and smile more.

Sasha knew he would solve her case sooner rather than later and that they would have to decide what would become of their relationship. But she couldn't worry about that now, not when he was here with her.

On Wednesday, he took time off to go with her to get her stitches out and was the first to sign her bright pink cast.

A true champion — Dare

Later that afternoon, Chief Randall called to tell Sasha he was withdrawing her protection detail because he didn't have the staff. "I can't keep this up without giving myself a heart attack. I need Tommy and the others back. I'm too old to be chasing people myself."

Apparently, Chief Randall had already contacted Darius, who shot her a text a moment later to ask whether she was okay with his staying at her place from now on.

As if she would object to that…

When it came to her case, he shared very little. She knew they were still looking for the guy who'd driven the stolen SUV and that the FBI had gotten involved. But he wouldn't tell her more.

"It's an ongoing case, so I really can't talk about it," he'd told her that night, holding her in his arms. "If we weren't sleeping together, you would only hear from me when I had questions or news to share."

Because Sasha knew it was important for him to maintain professional standards of conduct, she quit asking. He was already breaking the rules by being with her. She wouldn't push him to do anything more.

On Thursday morning, Scott, her manager, called to insist she do a slate of interviews. "The biggest news of the world championships is that you won't be there. People want to know what happened. Your sponsors really want these interviews, kiddo. You won't be competing or climbing for a while, and they need this from you to justify the big dollars."

Sasha didn't feel like she had any choice. She sent a quick text to Darius, explaining the situation and asking him if he thought it was safe for her to tell reporters the truth. Most people still didn't know that her cycling *accident* had been a deliberate act of violence.

Darius called her. "Please don't mention any of the suspects or Watts' death. So far, it's only gotten a mention in the local papers. If people learn it's related to an assault against you, I'm afraid it will blow up. We're hoping the driver doesn't know Watts is dead so we can take advantage of having his phone."

Sasha did five interviews over the phone that afternoon, maintaining the cover story of her bicycle accident, and answering their many questions.

Yes, she was lucky to be alive. Yes, she missed being in Bratislava with her climbing friends. Yes, her injuries were healing, and she would be climbing again soon. No, she wasn't upset that her five-year winning streak had come to an end. She was bound to fall off that pedestal sooner or later, right? Yes, she had the highest score moving into this final competition of the year, but she couldn't say with certainty that she would have won if she'd competed.

"They're more obsessed with trophies than I am," Sasha told Darius that night, the two of them snuggled together, replete and naked, on her bed. "I like to win, but there's more to life and climbing than trophies."

"Your work with the Team, for example."

Sasha loved that Darius understood. "Yes."

He traced his fingertips lazily up her spine. "When Nicole first told me that you joined the Team because it made you happy to save lives, some cynical part of me thought she was just a fan who saw you through rose-colored lenses."

"Really?"

"Yes. Here's this beautiful young woman with a stellar athletic career, lots of money, and fame, and she chooses to use her skill to rescue people."

"Is that so strange?"

He smiled. "It's not strange for you. But I cut my teeth

as a detective protecting celebrities—men and women—who never did anything without an ulterior motive. They were always working an angle."

"What a sad way to live."

"Tell me about it."

"Are you going to be able to join us tomorrow? The live stream of the competition starts at seven in the evening in Bratislava, which is eleven here."

"I'll try to come to Knockers for lunch, but I've got a pretty full day."

Sasha refused to feel disappointed. She ran her fingers over his bruised chest. "I know you're working hard to catch this guy. We can stream it tomorrow night if you have to miss it—that is, if you want to watch it."

"Of course, I want to watch, but you might have to explain a few things."

———

"SENDING IT NOW." Darius tapped a message into Watts' mobile phone, Deputy Marcs looking over his shoulder.

They busted Riggs. They think he did it.
What do you want me to do?

On Darius' screen, Kelso nodded. "I see it. We're tracking it. Now we wait."

Darius had no idea whether Tiger889 would respond or whether he was sending this text message to a burner phone that had already been abandoned. But they would soon find out.

The phone had been hooked up to the system, so the message included an encrypted recorder that would gather data and send it back to be validated and then securely stored with forensics. It was the most cutting-edge tech they had for situations like this. If they were lucky, they'd get a location for the phone.

"What happens if we get nothing, if he doesn't answer?" Marcs asked.

"This isn't our only iron in the fire. We'll find this bastard."

With the FBI's muscle behind him, Darius had served the various social media companies with warrants for identifying information for Tiger889—his ISP address, his email address, and any other information they might have.

"Thanks for your help on this one, Kelso. I'm going to head out for an early lunch. Let me know if you get anything."

"Will do."

Darius ended the virtual meeting and got to his feet, planning to spend the next couple of hours with Sasha watching the world championships. She put a brave face on it, but he knew it must be hard to be sidelined, especially given how it had happened. "Are you coming to Knockers?"

Marcs shook her head. "Some of us have to work. I've got a lot of shit that's piled up this past week."

"Sorry you'll miss it."

"Tell Sasha hi for me." Deputy Marcs left.

"I will." He slipped his concealed carry weapon into his pocket holster and drove to the pub. It was only a short distance from the substation, and he could have walked. But he would rather have his vehicle on hand should he need it than lose ten minutes running to fetch it.

He stepped through the door and found Knockers transformed. Extra TVs had been positioned where everyone could see them, clusters of yellow and pink helium balloons tied everywhere.

He waved to Marcia, the bartender, who was filling a mug with beer. "Hey, Marcia. How's it going?"

"Hey, Detective Silva. Good to see you again." Marcia smiled, her gaze on him for a moment too long, the mug overflowing, spilling beer onto her hands. "Oh!"

Rain waved to him. "You've come to join the madness. She's back at the Team table with most of the gang."

"Thanks. I know the way." Darius threaded his way between crowded tables, warmth blossoming in his chest when he saw.

Sasha sat, surrounded by her friends, an enormous bouquet of pink and yellow roses beside her.

Her friends were taking care of her.

All eyes were on the screen, where a young woman with a dark ponytail seemed to move up the rock wall like a spider, reaching the top in seconds.

Cheers went up, Sasha applauding.

"That's a new women's speed climbing world record! Way to go, Akari!"

Megs was the first one to see Darius. "Make room next to Sasha for the brave detective. Herrera, that means you. Yes, you. Move your butt."

Sasha turned, her face lighting up when she saw him, the brightness of her smile putting a hitch in his chest. "Dare!"

Yeah, he was a goner.

He sat beside her. "Deputy Marcs says hi. What's happened so far?"

"This is the women's speed climbing finals. Akari Kiyama from Japan just set a new world record. I think Maritza and Daryna Andrusenko are up next."

"Maritza Braun is one of Sasha's best buds," Megs explained, all but shouting so he could hear her. "I'll be cheering for her, and so will you."

Darius chuckled. "Got it."

Sasha took a sip of what looked like iced tea. "Speed climbing isn't her strength—or mine. It's always my worst event. My best time on a fifteen-meter wall was seven-point-one-two-eight seconds."

"That's such a narrow margin."

"It is, but it matters." While Sasha explained how scoring worked at the world championships, Cheyenne took Darius' drink order.

The chatter stilled as the two women stepped up to the wall and got ready, their hands on the first holds. Three loud beeps, and they were off, flying up the wall in seconds.

Sasha cheered when her friend topped out. "Way to go, Mari! Not a world record, but a solid seven-point-two-five-one. She's still in the lead. That's the best speed climbing time of her career."

"Go, Maritza!" Sasha drew out her phone and tapped in a message, presumably congratulating her friend.

On the screen, a reporter motioned a smiling Maritza off to the side.

"That was a new personal best. How do you feel going into the bouldering portion of the competition?" The reporter held the mic out for Maritza to answer.

"I feel great." Maritza shook out her arms. "I've been training hard all season and competing well. I'm going out there to do nothing less than my best."

The reporter asked another question. "Do you think you'd be in the lead right now if Sasha Dillon hadn't wrecked her bike and withdrawn from the competition because of her injuries?"

Darius glanced at Sasha, saw her cringe at the question.

Maritza's expression changed to an angry scowl. "Why

do you journalists keep talking about Sasha Dillon? Sasha isn't here. She is the past."

As Maritza stormed off, the brewpub exploded with loud boos and shouts.

"You're just jealous!"

"That's not true!"

"What a bitch!"

A man who'd clearly had too much to drink lurched to his feet and pointed unsteadily at the TV. "Come say that to my face, bitch, and I'll show you—"

"Sit down, Hank!" Bob Jewell shouted.

But Sasha's gaze was fixed on the screen, hurt and surprise on her face. "He shouldn't have asked her a question like that. She's under a lot of pressure. I'm sure she didn't mean that the way it came out."

But Darius wasn't so sure.

———

"I WISH the commentators would quit talking about me." Sasha didn't want her fellow climbers to think she was stealing their limelight.

"You are a five-time world champion." Darius put his arm around her shoulder. "If not for the attack, you'd be at the competition. How can they not mention you?"

"I suppose you're right." Sasha still felt the sting of Maritza's comment, her hurt deepened by the fact that Maritza hadn't responded to any of her text messages.

Megs must have overheard the two of them because she traded places with Creed and sat beside Sasha. "If Maritza and the other climbers get their feelings hurt because a reporter mentions you, that is *their* problem. Don't let Maritza's temper tantrum get under your skin. You're the most celebrated women's sports climber in history. You're not at the competition only because some asshats tried to kill you. How can the reporters do their job without mentioning you?"

An image of Sasha from last year's world championships filled the screen, as the two commentators discussed her career and her accident.

"You're right."

Megs patted her arm. "Of course, I'm right."

Darius stood. "I need to make a pit stop. Can I get you anything?"

"More water?"

He squeezed her shoulder. "You've got it."

Sasha watched him walk away.

Megs leaned closer. "He's a good man. I hope it works out for you two."

"So do I."

Rain brought a pitcher of ice water. "Darius said you needed more water, so I brought some for the whole table. We'll get your lunch dishes cleared away. Is there anything else I can bring you—dessert, coffee, beer, nachos?"

By the time the table had been cleared and glasses refilled, Darius returned, a frown on his face, phone in hand.

"Is everything okay?"

He nodded, but the frown didn't leave his face. He glanced up at the screen. "What did I miss?"

"Nothing. They're about to start the bouldering portion of the competition." Sasha explained how each climber had four minutes to top out. "The goal is to finish with both hands on the top hold in a controlled manner. You can't just throw yourself at it, tap it, and call it a win. You have to hold it."

The women's competition came first, and though Sasha still rooted for Maritza, her heart was no longer in it.

Sasha is the past.

Even as Sasha rejected that idea, some part of her wondered whether Maritza was right. Was her career over? Was this attack the end of her life as a serious competitor?

Stop it!

The only person who could decide what kind of future Sasha had in competitive climbing was Sasha herself.

In the end, Maritza came in first, managing to stick an awkwardly placed sloper that caused most of the women to fall.

Sasha tried to explain to Darius what had happened. "They had too much momentum going for that sloper. Their feet swung out, and that threw them off the route. It's hard to keep the motion of your body in check when you make big moves like that. I try to make sure one of my legs is providing counter-balance."

This time when the reporters wanted to interview Maritza, she shot an angry glance their way and ignored them, smiling and waving to the cheering audience, the news cameras following her as she walked off the floor.

Darius was on his feet, pointing at the screen. "Pause it! Can someone pause it?"

Without waiting for an answer, he jumped onto the table and leaped to the floor, dashing toward the giant flat-screen TV with his phone in hand.

Austin shot to his feet, too, and jogged off, shouting for Rain. "Pause the streaming! Yes, pause it! It's important!"

The room around them fell silent.

The image on the television froze, Darius snapping photo after photo, his actions drawing Sasha's gaze back to the screen.

Her blood went cold. "It's him. It's the man who drove the SUV."

He was there, in Bratislava, and he was standing with Maritza, the two of them smiling and talking.

Blood rushed into Sasha's head, the thrum of her pulse against her eardrums drowning out all sound in the room.

Megs said something, put an arm around her.

Eric came to sit on her other side, a big hand coming to rest on her back. "Breathe, Sasha. Just breathe. In and out."

Sasha tried to do as Eric said, but there was a knot in her throat and a hole where her heart should have been.

"In and out. There you go. That's right. You're okay. We're all here with you."

Gradually, her shock subsided, her heartbeat slowing, her scattered thoughts coalescing into a single question. Had Maritza betrayed her?

Then Darius was there.

He knelt before her. "I need to go, Sasha. Go with Megs and Mitch, okay? Someone will stay with you until I get there tonight."

She took hold of his hand. "That was him, wasn't it? He was talking to Maritza."

Darius nodded. "I need to move fast if I'm going to catch this son of a bitch."

He kissed her and was gone.

As if in a dream, Sasha stood, Megs and Mitch on either side of her as they made their way through the restaurant. She barely noticed the people watching as she passed or heard what they said to her.

Rain and Joe met her at the front, concern on their faces.

"I'm so sorry," Sasha said. "I'm ruining this beautiful party. Thanks for everything—the flowers, the balloons."

"You're not ruining anything, sweetie—and you're

welcome." Rain kissed her cheek. "You go rest and don't worry about a thing. None of this is your fault."

"Thank you," Sasha repeated, nothing around her seeming real.

She was buckled into the front seat of Megs' SUV before it occurred to her to ask. "Where are we going?"

"We're driving you home so you can rest. We will stay with you, okay?"

"Okay."

Chapter 20

DARIUS SPOKE with Kelso as he drove to the substation, where Marcs would meet him. "You got the photo to Interpol?"

"They have the photo and our files, including the footage that shows him at the wheel of the stolen SUV. They're running it through their facial recognition software. They've already contacted the Slovak Police Force and given them his whereabouts."

That was good news.

"If this bastard figures out we're onto him, he might bolt."

"I expressed our concern to the State Department. They've reached out to our embassy in Slovakia. There's not a lot you can do right now but wait."

Darius wasn't good at waiting. "If we get him, will someone from the US be permitted to be present during the interrogation?"

"Yes, and he..." Kelso's words trailed off. "I just got a reply to the message you sent this morning."

"What did he say?"

"Oh, nice. He said, 'Fuck off. Don't contact me again!' According to the data we're getting back, the phone is in Bratislava."

Darius brought his fist down on the steering wheel. "It *has* to be him. I'll check in when I get to the office. I need to bring local law enforcement up to date."

"Brief the locals, and get back to me."

Marcs was waiting for Darius outside the building, pacing back and forth in front of the entrance. "Tell me everything."

Darius walked with her to his makeshift office and showed her the images on his phone. "I was watching the sports climbing world championships with Sasha and the Team and saw this asshole on the screen."

"Son of a bitch!"

"Kelso, my FBI contact, told me they traced the message I sent this morning to Bratislava, where the competition is happening, so there's no doubt. This is our guy."

"So this asshole isn't a US citizen?"

"We don't know that yet. We don't know anything about him, not even his name. All we know is that he's there at the world championships with what's-her-face—Sasha's friend, the one who looks like she's going to win."

Marcs gaped at him. "This asshole was talking to one of her friends? Do you think this friend knew about it?"

Darius reined in his rage, willed himself to lock down his emotions. "We don't have any evidence one way or another yet."

"If the suspect is in Slovakia and we're in Scarlet, what can we do to help?"

"We get to work and build a case so that, if and when

they arrest him, we've got what we need to request extradition and convict the bastard."

While Marcs contacted TSA and asked for security footage for the day the text messages said the suspect had arrived, Darius called the office of the state's attorney general and got subpoenas for the flight manifests of every plane that landed that day.

If only they had this bastard's name…

When that was done, Darius found himself in unfamiliar territory. All he could do now was wait. Wait for the TSA footage. Wait for the flight manifests. Wait for Kelso to get back to him with a sitrep from Slovakia.

He stood in front of the whiteboard, his frustration rising. "Damn it."

He *hated* feeling helpless.

Marcs stood, walked over to him, touched her hand to his shoulder. "You've done everything you can, Silva. You can't be everywhere at once. You can't control the outcome of every situation. Think of it this way. While this loser is in Slovakia, we know he can't hurt our girl."

"True." Darius could be grateful for that. "I should have thought of this. I told you the day we met that motive was the key. Sasha was hit the week before the world championships. It didn't occur to me that someone might want to get her out of the way."

"Don't be hard on yourself." Marcs motioned to the door with a jerk of her head. "Come on. Let's get a cup of shitty coffee from the break room and maybe some kind of toxic snack food."

Darius chuckled. "I can see why Darcangelo and Hunter like you."

"It took you that long to figure it out?" Shaking her head, Marcs led the way to the small breakroom.

Darius took a clean mug from the dishwasher, poured coffee into his cup. "You should have seen the shock on Sasha's face. She saw him on the TV screen talking with her friend, and I watched her heart break."

"You really care about her, don't you?"

Darius wouldn't bother to deny it. "Yeah. She's special."

Marcs smiled. "You're smarter than you look."

Darius was about to offer some witty rejoinder when his phone buzzed. "It's Kelso. Silva here."

"They arrested him. He's in custody. His name is Hans Jakob Reiter, and he's an Austrian national."

"Hans Jakob Reiter." Darius passed the news to Marcs. "They arrested him."

"Yes!"

Kelso wasn't done. "He's in custody now in Bratislava. Interpol had a file on him with a short but serious list of priors—auto theft, assault, public brawling."

"A model citizen. How long will they hold him?"

"As it turns out, he had some Colorado agriculture on his person when they arrested him, so he's going nowhere. You've got the time you need."

That was a relief. "I take it marijuana is still illegal there."

"Very. He's looking at three years to a dime here in Slovakia."

Darius didn't like that. "I want him here, in the US, enjoying the hospitality of the Colorado State Penitentiary."

"That's up to the diplomats. We have an extradition treaty with Austria, but it's a complicated process. For now, they've offered to send over his records and his fingerprints. They've also invited us to be part of the interrogation virtually. One of the spooks assigned to protect the embassy staff in Bratislava will question him, but you can brief him ahead of time and message him with follow-up questions."

Kelso gave him the agent's contact information.

"Perfect. Thanks, man."

"Hey, it's nice to work with you again. It's been a while. Let me know what else I can do to help. I'll stay in contact with State and our agent from the embassy and update you on any new developments."

"Thanks." Darius ended the call, shared what Kelso had told him.

"One of our CIA guys is questioning him?" Marcs seemed to be happy about this.

"Yes, with our help. We've got a lot to do to get ready."

———

SASHA SAT ON HER RECLINER, Megs, Mitch, and Nicole sitting on her sofa and floor, watching a documentary about Yellowstone National Park, food from Knockers and the big bouquet Rain and Joe had gotten her arranged on the coffee table.

But Sasha could barely focus on the documentary, an image fixed in her mind of the man who'd tried to kill her talking with Maritza.

Had Maritza known? Sasha hoped with her whole heart that she hadn't. Then again, how could she not?

Darius had sent her a text to let her know the police in Slovakia had arrested him and that he would participate in questioning him.

Hans Jakob Reiter.

That was his name. But who was he? And what was his relationship to Maritza?

Maritza still hadn't replied to any of Sasha's text messages congratulating her for winning the world championship. Sasha hadn't watched the lead climbing part of the competition or the award ceremony, but Megs had followed it on social media and let Sasha know the outcome.

"I hope she's happy," Megs had said. "I doubt she'll have that trophy for long."

Nicole had made a point of reminding Sasha that she was safe. "One of the men who attacked you is in the morgue, and the other one is in jail."

Yesterday, she would have found comfort in that news. But today…

Maritza was one of her best friends. They had climbed together all over the world. They'd stood side by side on the winners' podium at dozens of competitions. Had Maritza's friendship been an act?

The thought left Sasha feeling hollow.

Buzz. Buzz.

Sasha looked at her phone, saw that Scott was calling. She let it go to voicemail. He'd called earlier to tell her that reporters wanted her response to Maritza's harsh words about her. But Sasha didn't want to talk to anyone right now, apart from Darius and her closest friends here in Scarlet, of course.

On her TV, bison plowed through deep snow, grunting as they moved, their shaggy fur covered in flakes.

Sasha had always known that competitive climbing had a dark underbelly. There'd been more than a few doping scandals. Climbers had been caught trying to bribe route-setters for beta on the routes before competing. One had tried to get a route-setter to create a route that played to his strengths. But none of this had ever touched Sasha personally. She'd tried to rise above it, believing that most competitive climbers were honest people who loved the sport as much as she did.

Had she been wrong?

Buzz. Buzz.

"Scott again?" Megs asked.

Sasha nodded. "I don't want to talk to the media right now. He just doesn't understand."

Megs took Sasha's phone and answered in a near-whisper. "Megs Hill here. Sasha is asleep. She's not feeling at all well. I'm sure she'll call you back when she's better. No, Scott, no interviews. The media will have to wait until she's up to it."

"How did he react?"

"No idea." Megs set Sasha's phone down beside her. "I hung up on him mid-sentence."

"Thanks, Megs."

"You're welcome."

"No, I mean thanks for all of it. I wouldn't be the climber I am without you. You inspired me in so many ways—climbing, the Team, your attitude. Your support has meant everything to me."

Megs rested her hand on top of Sasha's. "You're welcome, but please don't tell me I'm the wind beneath your wings, or I'll have to cry."

Sasha smiled. "You warned me that competitive sports climbing could be dirty. I should have listened."

Mitch, who sat on the far end of the sofa, leaned forward so he could see Sasha. "This isn't your fault, sweetie. None of us could have imagined this."

Megs nodded. "He's right."

"An hour before I left on my bike ride, Maritza and I were messaging back and forth. She knew I was going for a conditioning ride—and she knew where."

God, it hurt to say those words aloud.

"Hear me, Sasha." Megs' expression was fierce. "If Maritza played any role in this, Darius and the others will uncover it, and her career will be over. I know that doesn't lessen your sense of betrayal, but she will pay."

Tears filled Sasha's eyes. "I've known her for six years —as long as I've known you. We've traveled together, climbed together, laughed together. I considered her a close friend. Was it all an act?"

Nicole got up from the floor and knelt beside Sasha. "I know this sucks, but your real friends, the friends who would do anything for you—we're right here. We won't let you face this alone."

Sasha sniffed. "Thanks, Nic. You're right. My real friends are here in Scarlet. I'm lucky to have you all in my life."

Nicole squeezed her hand. "We all think we're lucky to have *you*."

Sasha tried to focus on that—and not the knot in her stomach.

―――

DARIUS PULLED into Sasha's driveway, turned off his vehicle, and sat there, wondering how he was going to do this. Sasha already suspected the worst. He'd seen it on her face at Knockers—the shock, the deep sense of betrayal. Now, he had to confirm that and break her heart again.

He drew a breath, climbed out of the SUV, and was glad to see Nicole's vehicle and Megs and Mitch's sitting at the curb.

He made his way to her door and knocked.

Megs answered. "We were just talking about you. Come in."

Sasha stood and hurried over to him, and he could see

she'd been crying. She wrapped her arms around him. "I'm so glad you're here."

"It's good to see you, too." Mindful of her ribs, he held her, the feel of her in his arms precious.

She was alive and safe, and he was so damned grateful for that.

"Maybe we should go," Megs offered, "unless you think we should stay."

Darius knew Megs was curious. "I'll leave that up to Sasha."

Sasha stepped back, the fingers of her left hand twining with his. "I'm fine if you all stay. I know you want to hear what happened as much as I do."

They settled around the dining room table with a fresh pot of tea that Nicole had just made.

"As you know, the Slovak police have Reiter in custody. Authorities there have charged him with possession of marijuana, which he bought while he was here. The State Department is putting together a case for extradition. I won't go into that, except to say that it's a long process with no guarantees."

Nicole frowned. "You mean he might never go to trial here?"

"That's a possibility." Darius took Sasha's hand. "Reiter has been cooperative. He gave the Slovak police access to his mobile phone and his laptop, which they retrieved from his hotel room there in Bratislava. The embassy staff member who interrogated him has already uploaded all of that information to Forensics. It paints a very clear picture."

Beside him, Sasha seemed to be holding her breath.

Darius thought the best thing he could do for her was to come out with it. "I'm so sorry, Sasha, but Maritza

Braun was the driving force behind the attempt on your life."

Sasha let out a little sob, her eyes filling with tears.

Megs rubbed Sasha's back, leaned in close. "There is nothing that hurts more than being betrayed by someone you thought was a friend."

"That fucking bitch." Nicole stood, stomped across the room to retrieve a box of tissues for Sasha, and returned, her face red with fury. "She better never come near me."

Sasha looked over at Darius, tears on her cheeks. "It was her idea?"

Darius nodded. "She and Reiter used bogus social media accounts to recruit Watts, preying on his loyalty to Riggs. They talked him into this over a period of months, with Braun acting as the mastermind. The original idea was for the two men to injure you enough to keep you from competing. Reiter says it was Watts' idea to kill you, but it's hard to say whether Watts came up with that on his own or whether the two of them worked him up to it."

Sasha reached for a tissue, dabbed her eyes. "This can't be real."

"I'm sorry, angel. I wish it weren't." Darius told her how Braun had gotten Reiter in touch with Watts on social media, how she'd bought Reiter's plane ticket, how she'd done her best to ensure they wouldn't screw up and leave evidence. "She was counting on the police going after Riggs and Watts and blaming the attack on them. Given that Watts did, indeed, play a role, she used them as a smokescreen to hide her involvement."

Megs still had a hand on Sasha's back. "Jesus fried chicken. So, she was the brain, and they were the brawn?"

"That's what Reiter alleges." Darius had no reason not to believe him.

"But how did they know *when* to steal the vehicle?"

"They got that information from you. Remember your chat with Braun not long before you took off for your bike ride?"

Sasha nodded. "Right. I remember. So, she told them."

"While the two of you were messaging back and forth, she sent a text to Reiter and Watts. They stole the car and parked near the roundabout to wait for you. Afterward, they ditched the vehicle, climbed into a rental that Reiter had parked near Boulder Falls earlier that day, and drove back into Boulder. Reiter dropped Watts off at Riggs' place and drove to DIA to catch a flight to Slovakia. He and Braun were surprised when you texted Braun the next day and they heard you were still alive."

Sasha was clearly reeling, the hurt on her face making Darius' chest ache. "I thought Maritza really cared about me. I thought we were friends."

"She cared about winning. Reiter says she knew she was moving beyond her prime and that this might be her last chance at the title. She told him she couldn't win if you were in the competition. The avatar of the middle finger? That's hers."

"Where is Braun now?" Mitch looked like he might want to settle the score with her personally.

"We don't know. When Reiter was arrested, she took off. She's in the wind. You don't have to worry about her coming to Scarlet. We put out an arrest warrant, and TSA knows to be on the lookout. My guess is she's on her way back to Germany. They won't extradite their citizens to the US."

"I think I'm going to be sick." Sasha lurched to her feet and darted from the room.

Darius hurried after her and held her hair while she threw up, a process that clearly caused her intense pain because of her ribs. Feeling absolutely helpless, he rubbed her back, held her hand, tried to offer her reassurance. "It's going to be okay, angel."

Damn it!

Afterward, Darius handed her a cold washcloth, helped her rinse her mouth and brush her teeth. "Come. You need to rest."

Chapter 21

SASHA AWOKE to find herself alone, Darius' side of the bed cold. She slowly sat up, put on leggings and a T-shirt, and made her way downstairs to find him talking on his phone in her office.

His gaze softened when he saw her. "I'll see you this afternoon in Denver. Thanks for the update, Kelso."

He was leaving?

Sasha's heart sank.

She wasn't ready to say goodbye. They'd never talked about their relationship, never spoken of what would happen when the case was resolved and the bad guys were in custody. She'd never told him how she felt about him.

He ended the call, slipped his phone into his pocket. "Hey. My phone kept buzzing. I didn't want to wake you, so I came down here. How do you feel?"

Sasha wasn't sure how to answer that, especially not now that she knew he was going home. "It still doesn't seem real. You're going back to Denver today?"

"The feds have taken over the case. My part is done. We're holding a joint press conference in Denver this afternoon at one. The Slovak police have held off on going public so we can break the news first."

"That's good, I guess."

"It gives us time to prepare for the media onslaught."

"Oh. Right." She hadn't thought about that.

"There's more." Darius drew her into his arms. "German police arrested Braun in Munich this morning. The State Department is working with them to question her. At this point, it looks like German authorities will put her on trial and sentence her there."

"Will I have to testify?"

"I don't know." Darius drew back, looked into her eyes. "I'm really sorry that things turned out this way."

Sasha touched her palm to his cheek. "Don't be sorry. Everyone thought it was Bren Riggs and Watts. But you stuck to the evidence. Because of you, the person behind all of this is in jail now. Thank you."

"You're welcome." He kissed her forehead. "You hungry? I thought I could make some omelets."

"That sounds really good."

While Darius chopped onions, red peppers, and mushrooms for the omelets, Sasha made coffee and checked her messages. There were a half dozen from Scott, once again asking for her response to Maritza's harsh comments yesterday.

"Bad news?"

"Just my manager. He's pushing me to do interviews. Apparently, the climbing world is waiting with bated breath for my response to Maritza."

"He's behind the times." Darius popped four pieces of wheat bread into the toaster, then went back to making omelets. "I've got a proposition for you. Why don't you come to Denver with me?"

"For the press conference?"

"You can give a statement, give the media something to chew on for a while. Then, rather than coming back to Scarlet Springs afterward, you can stay at my place for the week. You can avoid reporters, and we can spend some real time together. I've asked Irving for the week off."

Sasha's heart lifted. "I would love that."

Darius flipped the omelets. "That's the first smile I've seen on your face since yesterday."

Sasha decided to take a risk. "I don't want us to say goodbye."

"Who said anything about saying goodbye?"

They ate their breakfast, talking about personal things and not the case—where he'd learned to cook, his condo, how Denver compared to LA.

"When my colleagues in Denver complain about the traffic, I just laugh. Sometimes it took me two hours to drive eight miles."

Sasha gaped at him. "How could you get anything done?"

His gaze met hers over the top of his coffee mug, a grin on his handsome face. "With a lot of cussing—and, if it's really urgent, helicopters."

While he cleaned up, she took a quick shower and worked on her statement, running it by Darius to make sure she didn't give away anything she shouldn't.

He nodded as he read it. "You can cut out all the tech details. The feds and I will handle that. But, yeah, this looks good otherwise."

While he broke down the gear in her office and packed it into his truck, she put a week's worth of toiletries and clothes into her carry-on and then dressed in something nice and put on a little makeup. Then she canceled the week's appointments with Esri and texted Megs, Nicole, her parents, and her manager to tell them about the press conference and that she would be going away for a week's rest.

Darius drove first to the Inn, where he packed the rest of his stuff, giving Sasha a chance to check out the locally famous Matchless Suite.

She glanced around, impressed. "This is beautiful. So elegant."

"You should try the croissants."

They went downstairs, where Darius checked out, thanking Bob and Kendra for their hospitality. "I will happily recommend this place."

Bob shook his hand. "We appreciate that. Thanks for helping Sasha."

"My pleasure."

When they went outside, Sasha spotted Rose peering out her front window. "Here comes Rose."

Rose hurried out the door, down her front steps, and across the street. "You're leaving town already, Detective Silva? Hi, Sasha."

Darius put his bag and other gear in the back of the vehicle. "My work on this case is done."

Rose glanced over at Sasha. "You're going with him?"

Sasha knew Rose was fishing for gossip. "I'm giving a statement at a press conference in Denver. He's driving me."

"Ah." Seemingly at a loss for words, Rose stood there for a moment.

"He's less than half your age, Rose!" Bob bellowed from the front door.

Rose glowered at Bob, raised her chin. "Nice to have met you, detective."

Darius looked like he was fighting not to laugh. "Take care, Rose."

Then they headed to the sheriff's substation so that

Darius could gather all the case files and other materials from his office there.

Sasha glanced around, took in the meticulous notes on the whiteboard, the neatly stacked files. "This is so *you*."

Darius was about to reply when Deputy Marcs appeared in the doorway.

"So, you're leaving us and heading back to Denver."

"There's a press conference at one. Aren't you going to be there?"

"Are you kidding? Sheriff Pella is handling that himself."

Sasha didn't like that. "That's not fair. You did the work."

"That's okay." Julia shrugged. "The underlings put in the hours, and the bosses get all the credit. I'm used to it."

Sasha walked over to her, gave a careful hug. "Thank you, Julia. And thanks for saving Darius' life."

"Just doing my job."

Julia followed them out to Darius' vehicle and held out her hand, a smile on her face. "I learned a lot from you, Silva. You're right. I let my prejudice and my emotions cloud my judgment. If it had been up to me, we would have arrested Riggs and Watts for the crime and been done with it."

Darius shook her hand. "Thanks, Marcs. I learned a lot from you, too."

She stepped back, looking confused. "Like what?"

He chuckled, opened the door for Sasha. "Like when it's good to break the rules."

Julia laughed. "Glad I could help. Now, get out of my town."

"See you around, Deputy Marcs." Darius climbed into the driver's seat, Julia watching as they drove away.

⸻

DARIUS WAITED outside the women's restroom for Sasha, who'd gone in to check her hair and makeup. It was the first time he'd seen her try to accentuate her appearance, and he understood why. She'd been badly hurt, both physically and emotionally, and she didn't want it to show.

"Hey, man." Darcangelo came up behind him. "Congrats on closing this case so quickly."

"Thanks." Then Darius got an idea. "Hey, there are a lot of reporters and random bystanders out there. Would you mind playing security for Sasha? She's been through a rough time. I'd feel better if I knew someone had eyes on the crowd."

"No problem. Let me see if I can get Hunter to join us." He pulled out his phone, sent a text message.

"Julian!" Sasha stepped out of the bathroom, smiling when she saw them.

"Hey, there, Sasha." Darcangelo started to give her a hug, but Darius stopped him.

"Broken ribs."

"Oh, right." Darcangelo bumped fists with Sasha instead. "I'm really sorry about what happened. How do you feel?"

"I'm healing, but my ribs still hurt a lot."

Irving and Pella appeared, heading toward the door, Pella in uniform, Irving in a sports jacket and tie.

Irving saw them, introduced himself to Sasha. "You two ready?"

Darius nodded. "Yes, sir."

Hunter came around the corner. "I'm here. Hey, Sasha."

Another bright smile. "Marc!"

"Don't hug her, Hunter," Darcangelo warned. "Broken ribs."

"Right." Another fist bump. "Glad to see you doing so well."

They followed Irving and Pella toward the front doors, where they found Kelso waiting for them in a tailored suit and mirrored Ray-Bans.

Kelso introduced himself to Sasha first. "I'm happy we were able to help on this one, Ms. Dillon. We will do our best to see that you get justice."

Darius could see on Sasha's face that this touched her.

"Thank you."

Kelso turned to the rest of them. "This is the order. Sheriff Pella, Chief Irving, Silva, then I'll speak, and then Ms. Dillon can make her statement."

"Sounds good." Darius didn't miss Darcangelo's eye roll or the look he exchanged with Hunter. He knew what they were thinking, and it was true. The feds had a way of taking over investigations if there was any chance for publicity. It was inevitable, like gravity. But Kelso deserved props this time.

They walked outside together, Sasha flanked by Darcangelo and Hunter.

Sheriff Pella told reporters about receiving the initial call that Sasha had been hurt and talked a little about her rescue, his deputy's suspicion that this wasn't an average hit-and-run, and Marcs' request for aid from DPD.

Irving kept his remarks brief, talking about Darius' experience in LA and how important interagency cooperation was before turning the mic over to Darius.

Leaving out Riggs, Darius told reporters how investigators had focused on Kyle Watts until dashcam footage had revealed another unknown suspect. When he reached the point where they had identified Reiter, Kelso took over.

Kelso thanked all of the agencies involved, including the State Department, the Slovak Police Force, and the German Federal Police. Then he talked a bit about the proprietary technology they'd used to find the location of the phone.

Behind him, Darius overheard Darcangelo whisper to Sasha.

"*Try not to fall asleep.*"

He glanced back, saw Sasha fighting not to laugh.

"Yesterday, the Slovak Police Force took one suspect, an Austrian national, Hans Jakob Reiter, into custody. He was cooperative under questioning by US and Slovak officials. As a result, we were able to issue a second warrant, which led to the arrest in Munich early this morning of Maritza Helena Christine Braun, who was the mastermind of the assault on Ms. Dillon."

A handful of gasps told Darius that some of the reporters followed sports climbing and knew who Braun was.

Kelso went on. "According to Reiter, the motivation behind the attack was to permanently disable or kill Ms. Dillon so she couldn't compete in the world championships. In Ms. Dillon's absence, Braun won the competition."

Kelso explained a bit about the effort to extradite Reiter and the likelihood that Braun would be tried for her crimes in Germany. "Before I take questions, Ms. Dillon would like to make a statement."

Sasha's gaze met Darius' as she came forward, and he could see she was nervous. But he could also see her strength.

"I'm Sasha Dillon. I'm a competitive sports climber."

"We love you, Sasha!" someone shouted.

"You're the greatest!"

Then Sasha started at the beginning, telling the crowd what had happened, sharing the terror of it along with her suffering. "I never could have imagined that the violence of that afternoon was the work of a friend. Maritza and I have climbed together all over the world. We've competed against one another, and sometimes she's performed better than I have. Learning that she conspired to have me disabled or killed…"

Her voice quavered, and her words trailed off. "Learning that my friend conspired to have me disabled or killed hurt far more than any injury. Trophies and gold medals were never my motivation for climbing. But these past two weeks have reminded me that what matters most in life isn't winning. It's the friends who are there for you when your world comes crashing down."

Tears on her cheeks, she thanked Megs, Mitch, Nicole, and the Team. She thanked the doctors and nurses who'd cared for her. She thanked Joe and Rain and the staff at Knockers. Then she thanked the State Department, the FBI, the governments of Slovakia, Austria, and Germany, the Forest County Sheriff's Department, Deputy Marcs, and, last of all, Darius.

But what she read next wasn't in the statement Darius had read earlier. "Detective Darius Silva was almost killed trying to bring my attackers to justice. There is no greater sense of duty and no greater love than that. He was prepared to give his life for a stranger, for me. I will always be grateful."

The crowd exploded with questions as Sasha left the microphone, but Darius barely heard them over the buzzing in his own brain.

No greater love.

It *was* love.

He was in love with Sasha.

———

SASHA SAT in an empty conference room waiting for Darius, who was in a meeting with Kelso. Ignoring the nonstop buzzing of her phone, she uploaded a copy of her statement to her social media. Then she gave in and checked messages.

She had expected this. The moment she'd stepped away from the microphone, people had started blowing up her phone. Akari and Daryna texted her to tell her how sorry they were and ask if she needed help. Elias, too, had sent a message offering his support. Megs and Nic texted her to tell her how well she'd done. Then Scott, her manager, called, outraged not just by the news, but also by the fact that Sasha hadn't told him the truth about her accident.

"How am I supposed to represent you when you keep me in the dark?"

"I did what the sheriff and the police asked me to do."

"I'm sure they didn't mean you should keep information from *me*."

"If I'd told you, would you have been able to keep quiet, or would you have leaked it to friends in the media? I know the answer to that."

Scott tellingly changed the subject. "This is a completely different situation than missing the world championships because of a bike accident. This is *huge*. It's the biggest news in climbing this year. I'll call your sponsors, set up a slate of interviews—"

"I told you already. I'm taking a week off."

"You're … what? You've been out of action for more

than a week already. This was your first public appearance since—"

"I just found out that someone I considered a close friend tried to kill me just to win a title. I'm still healing physically and emotionally. *Do not* push me!" Sasha had never raised her voice at Scott before. "I need time."

A hand came to rest on her shoulder.

She glanced up.

Darius.

Scott conceded. "Okay, you need time."

"I will be out of touch for a week at least. I'll check in with you when I'm able."

"All right." Scott wasn't happy. "Time waits for no one, but I understand."

Clearly, he didn't, but that was his problem.

"Thanks, Scott." She ended the call.

"Is everything okay?"

Fighting tears, she stood, slipped into his arms. "Nothing is okay, except this."

"Maybe you need to turn off your phone for a few days."

"Good idea." She sent a quick text to Megs and Nicole, letting them know she was shutting off her mobile. Then she turned it off—something she never did.

The drive to Darius' condo was short. "I wanted a place close to the office and the highway system that was quiet, so I ended up in East Wash Park."

His condo was in a secure high rise on the east side of Washington Park, which Sasha had never seen.

"That's a big park. So many trees—and a lake."

"It's more than a hundred fifty acres with *two* lakes." He chuckled. "You don't know Denver very well, do you?"

"I don't know Denver at all."

He parked in the underground garage, grabbed their

bags out of the back, and they rode the elevator to the sixth floor. "Second door on the left."

He unlocked the door and stood back to let her enter.

"Home, sweet home." Sasha couldn't help but smile. "I like it."

Darius' home reflected his personality—ordered, classy, and a little Spartan. There was no art on the walls, no photographs on the shelves, no houseplants. But everything about it spoke of good taste.

A blocky sofa of black leather sat in the living room across from a gas fireplace, a matching loveseat beside it. There were wood floors throughout, with granite countertops and stainless steel appliances in the kitchen. The primary bedroom had its own bathroom, with a large tub, a walk-in shower, and twin sinks. There was a second bedroom and a second bathroom, as well as a small office. A balcony stretched from his living room to his bedroom, facing west.

Sasha stepped outside, took in the amazing view—the park with its lakes, the downtown Denver skyline, and, far to the west, the mountains. "Standing here, it doesn't feel like you live in a big city."

He slipped his arm around her shoulders. "I bought the place for this view."

"Smart man."

Darius made Sasha a cup of tea, and they settled in the living room in front of the fire. It took them a moment to get situated so that Sasha could lean against his chest, but in the end, they made it work. "Are you comfortable?"

"Yes. You?"

"I'm fine." He kissed the top of her head. "How are you feeling, really?"

Sasha tried to put the confusion inside her into words. "I feel like an idiot."

"You are *not* an idiot."

"Then I must be the most naïve person alive." She found herself fighting tears. "I knew Maritza had a jealous streak. I heard her say unkind things about other pro climbers. I overlooked all of that. I guess I wanted to believe the best about her. I thought she was my friend."

Darius held her closer. "Don't blame yourself. She deceived you—and then she betrayed you. That is on *her*, not you."

Sasha wiped her cheeks. "It's time for me to grow up, to get tougher and smarter and stop being a stupid little girl who thinks everyone is good. I need—"

"Sasha, *stop*. You're taking this out on yourself. Braun is the one to blame, not you. Please don't let that hateful, jealous *criminal* change who you are. People love you. They love your big, open heart, your kindness, your willingness to put others first, your humility, and your beautiful smile." He chuckled. "The first time I spoke with Mitch, he told me that your smile lights up the room. He's right. If someone managed to bottle sunshine and pour it into a person—that would be you."

She sat up, looked into his eyes. "That's so sweet."

He wiped her cheek with his thumb. "You see people as innately good because you're good. The world needs you—hell, *I* need you—to stay just the way you are."

"Do you really mean that?"

He seemed as serious as she'd ever seen him. "I do."

"Thank you." She snuggled against his chest, closed her eyes, and willed herself to let the rest of the world go.

Chapter 22

SASHA LEANED FORWARD against a towel draped over the side of the tub, careful to keep her cast out of the water, while Darius kneaded the tension from her neck and shoulders, turning her muscles to putty.

"You're really tight here." He focused for a moment on her left upper trapezius, his hands gently working the muscle.

It was in her mind to say that she'd been using her left arm more and that she was probably compensating for her broken ribs, but all that came out was, "Mmm."

These past few days were exactly what she'd needed. Time alone with Darius. No buzzing phone. No media. No decisions to make beyond what to order for dinner. No contact with the outside world apart from the ten minutes she spent checking email and messages each morning.

Today, they'd slept in, had a late breakfast, then talked most of the afternoon. After that, they'd gone for a long walk in the park, where they'd watched flocks of geese settling on the lakes, the setting sun turning the water to gold. On the way back, they'd grabbed some Thai takeout, which they'd eaten in the living room in front of the fire, Darius showing her photos of his family.

Somehow, that had led to sex. Then again, when Sasha was with Darius, everything led to sex.

"Better?"

"Yes. Thanks." She leaned back against his chest, the hot water soothing. "If you get sick of being a detective, you could always become a massage therapist."

He chuckled, a soft sound deep in his chest. "And if the only person I want to massage is you?"

She closed her eyes, smiled. "That's not a very successful business model, but it works for me."

For a time, they sat in an intimate silence, just savoring the moment, Darius lazily fondling one of her breasts.

Sasha's thoughts drifted to the photos of Darius' family. "You, Gus, and Max look so much alike. Even if I didn't know you, I'd know you were brothers."

"Do you and your brother look alike?"

"We're both blond-haired, but Sean has brown eyes and is six feet tall. I'm the short one in the family."

"Is he athletic, too?"

"He's spent his life gaming and sitting at a desk, so he's pretty out of shape. But when we were kids, he was athletic. He liked climbing, too, but he wasn't obsessed with it like I am."

But talking about Sean made her think of her parents and the angry message her mother had left this morning, accusing Sasha of deliberately keeping her in the dark.

We had no idea you'd almost been killed. We thought you'd crashed your bike.

Darius seemed to read her mind. "Don't let your mother's message bother you. Your parents are in the wrong. They should have been here, and they chose not to come."

Sasha was tired of defending her parents, so she didn't bother. "They're pestering me to move back to California again. They think my living in Scarlet is the problem. They don't know that it was the people in Scarlet—and a certain hot detective from Denver—who got me through this."

"Want to hear a confession?"

"A confession? This sounds juicy. Do tell."

"Two weeks ago, I might have agreed with your parents. I saw Scarlet as a small town full of... *eccentric* people. One square mile surrounded by reality. I couldn't fathom why a woman with your good looks and talent would choose to live there. I was wrong about the town and *most* of the people."

"Really?"

"Sorry." He kissed her hair. "It's true."

Sasha wasn't surprised. Lots of people felt that way. "I'm glad your opinion of the town and *most* of its people has changed."

"I saw how they showed up for you every day in big ways and small. Most of us don't have that kind of community. If I were surrounded with that kind of friendship, I wouldn't want to leave, either."

"Thanks. That means a lot to me." Sasha wondered if he realized how much the people of Scarlet had come to care about him, but she let it go. She didn't want to make him think she was pressuring him to stay with her or move to Scarlet. She knew that wasn't practical, given where he worked.

Besides, his slow, persistent teasing of her breast was turning her thoughts in other directions. "Want to hear my confession?"

"Hit me."

"I can't wait until my ribs are healed so we can have sex without holding back."

"I get turned on just thinking about that." He was telling the truth, his cock growing hard behind her.

Sasha's blood grew hotter. "I want to have sex without spending fifteen minutes trying to figure out the logistics every time."

He nuzzled her ear, his voice deep and sexy. "How about you lean on the edge of the tub like you did before but get up on your knees? I promise I'll take care of everything else."

—

ON WEDNESDAY MORNING, Darius took Sasha to his favorite breakfast place. A little family-owned Creole joint decorated with Mardi Gras posters, it served the best damned eggs Benedict in Denver.

They got a seat next to a sunny window, where a friendly Black server named Angelica quickly took their orders. Darius suggested beignets, eggs Benedict, and mimosas, and Sasha was happy to try it all.

"I've never had eggs Benedict—or mimosas for that matter."

Angelica gaped at her. "Girl, it's about time."

Darius seconded that. "You won't be sorry."

Angelica brought their drinks first—coffee, orange juice, champagne, and two flutes. "Your beignets should be right out."

Darius opened the champagne, poured a little into their flutes, then topped it off with orange juice. He handed Sasha her mimosa, and raised his glass. "To you."

Sasha took a sip, her eyes going wide. "That's really good."

"I'm glad you like it."

"Do you come here often?"

"Mostly on special occasions—if I have family in town or a reason to celebrate."

"So, not very often, then."

"Not as often as I'd like."

Their beignets arrived, Darius suppressing a smile at the powdered sugar on Sasha's upper lip. Then the eggs Benedict came.

"How am I supposed to eat all of this?"

Angelica smiled. "One delicious bite at a time."

They were in the middle of breakfast and talking about the horrors of reconstituted scrambled eggs when Darius' phone buzzed.

Deputy Marcs.

Hoping Sasha hadn't seen the name, Darius excused himself and walked outside. "Marcs, what's up?"

"I can't reach Sasha, but I thought she'd want to know that karma just took a big bite out of Braun's ass."

Darius needed to hear this. "I'm listening."

"The International Association of Sports Climbing just held a press conference in Bratislava. They reviewed the case and have stripped Braun of her title."

Darius felt a savage stab of satisfaction at this news. "I'm glad to hear it."

"The guy in charge said the record would state that no championship trophy was awarded for women this year, so Sasha's winning streak is intact."

Darius wasn't sure Sasha cared about that, but he did. "Glad to hear it."

"There's more. They also banned Braun from competing for the rest of her life. She's out of competitive sports climbing forever."

That was as it should be. "Braun wanted fame, and she got it."

"She sure as hell did. She wanted to be the world

champion, but now she'll be remembered only for trying to kill a competitor."

"Thanks, Marcs. Anything else?"

"We compared Reiter's prints to the ones lifted from the stolen SUV, and they were a match. So, there's your hard evidence connecting him to the scene. The DA is working on a plea deal for Riggs, hoping to get him into drug treatment and keep him out of prison. He believes, as we do, that Riggs only called Watts to bail him out."

"That's all good news."

"Tell Sasha we're all thinking of her."

"I will."

When Darius returned to the table, he saw Sasha signing a menu for Angelica. He sat, spread his napkin on his lap. "Are you a fan of competitive sports climbing?"

"I am now." Angelica beamed at Sasha. "I hope you feel better soon. And thank you, sir, for doing your job."

"Thanks." Mystified, Darius watched her walk away.

Sasha leaned closer, lowered her voice so she wouldn't be overheard. "When you left the table, Angelica hurried over and told me she could see the faded bruises on my face. She asked if I felt safe with you, if I wanted someone to call the police. I had to tell her what happened. I didn't want her thinking that you abused me. She told me she remembered seeing something about that on the news, and then she asked for my autograph."

"Good for her." Darius glanced across the room, saw Angelica carrying a tray of drinks to another table. "I wish more people had that kind of courage and attention to detail. It would save women's lives."

"What was the call about—work?"

Darius understood Sasha well enough to know she wouldn't derive the same vengeful pleasure he and Marcs had about Braun's comeuppance. At the same time, he couldn't lie to her. "That was Marcs."

"Julia?" Sasha's expression changed to one of worry. "Is everything okay?"

Darius took a sip of his mimosa. "Reiter's fingerprints matched a set taken from the SUV."

"That leaves no doubt then."

"Also, the IASC just held a press conference. They reviewed the evidence and have stripped Braun of her title."

Sasha's eyes went wide. "Oh! Well. What else could they do? Her sponsors dropped her. They couldn't keep her on their payroll, and the IASC can't have her as the public face of women's sports climbing."

Angelica must have overheard. She picked up their empty beignet plates. "No one wants a wannabe murderer on their box of Wheaties, know what I mean?"

That made Sasha smile.

"They announced that there was no world champion in the women's events this year, so you're still the reigning world champ."

As Darius had predicted, this didn't seem to carry much weight with Sasha.

"They didn't have to do that. They could have given it to Daryna. She climbed well and came in second."

"There's more. They also banned Braun from competition for life."

Sasha set her fork aside, her gaze falling to the table. "Imagine wanting something so bad that you destroy any chance you have of getting it. Her life as a professional climber is over. I can't help but feel pity for her. I can't imagine how she must feel now. The climbing community will ostracize her."

Darius didn't feel sorry for Braun at all. She'd done this

to herself. But he didn't say that. Instead, he reached across the table, took Sasha's hand. "Are you okay?"

Sasha drew a breath, nodded, her smile returning. "It's a beautiful morning. I'm alive and enjoying a champagne breakfast with the man I love and…"

Her words trailed off, her eyes going wide when she realized what she'd said. Her face flushed pink, and she stammered. "I… I'm… "

Darius' heart gave a hard thud, and for a moment, he couldn't speak. When he could, he found himself wanting to tell her that he hadn't expected to find her, that he wasn't sure he was ready for this, that he might not be good at relationships. It had been so long since he'd had anyone in his life. But what he *really* wanted to tell her was that he loved her, too. He just couldn't find the courage.

He set his fork aside, took her hand, and raised it to his lips, the vulnerability on her face making his heart ache. "That sounds like the perfect morning."

ON SUNDAY, her last day in Denver, Darius took Sasha to the art museum, where they enjoyed an exhibit featuring American post-Impressionist artists. But Sasha's mind was on the man beside her and not so much on art. Afterward, they strolled down the Sixteenth Street Mall, stopped for some Italian food, then drove back to his place, where they made long, slow love to one other.

Afterward, they lay together on his bed, Darius stroking her hair and holding her as best he could with their injuries.

Sasha didn't want to bring this up, but she was running out of time. She'd told him she loved him during breakfast on Wednesday, and she knew he'd heard her. His reaction hadn't been negative. She'd seen the surprise on his face, but he hadn't shared how he felt about her. And now their stolen week together was almost over, and she was about to return to Scarlet. She wanted Darius in her life. Did he feel the same way?

There was only one way to find out.

She traced the line of dark curls that ran from his navel to his groin. "Where do we go from here, Dare? I said it the other day at the restaurant. I love you. I mean that, but I don't want to rush this or push you away. What do we do?"

He kissed her head. "That's why you've been so quiet all afternoon."

"I keep imagining life as your girlfriend, and I guess I should stop because I'm not sure that's what you want. So much has happened in such a short time."

For a moment, he was silent, his fingers tracing a path along her spine. Then he sat up, helped her to sit, his gaze turning to the window, his expression so troubled that Sasha was sure he was about to let her go.

He looked into her eyes. "Some part of me broke after Becca's murder. It's been hard to get close to people. Women I've dated since have all said I was cold or closed off or emotionally unavailable. I'm not sure I'm capable of being the man you need and deserve. I guess it makes me selfish, but I don't want this to end, either."

Sasha had expected rejection, so it took her a moment. "You … you don't?"

"God, no." He chuckled, ran his thumb over her cheek. "It's been so long since I've felt this way about any woman, so long since I've been able to talk with anyone like this. You changed everything, Sasha. But this won't be easy."

"Nothing worthwhile ever is." She twined her fingers

with his. "I already know you work lots of late nights and weekends. While we're doing disclaimers, I should mention that I travel a lot. To maintain my sponsorships, I have to take on a certain number of high-profile climbing projects every year, and I'm not always the one who chooses them. I can be gone for six to eight weeks at a time. I face risks that most people don't. I could get seriously injured or even killed. Elite climbers die every year."

His brow furrowed. "God, don't even say that."

"It's true."

"*Geezus*. Okay, right." It was his turn again. "I see some awful shit, and sometimes I come home upset and angry and just need my space."

"I understand that." Sasha thought of the young man who'd found his girlfriend murdered and lying in her own blood. How horrifying that must have been. "After all you've been through, it must take real courage to do your job. Some part of you has been fighting all these years to make things right, and you *do* make things right. You did that for me. But you also get to have a life and make things right for yourself."

"I'm not sure how to do that, but this feels like a good start."

It wasn't a declaration of love, but it was good enough —for now.

"Climbing has taught me one thing."

"What's that?"

"If you take one step at a time, you can reach the sky."

He leaned closer, kissed her forehead. "Then that's how we'll do this—one step at a time, one day at a time."

They took a shower together, Darius dropping to his knees, making her come hard and fast with his mouth, before sliding into her from behind and making her come again.

"Sex with you is so... damned... *good*," she said, her legs wobbly, her cheek pressed against wet tile.

They dried each other off, got dressed, and ate Italian leftovers. Then it was time for Sasha to pack up and head back to Scarlet.

Darius stopped at a gas station to fill up, so Sasha sent a quick text to Nicole asking her to leave her key in her mailbox.

`I'm giving a key to Darius. I'll make you a`
`new one.`

Nicole answered quickly.

`I'll head over now. You're giving him a`
`key? Wow!!! Can't wait to hear the details!`

It was a Sunday evening, so traffic was light—not a good thing when Sasha wanted the drive to last. Far too quickly, they reached the roundabout. A few minutes later, they pulled up to Sasha's house.

Darius turned off the engine. "I'll carry your bag inside, make sure you're safe."

"Thanks. I'll just check the mailbox."

Once they got inside, Darius made her a fire. Then he stacked more wood on her deck. She offered him a cup of coffee for the drive home, but she knew all of this was just the two of them trying to delay the inevitable.

All too soon, he stood on her doorstep. "I've got something for you."

He held out his hand, a key and a remote on his palm. "The key is for my apartment. The remote is for the parking garage. Whenever you're sick of beautiful scenery and fresh air, you're welcome to stay at my place."

Sasha laughed, held out the key to her house. "I was going to give you this."

He grinned, took the key. "I'm going to use it."

"You'd better."

"I'll call when I get a grip on things at the office, and we'll go from there."

"That sounds good."

Darius kissed her long and slow. "Stay safe."

"You, too."

He turned and walked back to his vehicle, Sasha watching as he drove away, taking her heart with him.

Chapter 23

SASHA STOWED her carry-on bag in the overhead compartment, pleased not to feel the slightest objection from her healed ribs or wrist. She closed the compartment, handed her parka to a flight attendant, and took her seat near the window. She rarely flew first class, but after all the publicity surrounding the attack, she was taking extra precautions. So many more people seemed to recognize her now.

She took her phone out of her handbag and sent Darius a quick text.

Boarded. Should arrive at DIA by 9:10 PM. The doc says I'm cleared to climb.

Great news! Have a safe flight! I'll meet you there.

Sasha put her phone in airplane mode, slipped it into her handbag, and buckled up, just as a flight attendant offered her complimentary champagne.

"Just water. Thanks."

She looked out the window, unconsciously doing PT exercises with her right wrist, the sullen, gray clouds promising rain again. She couldn't wait to see the blue Colorado sky, snow-covered mountains, and Darius.

The flight attendant returned with a bottle of bubbly water, a cup, and a napkin. "I saw you on TV and heard what happened. I'm glad you're okay. My name is Grace. If you need anything…"

Sasha took the water. "That's sweet of you. Thank you, Grace."

She'd been in New York for almost a week, arriving last Sunday. On Monday, she was a guest on *Good Morning America*. She'd spent Tuesday and Wednesday being interviewed for *60 Minutes*, which was filming a program about her ordeal and the dark side of sports climbing. On Thursday, she'd spent the day talking with a reporter from the *Times*. Today, she'd had a visit with the nation's foremost sports medicine specialist. He'd given Sasha a complete physical, done scans of her ribs and wrist, cleared her to climb again, and asked her to sign the wall in his waiting room.

Lately, it felt like all she'd done was interviews. Scott had arranged a media blitz that had thrilled her sponsors —and consumed much of Sasha's spare time. Over the past six weeks, she'd spoken with dozens of reporters, most of them asking the same questions. She was relieved to have it all in her rearview mirror and more than ready to put the attack—and Maritza's betrayal—behind her.

Not that she'd ever truly be able to forget what had happened. Her body had healed, and therapy had helped her mind to heal, too. But even if she were able to forget the attack, the public wouldn't. Everyone she met brought it up, even strangers like Grace. Besides, neither Maritza's nor Reiter's cases had yet been decided, so she still got regular updates from the State Department.

She knew that Maritza had been released from custody and was awaiting trial on criminal charges in Germany, while Reiter was trying to cut a deal with the State Department. Reiter had offered to testify against Maritza if he could skip extradition and be tried for his role in the attack in Austria. In the meantime, he still had to face illegal possession charges in Slovakia.

"They just don't want to end up in a US prison," Darius had explained.

It enraged Sasha. "Why do they get a choice when they didn't give me one?"

From behind her, Sasha heard the airplane door close.

She didn't like to fly. As the flight attendants started their in-flight safety speech and the plane taxied toward the runway, she did her best to focus on the man who would be waiting for her when she landed.

Sasha hoped Darius got the subtext of her message. The doc had cleared her, which meant they had no reason to hold back in bed. They'd had to be careful these past two months, but now—

The plane took off, leaving Sasha's stomach on the ground below. She watched New York City recede until it was lost below the clouds, then tried to find a movie to distract her. She picked the latest superhero flick, but before long, she had fallen asleep.

She woke when Grace asked for her meal preference— parmesan chicken or breaded halibut. Neither sounded particularly appetizing to Sasha, not when they came from the galley of an airplane, so she took an energy bar out of her handbag and nibbled that instead.

There were still two hours and forty-five minutes until the plane landed, and Sasha could barely wait.

⸻

DARIUS GLANCED AT HIS WATCH. He needed to leave for DIA in an hour.

He climbed out of his vehicle, smoothed his trousers, and walked into the Scarlet Springs Municipal Building, an old one-story wood structure, its wooden floor creaking as he walked to the reception desk. "Darius Silva here for a meeting with—"

A door opened, and Megs stuck her head out. "Silva, in here."

He gave a nod to the receptionist, who smiled. "Thanks."

Inside, he found a handful of people he recognized, and some he didn't, sitting around the conference table. He shook their hands. "Megs. Bob. Marcia. Joe. Good to see you all again."

An older man in a blue dress shirt and tan slacks got to his feet. "I'm Michael Taylor, the mayor of Scarlet Springs. I think you've met my son, Austin, the ranger."

"Yes." Darius shook his hand. "Good to meet you."

Also present were Chip, a Scarlet resident, Janice, a nurse at the local hospital, and Jake, the co-owner of the climbing gym.

"Good to meet you." Darius sat, accepted a glass of water.

Megs broke the silence. "Bob, Marcia, Janice, Chip, Jake, and I make up Scarlet's Town Council, with Michael serving as the tie-breaking vote. Sorry to be so vague on the phone, but I wanted to keep this quiet."

Darius bit back a grin. He wasn't sure it was possible to keep something important quiet in Scarlet. "Julia Marcs told me that Chief Randall has finally agreed to retire, and you're looking for his replacement."

Megs raised an eyebrow. "Well, that saves time. Let's get right to it."

Michael described a police department that had fallen into poor order and a town that had changed. "Seasonal tourist traffic continues to increase and brings crime with it —mostly theft and vandalism. But there are also encampments of transients just outside of Scarlet and along the banks of the creek that runs through town."

Megs took over. "These aren't all men down on their luck. Some have fallen into hard times, but many are criminals—sex offenders who refuse to register, escaped cons. Others are men who served their time but haven't changed their stripes."

"Criminal transients." Darius knew the type only too well.

"Exactly."

"Now, Chief Randall has served this town well, but when he came on board, fewer than a thousand people lived here." Michael chuckled. "There was no Internet, no cell phones. Marijuana was illegal. Tourists mostly passed us by. It's time to modernize our police department."

"He's been here a while, then."

"Since Carter was president." Michael laughed at Darius' surprised expression. "The incident with Sasha showed Chief Randall that it is time for him to go. Posting officers at Sasha's place left him short-handed, and he was overwhelmed."

"That's putting it kindly," Megs muttered.

Michael gave Megs a sideways glance, obviously the diplomat on the council. "He has agreed to step down at the end of the year with well-deserved accolades and a nice pension, and we want to offer you the position."

Darius had assumed as much.

He opened his mouth to speak, but was cut off by

Chip, who spoke so quickly that Darius couldn't get in a word. "You've got only nine staff, but the town has put together a budget for equipment upgrades, uniform upgrades, training, and the like. We're willing to match your current salary and include a generous pension plan. It will be your department to shape the way you see fit. You can evaluate the staff, and fire or hire—"

"Can I speak?"

Heads nodded.

"First, I want to thank you for your confidence in me. To my knowledge, you've never looked at my résumé or spoken to my bosses, so that means you're going by your gut instinct here."

Megs waved him off. "We know everything about you we need to know."

"Not everything." Darius took a breath. "When I was nineteen, my girlfriend was brutally raped and murdered, and I was arrested and charged in her death."

Jaws dropped.

"I was exonerated when another young woman died in the same way. A man who lived in our apartment building —an unregistered sex offender—was convicted of their murders and died in prison. That's why I became a cop. If you'd done a background check on me, you'd have learned all of this."

For a moment, no one said a word.

Then Marcia spoke. "So, will you take the job?"

Darius couldn't help but smile. "I'm interested, but I need to know more about your vision for the police department and for Scarlet."

All heads turned to Joe.

Was the brewpub owner the real power in town?

Joe met Darius' gaze. "I know you've worked in big cities most of your life, and I'm sure that our little town isn't somewhere you've imagined yourself working or living. As I recall, Megs didn't want to live here, either."

"You recall correctly."

"I'll tell you what I told her." Joe stroked his beard. "My ancestors owned the now-dormant silver mine up above Caribou, and they bled this town and its people dry. Since I inherited the mine, I've worked hard to rebuild Scarlet and give back what my family took."

Darius hadn't known any of this.

Joe went on. "What do we want? We want a town that's safe and welcoming to all. We want a community that's self-reliant and strong. We want a police department that's actively involved with our residents and a chief who can shift gears to meet emerging dangers like the transient camps. We want someone who's forward-thinking, someone who can join minds with us to make Scarlet the best town it can be."

"Damn, Joe." Bob gaped at him. "Nice speech. You should run for mayor."

More laughter.

Darius made eye contact with everyone at the table. "I am interested. You're right, Joe. I never imagined living in a small town. Part of that comes from being a murder suspect. Let's just say that I quickly learned to value anonymity."

"I bet." There was understanding in Megs' eyes. "What's changed your mind—besides Sasha."

Darius had spent the better part of two months thinking over what he was about to share with them now. "I saw how you rallied around Sasha, how the town pulled together. I've seen how you care for Bear. You welcomed me like a friend from the moment I arrived. I've never experienced that sense of ... belonging."

Darius spoke only the truth. He had a family that loved

him. He'd had friends growing up, and he'd had colleagues. But he had never *belonged* anywhere.

"So, you'll do it?" Marcia looked ready to break out the champagne.

"Before I can make a decision, I need two things. First, I need to see specifics—the budget, an inventory of gear, a review of the staff—and maybe get a tour of the department."

Michael opened a manila folder. "I've got some of that here."

"What's the second thing?" Megs looked ready to run out and get it for him.

"I need to talk to Sasha."

SASHA RODE UP THE ESCALATOR, her gaze seeking Darius in the crowd. Just before her plane had landed, she'd changed into that little black dress he liked and a pair of heels, her legs bare, nothing beneath her dress but a black, lacy bra and matching panties. Sure, it was November, and she'd be a little chilly. But she wanted to surprise him.

She reached the top of the escalator, her heart swelling when she spotted him, standing there in a dark wool overcoat, a frown of concentration on his face as he watched for her.

"Dare!" She waved.

He saw her, and his frown became a broad grin.

She threaded her way over to him, leaped into his arms, and planted a kiss on his lips, his familiar scent filling her head. "Oh, I've missed you!"

"I've missed you, too." He buried his face in her hair. "God, you smell good."

He stepped back, his gaze sliding over her, one emotion chasing the next across his face—hunger followed by concern. "That dress. Aren't you cold?"

She lowered her voice to a whisper. "I want you *now*. Get me home!"

"Let's go." He took her bag and led her toward the west parking garage, no need to speak, both of them focused on the same goal with single-minded intensity.

It *was* cold outside, a chilly wind from the mountains seeming to go straight up her dress, but the cold was no match for the heat in her blood. She'd thought about him so much that she was already intensely aroused.

The inside of his vehicle was warm, and he turned on the seat warmers. "Better?"

She slid a hand up his inner thigh. "Can't we just do it here?"

"In the parking garage?" He glanced around, laughing. "There are cams everywhere—and people walking by. I'd lose my badge."

"Then *hurry*." She squeezed her thighs together to assuage the ache, but it only made things worse.

He drove out of the airport, exiting onto the highway. "Put your seat back, and spread your legs."

Without hesitation, she did as he asked, planting her feet on the dash.

He slid a hand beneath her panties to stroke her, going by feel, his gaze on the road. "You're already wet."

"I want you." She closed her eyes, loving the way he knew her.

He teased her clit, penetrated her with his fingers, her hips rising to match each thrust. It felt so good, his fingers never losing their rhythm.

She came just as they reached his street, her thighs

trembling, her head spinning with the rush of climax, her panting cries fading into breathlessness.

He hit the remote for the parking garage, drove inside, shut off the engine.

Sasha sat up, collected herself, looked up to find him watching her, lust naked on his face—an instant turn-on.

She adjusted her panties and climbed out. Darius was already getting her bag from the back. She fell in beside him, the two of them walking quickly to the elevator. When the elevator doors closed, she moved toward him.

He gave a shake of his head, looked up, his eyes dark. *Cams.*

Damn.

The ride to the sixth floor took what felt like a month, the two of them walking in silence to his door. He unlocked it, and she followed him inside.

He shucked off his coat, kicked the door shut with his foot. "*Sasha.*"

Jerking down his fly, he backed her up against the hallway wall, lifted her off her feet, pushed the crotch of her panties aside—and buried himself inside her.

"*Ahh.* Yes!" She held on tight.

This is what she'd longed for. She loved feeling his strength like this, loved the sensation of his cock driving inside her, loved the way he moaned against her throat.

She came hard and fast, Darius coming apart in her arms as he joined her. They sank slowly to the floor in a heap, laughing, his trousers around his knees, her dress over her hips, her panties askew.

He dragged her closer, kissed her. "Welcome home. You hungry?"

"Starving!"

Chapter 24

THEY ORDERED sushi and plum wine from a local restaurant and ate their dinner sitting on the living room floor with the coffee table serving as their dining table, a fire burning in the fireplace.

Sasha set her chopsticks aside, dabbed her lips, her hair adorably tousled. "Sorry my heels scratched your wall."

Darius chuckled. "Don't worry about it. The scratches can stay as a reminder of one of the best fucks of my life."

"Do you mean that?"

He looked into her eyes so she could see he was serious. "Hell, yes, I do. You blow my mind, Sasha."

He'd never felt this way for any woman—ever.

She gave him that beautiful smile of hers. "I could say the same about you. How was your day?"

And now they came to it—his news.

Darius had thought long and hard about all the things he wanted to say to Sasha, but the moment he opened his mouth, his brain went blank. "I ... I met with the Scarlet Springs Town Council today."

"The Town Council? Is it about the case?" Sasha tilted

her head, clearly curious. Then her eyes went wide. "They're going to give you and Julia awards."

Darius chuckled. "I imagine Marcs will get an award for saving my life, but, no, that's not why I met with them. It seems that Chief Randall is finally going to retire after thirty-nine years, and they offered me the job."

"They offered *you*…?" Sasha's eyes went wide, but her astonishment quickly faded. "You turned them down, of course."

Darius shook his head. "I'm considering it."

"You are?"

Darius laughed at the stunned look on her face. "I asked for more information about the department and the job and said I needed to talk it over with you."

"I'm sorry, but … what?"

He reached across the coffee table, took her hand. "They'll match my DPD salary, which is a stretch for them. They've also put together a budget for upgrades, training, and building repairs."

Sasha looked worried. "As much as I would love for us to live closer to one another, I don't want you to give up your job or your life here. You'll end up feeling claustrophobic and unhappy and resent me, and that could ruin what we have together. I don't want that. Besides, you hate Scarlet."

"I don't hate Scarlet."

She frowned. "Who are you, and what have you done with Darius?"

Darius poured a little more plum wine into her glass. "After I was exonerated in Becca's murder, I wanted to disappear. I wanted to live where no one knew me, where nothing from her murder could touch me. Big cities make that easy. You drive into LA or Denver or Manhattan, and you disappear into the throng, one of millions. No one knows you, and no one cares. After that very public ordeal, I needed anonymity."

She squeezed his hand. "Small towns don't offer that, do they? That's what you meant when you said you'd feel claustrophobic."

"Exactly. I imagined Scarlet being a little town with small-minded people, where every molehill becomes a mountain and everyone meddles in everyone else's business."

"Well… I won't lie. That *does* happen."

"What I couldn't see were the connections between people. You're not just a bunch of yokels getting in each other's way. You truly care about one another. The way everyone pulled together to help you… The Team… I've never seen that kind of community before. It shows how fucked up I am… or was."

"You aren't fucked up. Your life and sense of safety were destroyed by what happened in the aftermath of Becca's murder. Tempe and the university were your community—and they turned against you when you'd done nothing wrong."

She started to say more but stopped herself.

"Go ahead. Say it."

"The first time I stayed here, you said something about the people of Scarlet helping me and how, if you had those kinds of friendships, you wouldn't want to leave the town, either."

"I remember. We were in the tub."

She nodded. "I wanted to tell you then that the people of Scarlet had already adopted you as one of their own, but I was afraid you'd think I was pushing you to like the place. It's true, though. Everyone who knows you in Scarlet cares about you."

His pulse picked up, and he steeled himself. He needed

to tell her. "Since Becca's death, I haven't felt like I belong anywhere. The only place I've felt at home was on the job. But when I look into your eyes, a part of me wants to believe I could belong in Scarlet, too. I want to believe I could belong with *you*, Sasha. I love you."

His heart thundered in his chest, but he'd said it.

Tears welled up in Sasha's eyes. "*Dare.*"

It got easier from there. "From the first moment I saw you in the hospital, something about you broke through the barrier I'd built around myself. You're the most genuine woman I know, and your smile—it's a gift. It lights up my world."

She laughed, tears spilling down her cheeks. "Am I dreaming?"

"Let's see." Darius slid his fingers into her hair, kissed her. "Did you feel that?"

"*Mmm.* Yes."

"Then you're not dreaming, angel." Because he'd said it once, he found it easier to say again. "I love you, Sasha. I love you with everything I am."

And for the first time in more than fifteen years, Darius felt whole.

———

SASHA WOKE to Darius planting little butterfly kisses along her nape, the hard length of his body pressed against hers.

"Good morning, beautiful." He cupped one of her breasts, teased its nipple.

"Good morning." She turned in his arms, drew his head down, and kissed him.

Last night's sex against the wall had been fast and frantic, but there was no hurry now. Hands slid over soft skin, exploring, caressing, the two of them lingering over the tiniest pleasures, each lost in the wonder of the other.

A catch of breath. A whimper. A quick inhale.

Sasha came first, climax washing through her as pure and golden as sunlight, her heart bursting with love at the sight of bliss on Darius' face as orgasm claimed him, too.

Her man. Her beautiful, wonderful man.

Afterward, they held each other, then showered and made breakfast together, the sky outside blue and cloudless.

As they finished their coffee, he slipped his fingers through hers. "What do you want to do today?"

"I want to climb. I want to spend the afternoon at the rock gym. It's been two months, and I can't wait to get vertical."

He grinned. "I thought you might say that."

A half an hour later, they were on their way toward Scarlet, Sasha's bag in the back, Darius with his duffel packed for the weekend. Sasha sent a message to Megs, telling her she planned to climb today, then the conversation turned to the Town Council's job offer and what it would be like if Darius moved to Scarlet.

"What would you do with your condo?"

"Keep it. Use it as a vacation rental. We can stay in Denver when we want to get away. It's a lot closer to the airport, so you could stay there before and after you travel and skip the drive up the canyon."

"Oh, I like that idea. Have you thought about where you're going to live? I have lots of room at my placc."

"I don't think we should live together—not yet. Who am I kidding? We'll probably spend most nights together anyway, but I don't want to rush this. You're too damned important to me, Sasha. I want to do this right. I want us to have time to get to know one another. I haven't lived with a woman since…"

He didn't have to finish.

Sasha took his free hand. "I understand."

"If you can still stand the sight of me in six months, then…"

"And if we break up?" Sasha didn't want to think about this, but it was important. "Would you regret leaving the DPD and moving up there?"

He changed lanes and took the Boulder exit, leaving I-25 behind. "I've already thought about that."

"Scarlet is small. We would run into each other a lot—at Food Mart, Knockers, the climbing gym. People might take sides."

"I've already considered that, too."

"And?"

Darius squeezed her hand. "I would rather risk it all and fail than miss out on this chance with you."

Sasha's heart soared.

———

THEY ARRIVED at the climbing gym to find the parking lot full to overflowing, cars parked along the street in both directions.

Darius chuckled. "I guess word got out that you were coming today."

Megs spotted them and motioned to Darius.

He rolled down his window.

"Bowen and Jake saved you a parking space up front."

"Thanks."

Darius drove through the parking lot, astonished to see people walking into the gym with lawn chairs. "You are popular."

Sasha was all smiles, waving to people as they passed. "This is crazy!"

Darius parked, and they walked inside, the gym exploding with applause. People sat on the floor or in lawn chairs, everyone facing the rock wall. He was surprised to realize how many of them he recognized. Most of the Team was here. Marcia and Cheyenne, too. Hank. Rose. Bob and Kendra. Even Bear, who looked a little lost.

Eric Hawke passed them with Vicki and their two kids. "Hey, Silva."

"Are we violating the fire code, chief?" Darius joked.

Eric glanced around, grinned. "Twice over, I'd guess."

Then Bowen hurried over to them, gave Sasha a kiss. "I had our route-setter freshen things up last night. Five-ten through Five-fourteen—they're all brand new."

"Thank you, Bowen. I think I'll warm up on the bouldering wall."

"You do whatever you want, baby girl." Bowen gestured to the room around them. "*Mi casa es su casa.*"

Darius knew Sasha was excited, but he could see worry in her eyes, too. He leaned closer, kissed her cheek. "You'll do great."

Bowen shouted to the crowd. "She needs to warm up. Make room, people!"

Sasha dropped her gym bag by the front desk, then stretched, the room silent. "This feels weird, folks. Talk to each other, for God's sake!"

Laughter.

Megs helped her stretch, the two of them talking together, trying to decide whether Sasha should tape her wrist. Darius found himself grateful that Sasha had Megs in her life. Megs was the only person on earth who could fully understand what it was like to be a woman climber on top of the sport.

When Sasha was ready, she walked over to the bouldering wall.

People turned their lawn chairs, some applauding.

She tested a few holds, moving slowly and deliberately upward, even hanging by her right hand for a moment, with Megs and Nicole encouraging her from below.

"How does that feel?" Megs called up to her. "Any pain?"

Sasha smiled. "No. It feels great."

She topped out to cheers, then downclimbed and walked over to the big rock wall, people turning their lawn chairs once again. She chose her route and roped in, Nicole tying in to belay her, Megs standing near Nicole like a worried mother.

Bowen seemed barely able to contain his excitement. "She's going to try to on-sight a five-fourteen."

Sasha motioned Darius over, and he made his way through the throng.

"Kiss me for luck?"

He lowered his lips to hers. "I don't think you're going to need luck."

Then he stepped back, stood next to Megs.

Sasha shook out her hands, and then she was off, a hush falling over the room as people raised their phones and started to film.

But, hey, no pressure, Sasha.

Darius had never watched her climb in person, and it stole his breath. She moved with a mastery that few people would ever have, part world-class athlete and part artist.

Beside him, Nicole took up the slack, encouraging Sasha. "You've got it."

Megs spoke, whether to herself or Darius, he couldn't say. "Find the flow."

Higher Sasha went, now on an overhang, her ponytail pointing at the ground.

"I didn't know people could do that," Hank muttered.

She raised a heel almost even with her head, shifted her other foot, reached for a crimper so small that Darius could barely make it out. Then she stretched with her right arm, caught a larger hold, shifting to the right, one leg moving to the left for counterbalance.

"That was the crux," Megs whispered. "You've got this."

And then Sasha was vertical again, moving quickly, smoothly.

When she topped out, she punched her fist into the air. "Yes!"

"She's back!" Megs shouted.

The gym exploded in cheers, Bowen clearly beside himself. "Her first day back, and she on-sights a five-fourteen!"

Nicole began lowering Sasha to the ground.

Megs looked over at Darius, a sheen in her eyes. "I won't cry if you don't."

Darius blinked, coughed the lump out of his throat. "Deal."

The moment her feet hit the ground, Sasha jumped into Darius' arms, Nicole bear-hugging them both.

Darius held her tight. "How did that feel?"

She beamed up at him. "It was perfect!"

———

SASHA SPENT THE AFTERNOON CLIMBING, taking turns being on belay with Nicole, Megs, Mitch, and Darius, the crowd thinning as the day waned. It felt so good to move again, to get her heart rate up, to feel the burn in her muscles. Then the party moved to Knockers, the Team table all but full.

Sasha was touched by how welcoming everyone was to

Darius, Eric making room for the two of them next to him and Vicki. "Dare flashed a five-eleven today. I filmed it, so I've got proof."

"Dare, huh?" Eric clapped him on the shoulder, grinning. "Not bad for a guy who says he doesn't really climb."

Darius looked a little embarrassed. "It wasn't graceful."

As Chey took their orders and brought their drinks, Sasha watched Darius talking and laughing with the others. Gone was the man who rarely smiled and kept the world at arm's length. He joked with Eric and Austin as if they were old friends.

The sight of him so happy and open put an ache in her chest.

Then Megs traded places with Eric and handed Darius a manila envelope. "This is the rest of the information you wanted."

Darius took the envelope. "My answer is yes—but I've got two more conditions."

Sasha found herself holding her breath.

"When I first got here, I decided Scarlet was more like Mayberry than Vail, albeit Stoned Mayberry."

Megs nodded thoughtfully, her expression serious. "You're not wrong."

"Now, Mayberry had a sheriff, but Forest County already has a sheriff. I'd like to change my job title from chief of police to town marshal. That's cooler."

Everyone at the table was listening now.

"Much cooler," Eric agreed.

Megs nodded. "I'm sure that won't be a problem. What's your other condition?"

"I want to wear a cowboy hat as part of my uniform."

Megs answered in a deadpan voice. "A white cowboy hat, I assume?"

"Of course." He held out his hand, and they shook.

Megs smiled, turned to the rest of the table. "Hot damn! Folks, we've got ourselves a new police chief… er… town marshal."

Cheers.

Darius and Megs chatted about the details.

"I have to give my notice at the DPD. They've been good to me."

"Understandable. We don't need you to start until January."

Then Joe and Rain brought their food, along with a bottle of Joe's prized McCallan and a tray of shot glasses.

"I hear Sasha crushed it at the gym today and that we have a new town marshal." A big smile on his face, Joe distributed the glasses to everyone who wanted one and poured liberal shots. Then he and Rain raised their glasses. "Congrats, Sasha. You will always be our champion. And Darius, welcome home! Cheers!"

"Cheers!"

"Welcome home!"

"Glad to have you, chief… er… marshal."

After they finished eating, some of the Team hit the rock wall, but Sasha stayed with Darius, the two of them talking with Joe about a rental cabin he thought Darius might like. Then the Timberline Mudbugs took the stage, and couples left the table for the dance floor.

"Excuse me." Darius stood and walked away.

Sasha thought he was just going to the restroom until she noticed him standing beside the stage a few minutes later. When the song ended, the lead singer leaned over to talk with him. Then Darius walked back to the table, his lips curving in a sexy smile when he caught her watching.

"What was that about?"

He sat, took her hand. "I guess you'll have to wait and see."

When the following number ended, the band's lead singer stepped up to the mic. "Listen up, everyone. Quiet! We've got a song dedication."

Sasha narrowed her eyes at Darius. "You didn't."

He chuckled. "Listen."

"We're all thrilled that Sasha is back to climbing again. Way to make a comeback, girl. You showed them."

The room exploded into whistles and cheers.

"Hear, hear!"

"Brava!"

"We've got a song dedication for Sasha from Darius, who says her smile lights up his world. You boys ready?"

The band broke into a newgrass version of *Here Comes the Sun*.

Sasha looked into Darius' eyes, fighting not to cry. "Thanks. For everything."

"Thank *you*." He took her hand, raised it to his lips.

She listened to the music, the feel of his hand in hers precious. "So, you're now the town marshal of one square mile."

"One square mile surrounded by reality." His gaze softened, a smile on his lips. "But now it's *my* square mile—and you're at the heart of it."

The love Sasha saw in his eyes gave her heart wings.

Epilogue

Ten Months Later
Chamonix, France
IASC World Championships

SASHA WAVED TO DARIUS, who sat with their families in the stands. Then she turned to face the climbing wall, willing herself to focus on the route, doing her best to shut out distractions. Her hands shifted, mimicking the motions she would make, as she mentally worked through one move after the other.

There was a dyno low on the wall, followed by a thin section with crimpers that her fingers, raw from a week of intense competition, weren't going to like. After that, there were some sloping forms that would challenge her because of her height, forcing her to make big moves. That section led to a forty-degree overhang with a stretch of pinches and underclings that would require raw strength. That was the crux. After that, a series of mixed holds led to a final dyno to the top.

How many times in her life had she done this?

So many.

She stopped that train of thought because she knew it would make her emotional. Instead, she searched the route for places where she might get a little rest. She used her last few seconds to think through that crux.

"Back to iso," one of the judges called.

She and the other climbers made their way back to isolation, where they surrendered their cell phones before being locked in, men in one room and women in the other. Isolation prevented anyone from getting additional beta on the route or watching online to learn from their competitors' mistakes.

Before the attack, time in iso used to feel like a backstage party, when she got to hang out with her international friends. But she'd been wearing rose-colored lenses then, assuming that everyone adored her as much as she adored them. That hadn't been true.

Daryna and Akari were once again in the finals with her. A young German climber, Elise, had made it, too. Last year, Elise had won the youth world championships, and now she was competing against adults. Ye-Jun Kim, a South Korean, was a newcomer. Inés Allard, who was French, had the support of the hometown crowd. Olivia Campbell, who came from the UK, and Marta Diáz, from Spain, rounded out the eight women who'd reached the finals.

They had at least a forty-minute wait until the men's competition was over, so Sasha focused on hydration and calories.

Daryna sat beside her. "How is your skin?"

Sasha set down her water bottle and held up her hands. She'd had to tape three fingers on her right hand and two on her left. "I need to retape them. I'm afraid they'll start bleeding the moment I hit the first crimper."

Daryna had tape on two of her fingers. "Someone needs to invent liquid skin that you paint on like nail polish that magically heals you."

"I'd buy a gallon of that."

One by one, the other women drifted over, but Sasha just wanted to be alone. She waited until they were deep in conversation. Then she walked over to a bench, stretched out, and closed her eyes as if sleeping, using the time and space to run the route through her mind. It wasn't that she didn't like the others. Far from it. But the conversation always seemed to turn to Maritza in the end.

Sasha had worked hard to put the attack behind her. Maritza had been sentenced to seven years in prison, while Hans Reiter had gotten twelve. Both had been banned from entering the US. It didn't feel like enough to Sasha, but she'd done her best to put them out of her mind for good, focusing on climbing and her new life with Darius.

She was now the strongest she'd ever been, and she was determined to make this her best year of climbing yet. She'd competed around the world, consistently winning gold. Then in May, she'd achieved her dream of setting a new women's world speed record for free-climbing El Capitan. If she could win today's event, she would prove to herself and the world that she had triumphed over the tragedy of last year.

It all came down to this competition.

Don't psych yourself out.

It was just another wall. Another route. Another climb.

About forty-five minutes had passed when the doors opened, and the judges called them out. One by one, they ran out onto the floor, where an announcer introduced them to the crowds, Sasha going last because she'd be climbing last.

"Sasha Dillon, United States of America!"

The crowd roared, the sound giving her a burst of adrenaline.

Sasha walked onto the floor, waving, her gaze seeking Darius once again. He sat in the second row, waving to her, Max and Gus in front of him, his parents to his left and her family to his right. Her mother blew her a kiss, so Sasha blew one back.

At least her parents were here this time.

———

DARIUS WATCHED Sasha walk out onto the floor, roped in, the judge who would belay her following her, carrying her rope in a clear, plastic container.

"If she gets to the top, she wins?" Melissa, Sasha's mother, asked.

Sean answered. "Yes, though she doesn't have to make it to the top. She just has to make it higher than that last climber."

Darius had had enough. "Please, everyone. Quiet. *Not a word* for the next six minutes."

The following six minutes would determine whether Sasha reclaimed her title or went back to Scarlet in second place.

Sasha walked up to the wall, paused for a moment, then stepped onto the route. Darius knew she was sore and tired and that the skin on her fingers was broken and tender, but no one would be able to tell she was in pain by the way she moved, every motion smooth and graceful. He found himself holding his breath as she got into position for the first dyno—and launched herself upward.

She stuck the dyno, slipped the rope into the clip, and moved into the diagonal section with the crimpers. She'd told him that climbing with raw fingers was like trying to walk normally with broken blisters on your feet. Still, she kept going, pausing to chalk her fingers again, shaking out her hands.

The big screens gave the audience a different view, cameramen moving to capture closeups and views of the climbers' bodies and faces. Sasha looked as calm and cool as ever, her attention entirely on the task at hand.

Next came the section of big sloping forms—red plastic shapes with tiny holds in different places, some of which were intentionally hard to see. They were far apart and would force Sasha to get creative, but that's what she did better than anyone else.

Find the flow.

That's what Megs and Nicole always said to her at the climbing gym, and the words came into Darius' mind now. She caught her foot beneath one of the forms, used it to hold on while she reached… reached… reached for a hold she couldn't see. When that didn't work, she took a moment to shake out her hands. Then she used her knee to wedge herself into a higher position, using counterpressure to gain a few more inches.

Come on, angel. You can do it. I know you can.

Finally, her fingers closed over that hold, and Darius exhaled.

The next section led to the crux—a forty-degree overhang with brutal pinches and underclings. Only Daryna had made it to this section, but she'd fallen before she'd gotten through it.

Making clever use of her heels and toes, Sasha moved into the overhang, shifting from one pinch and undercling to the other, shaking out her hands whenever she could.

Higher. Higher. Higher.

In front of Darius, Max covered his eyes and got an elbow in the ribs from Gus, who pointed at Sasha.

Sasha shifted her hips, reached diagonally—and grasped that last pinch.

Darius exhaled as she chalked up, slipped the rope through the clip, and moved to her left for the last section. It took her a good thirty seconds to get into position, the clock ticking. She reached for the next hold, the tension in the sports hall growing.

Darius knew she must be exhausted by now, her muscles pumped, her fingers hurting, possibly even bleeding. But when a camera cut in for a close view of her face, all he could see was determination and concentration.

God, he loved her.

She was only six feet from the top now, and she took her time, carefully shifting from one hold to another, most so small Darius couldn't see them. As she got ready for the final dyno, both Max and Gus covered their eyes.

You've got this, Sasha.

With an intense burst of energy, she threw herself upward, clinching the dyno.

The arena exploded, people leaping to their feet, even her competitors giving her an ovation. Max and Gus hugged each other, jumping up and down. Darius knew that people back home in Scarlet were doing the same.

Heart pounding with happiness for her, Darius applauded with everyone else, watching as the woman he loved was lowered, victorious once again, to the mat, her arms raised over her head, a bright smile on her face.

Gus turned to Darius. "I hope they have televisions in German prisons."

"So do I."

He left his seat, made his way down to the barrier, where he showed his tag to one of the security guards, who let him through. Sasha hurried over to him and threw herself into his arms. He held her tight, ignoring the cameras. "Congrats, angel. I love you."

———

SASHA SAT in the passenger seat, the sun setting as Darius drove them home to Scarlet Springs. She'd spent the past few weeks flying from one event, interview, public talk, and magazine cover shoot to the next. It's not what she would have chosen to do, but she needed to fulfill her contractual obligations to her sponsors, who wanted her to stand in front of as many cameras as possible wearing their logos.

In its own way, it was as exhausting as competition, flight after flight, hotel after hotel. The hardest part about it was being away from Darius for so long. As town marshal with a small staff and limited vacation time, he hadn't been able to join her, the two of them checking in each night by phone or video chat.

Still, Sasha had done her best to enjoy it. So many people had first heard her name after the attack last year, and they just wanted to congratulate her. Her manager's publicist had come up with the hashtag #Undefeated for Sasha's victory tour, and it had stuck. She'd lost count of the number of people who'd shouted "Undefeated!" as they passed her on streets or in airports, smiles on their faces.

She'd been inundated by book offers, modeling contracts, and even an offer to make a TV movie about her life. She'd turned them down. All she wanted was to go home with Darius and smell the mountain air again.

Darius listened to her talk about the agent who'd come to her hotel in LA and tried to sign her, shaking his head. "I don't know if Maritza realizes this, but she did more to boost your career than anyone."

Sasha had had the same thought. "Ironic, isn't it?"

They hadn't told anyone Sasha was coming home today. She needed to rest before she found herself on the receiving end of a Scarlet Springs celebration. The only people who knew were Megs and Mitch, who had invited them to a quiet dinner tonight.

"Did you read through it?" Sasha had sent Darius a statement she planned to send to the media tonight.

"I did." He took her hand, squeezed it. "I thought it was great—short and sweet, humble and honest. In other words, very you. Just be certain you're not doing this for my sake. Yes, I miss you when you're gone, but I knew what I signed on for before I moved to Scarlet."

"I'm sure."

They stopped at their house so Sasha could take a shower, change, and drop off her luggage. Darius had moved in a few of months ago, and there were still boxes sitting unpacked here and there. With the holidays fast approaching, the boxes would probably be there through New Year's.

When Sasha felt clean again, they took a bottle of wine from the fridge and drove the short distance to Megs and Mitch's house, where Megs met them at the door.

"There she is—undefeated and with wet hair."

"Hey, Megs! Mitch!"

The four of them sat in the dining room, enjoying Mitch's chili, salad, wine, and friendship. Darius and Megs talked about town business, and then the conversation switched to the world championships and Sasha's victory tour.

"You should have heard the roar in Knockers when you stuck that final dyno."

Mitch chuckled. "I thought the walls were going to come down."

They'd watched all of her TV appearances.

"I recorded them," Mitch admitted.

Sasha knew it was time. She took out her phone, opened a document she'd saved to her files. "I'd like you two to read this before I post it."

They both glanced at the document and then stood and went in search of their reading glasses. When they sat at the table once again, glasses perched on their noses, they bent their heads together and read.

Sasha saw Megs' grip tighten on Mitch's arm—the only sign of surprise from either of them. But when their heads came up, there were actual tears in Megs' eyes.

"Oh, honey." Megs swallowed, took Sasha's hand. "Are you sure?"

Sasha nodded. "I told myself a long time ago that when competition was no longer fun, I would leave it and go back to climbing for the joy of it. I want to retire while I'm at the top of my game and my body is still strong. I want to enjoy my life and stop spending so much time on airplanes."

Megs squeezed her hand. "If there's anyone on this earth who understands, it's the two of us. Do your sponsors know?"

"Yes. My contracts run out at the end of the year."

"Good. You don't want to blindside them."

"No."

"You've got money saved?"

"More than six million."

Megs' gaze shifted to Darius. "And what does our town marshal think of this?"

Under the table, Darius squeezed Sasha's hand. "I just want Sasha to be happy. If she thinks it's time to leave professional climbing, then I support her."

Mitch poured more wine. "What do you plan to do

with your time?"

Sasha met Darius' gaze, the warmth in his eyes encouraging her. "I was wondering if I could talk with you about changing my role with the Team. I'd like to become your apprentice, Megs. I'd like to learn how to manage the operation."

Megs closed her eyes, exhaled as if she were relieved.

When she opened her eyes again, Sasha could see a gleam of humor. "Did you hear that, Mitch? Sasha wants to train to take my place in the unlikely event I don't live forever. What do you think?"

Mitch laughed. "Well, if she's going to take your place, one thing is certain. She's going to have to learn to be a lot meaner."

Sasha laughed, then tried to imitate Megs' deeper voice. "I might could do that."

"When are you sending out that press release?" Megs asked.

"Watch." Sasha copied the text, pasted it into a box on her Facebook page, and clicked *Post*, a lump in her throat. "There."

Megs stood, came around the table to hug Sasha. "You know, Mitch and I don't have kids, but if we'd ever had a child, I would want her to be just like you."

———

DARIUS SAT with Sasha in their newly installed hot tub, both of them naked, nothing but stars above them. They scanned social media for responses to Sasha's announcement that she was retiring from professional climbing.

"Apparently, I'm pregnant. Did you know? I didn't."

Beneath the water, Darius' hand caressed her flat belly.

"I had no idea."

"This guy says you made me stop climbing. You bad, bad man."

Darius made a disapproving grunt. "I knew someone would think that."

Sasha set her phone aside and turned to face him. "I don't care what they think. I did what was best for me, for us, and now I'm ready for the next chapter in my life."

Darius kissed her. "Don't worry about me. I've dealt with worse."

She leaned against his chest, her palm against one of his pecs, the feel of her precious. God, he had missed her.

Then he remembered. "I have it on very good authority that the Town Council is going to rename Third Street after you—Sasha Dillon Street."

Third Street had been chosen because the climbing gym was there.

She gaped at him. "Really?"

"Really." Darius wondered if she truly understood how much she meant to this town. He thought he'd known when he moved here, but the devotion he'd seen these past couple of months had blown his mind.

She was a hometown hero.

Sasha's expression changed from surprise to worry. "Are you truly happy here?"

Darius was taken aback by her question. "Am I happy?"

"So much of this past year has been me chasing titles and big dreams. But you've sacrificed so much. You moved to a new town, started a new job. You've held things together while I've been away. I just hope you're not disappointed."

Darius laughed. "Disappointed? How could I be disappointed?"

"Well, you—"

He pressed his fingers to her lips. "I love my new job. Being the town marshal is a lot more interesting and fun than being a detective. Do you know how nice it is to get up in the morning and know that I most likely won't have to see a dead body or tell someone that the person they love is gone?"

"I hadn't thought about that."

"In Scarlet, a crime wave is Hank going on a bender or a couple of tourists shoplifting."

That made her laugh. "Poor Hank."

He'd once blown up his own house trying to extract hash oil using butane and had lost his driver's license and done time after driving drunk into the creek. It seemed to take a village to keep him sober, safe, and out of jail.

"Here, I'm able to do more than solve crimes. I get to make people's lives better."

"Like when you and Eric rescued that puppy from the creek."

"Just like that. I feel connected to this community and its people in a way that I never did in the big city. Plus, I get to wear jeans and a cowboy hat to work."

"I'm so glad it turned out this way."

"It was the job change I didn't know I needed—until you."

"I've been away so much."

"I spent eighteen years living completely alone, no attachments, no real relationships. Do you know how good it feels to come home and know that this is the space I share with you? Even when you're gone, I feel grateful. Love is what makes a home, Sasha. You've given me a home—and so much more."

Then Darius drew Sasha close and kissed her, the stars wheeling silently overhead.

Thank You

Thanks for reading *Bound to Fall*. I hope you enjoyed Sasha and Darius' story. Follow me on Facebook or on Twitter @Pamela_Clare. Join my reader's group on Facebook to be a part of a never-ending conversation with other Pamela Clare fans and get inside information about my books and about life in Colorado's mountains. You can also sign up to my mailing list at my website to keep current with all my releases and to be a part of special newsletter giveaways.

Also by Pamela Clare

Contemporary Romance:

Colorado High Country Series

Romantic Suspense:

I-Team Series

About the Author

USA Today best-selling author Pamela Clare began her writing career as a columnist and investigative reporter and eventually became the first woman editor-in-chief of two different newspapers. Along the way, she and her team won numerous state and national honors, including the National Journalism Award for Public Service. In 2011, Clare was awarded the Keeper of the Flame Lifetime Achievement Award for her body of work. A single mother with two sons, she writes historical romance and contemporary romantic suspense at the foot of the beautiful Rocky Mountains. Visit her website and join her mailing list to never miss a new release!

www.pamelaclare.com

Printed in Great Britain
by Amazon

77081720R00182